INFUSED

INFUSED

by
algernon michael roark

Copyright © 2019–2020 by Michael Magnus

Edited by Holli Tri | Inkwater.com
Cover and interior illustrations by Ginger Triplett
Cover layout and interior design by Masha Shubin | Inkwater.com

This is a work of fiction. The events described here are imaginary. The settings and characters are fictitious or used in a fictitious manner and do not represent specific places or living or dead people. Any resemblance is entirely coincidental.

All rights reserved. No part of this book may be reproduced or transmitted in any form or by any means whatsoever, including photocopying, recording or by any information storage and retrieval system, without written permission from the publisher and/or author. The views and opinions expressed in this book are those of the author(s) and do not necessarily reflect those of the publisher, and the publisher hereby disclaims any responsibility for them. Neither is the publisher responsible for the content or accuracy of the information provided in this document. Contact Inkwater Press at inkwater.com. 503.968.6777

Publisher: Inkwater Press | www.inkwaterpress.com

Hardback ISBN-13 978-1-0879-3856-1
eBbook ISBN-13 978-1-0879-3907-0

1 3 5 7 9 10 8 6 4 2

It is with much pleasure that I dedicate this work to Gloribella Frank, a woman whom I consider a great culinary Icon in her own right. Ms. Frank taught me the importance of presentation as it relates to the adage: you first eat with your eyes. So, in honor of her, this story is told in the same tone and manner, in which it would be imparted from her own pen.

Contents

ACKNOWLEDGEMENTS XI

PREFACE XIII
- Pot Roast Pork xiv
- Rice and Peas xiv
- Infused Water xv

CHAPTER ONE 1

CHAPTER TWO 7
- Cornmeal Porridge 12
- Coconut Apple Pancakes 13

CHAPTER THREE 15
- Vegetable Fries 18
- Dipping Sauce 19
- Jerk Turkey Bowl with Buckwheat Edamame Salad 20
- Buckwheat Edamame Salad 21
- Mango and Strawberry Trifle 22
- Beef Pumpkin Soup 28

- ☐ Sweet Potato and Salmon Cakes 29
- ☐ Pork and Beans Croquettes 30
- ☐ Tuna Cucumber Boats 31
- ☐ Kabocha Pumpkin Salad 31
- ☐ Poultry Brining 32
- ☐ Pickled Cucumber Salad 34
- ☐ Buckwheat and Black Bean Muffins 34
- ☐ Rum and Raisin Banana Mango Cream Pie 35
- ☐ Eggplant Mozzarella Sandwiches 35
- ☐ Red Kidney Beans and Pork Belly Stew 36
- ☐ Basmati Rice 37
- ☐ Ginger Beer 37

CHAPTER FOUR 41
- ☐ Fried Green Plantains 41
- ☐ Spinach and Feta Cheese Lasagna Rolls 44
- ☐ Pulled Pork and Plantains 45
- ☐ Tzatziki Sauce 46
- ☐ Caper Sauce 47
- ☐ Crispy Fried Tilapia 47
- ☐ Glazed Carrots 48

CHAPTER FIVE 49

CHAPTER SIX 61
- ☐ Quiche in Mugs 61
- ☐ Fish and Baked Sweet Potato Chips 63
- ☐ Curried Beef 67
- ☐ Mushroom Celery Rice 68
- ☐ Split Pea Curry 69
- ☐ Cauliflower Crust Pizza 75

CHAPTER SEVEN 79
- ☐ Ackee and Codfish 83

CHAPTER EIGHT 89
- ☐ Sweet Potato Ham Casserole 91

- Sausage and Black Bean Casserole 92
- Greek Macaroni and Cheese... 92
- Beef Pumpkin Savory Pie 93
- Lemon Carrot Cake 94

CHAPTER NINE 101
- Watermelon Delight... 105

CHAPTER TEN 111
- Scotch Bonnet Curry Goat Wrap....................................112
- Popcorn Turkey 113
- Turkey Teriyaki and Cilantro Rice 114
- Cilantro Rice 115
- Mustard Mackerel and Banana 115
- Salmon Burgers 116
- Grilled Zucchini Brown Rice...117
- Columbus Day Hash 117
- Roasted Cauliflower Stuffing 118
- Bean and Pepper Stuffed Bell Peppers 118
- Almond Mango Bars 119
- Roasted Sweet Potato Salad with Bacon 120
- Grapefruit Bubbles 120
- Jicama Carrot Salad 121
- Orange Cran-Apple Splash.. 121
- Pickled Red Onions 121
- Grilled Snow Peas Buckwheat and Salmon Bowl 122
- Peach and Mango Delight... 123
- Party Bacon Sandwiches.. 123
- Pepper Pot 125

CHAPTER ELEVEN 127
- Dates and Rum Bars 128
- Origami Pancakes 129
- Origami French Toast 129

CHAPTER TWELVE 139

CHAPTER THIRTEEN 143
- Calabaza Corn Cakes.. 145
- Sweet Potato Whole Wheat Pasta Salad..................... 145
- Date Blueberry Pudding 147
- Sugar Free Hummingbird Cake.......................................147
- Buckwheat Black Bean Stars 148
- Green Lima Bean Soup..149
- Grilled Eggplant Sandwiches... 150
- Garlic Roasted Salmon and Bulgur 151

CHAPTER FOURTEEN.. 163
- Roasted Garlic and Pumpkin Soup 170
- Slow Cooker Lamb..171
- Wild Rice Arugula Salad 172

CHAPTER FIFTEEN 173

CHAPTER SIXTEEN... 179
- Fried Chicken in Grapeseed Oil 181

CHAPTER SEVENTEEN.. 187
- Buffalo Chicken Zucchini Boats.....................................191
- Coconut Buckwheat with Cilantro and Lime 191
- Cornmeal Crusted Chicken Delights 192
- Fresh Dill Salmon Dip.. 193
- Spicy Lentils with Buckwheat Noodles....................... 193
- Crockpot Kale.. 194
- Goat Curry Chayote Meatloaf.......................................195
- Zucchini Lentil Fritter 198
- Grilled Eggplant Fritters... 198

CHAPTER EIGHTEEN 201

EPILOGUE..213

RECIPE INDEX... 215

Acknowledgements

Many, many thanks to family, friends and everyone with whom food was always one of the focal points of our conversations and interactions. Your encouragement and enthusiasm helped to make this book a reality. To my associates and tasters, I owe you a great deal, I was very lucky to have you all.

Preface

The riveting and rustic figure of a woman cooking on a wood-burning stove in an open yard was branded deeply into my soul. It was an image that only the lenses of a particular part of the mind could fully process and assimilate in a meaningful way. The meandering puffy gray smoke rose from the stove like a charmed snake from a basket as she fanned the fire to get a perfect flame of amber and blue. Then, one by one and in batches, the ingredients and utensils were gathered for the mixing and combining of flavors. The sizzling of oil, the aroma of garlic and the emission of steam laid bare this woman's love for her craft in making a meal of rice and peas with pot roast pork---one of the best dishes that mortals could ever imagine tasting.

POT ROAST PORK

3 pounds of pork shoulder
1 tablespoon black pepper
¼ tablespoon ground thyme
5 cloves minced garlic
1 onion (chopped)
½ teaspoon salt
1 tablespoon gravy master
1 quart low-sodium vegetable stock
2 tablespoons vegetable oil
cornstarch

METHOD

Clean pork and remove 95% of the fat and bone in the middle. Cut pork into quarters and marinate for 24 hours in the next 6 ingredients: black pepper, thyme, garlic, onion, salt, and gravy master. Remove bits of garlic and onion from pork and set aside. Heat vegetable oil and brown quarters of pork in a 3-quart Dutch oven on the stovetop. Cover pot and let the meat develop its own liquid over medium heat. After about 15 minutes, the pork will have its own juices. When the juices are really low, add a cup of vegetable stock and cover the pot once more. Keep on repeating the process until the meat is tender and brown. In the final stage, add the bits of onions and garlic and more vegetable stock if needed. Cook until onions and garlic are tender. By then gravy should begin to form, and if pork is fully cooked, remove from pot and drain fat, then add a thickening agent to the juice, such as cornstarch. Mix about a teaspoon of cornstarch in a ½ cup of cold water and low-sodium vegetable stock then add mixture to the pot. Keep stirring until the thickness and consistency are achieved. Return the pork to the pot and cook for another 15 minutes. Stir thoroughly and remove from flame.

RICE AND PEAS

1 8-ounce can coconut milk
1 pint cold water
½ cup red kidney beans
1 bay leaf
4 large grains of whole allspice
3 cloves garlic

2 cups long grain parboiled rice
2 stalks scallions
1 teaspoon ground thyme
1 teaspoon salt

METHOD

Soak kidney beans in cold water for 4 hours, then drain. Add kidney beans, water, and coconut milk to a medium pot, and bring to a boil on medium heat. Add 2 cloves of crushed garlic. Let the beans cook until tender but not falling apart. When beans are cooked, add the rice and other ingredients, including the remaining clove of garlic. Stir pot only once and make sure rice is proportionate to liquid content. Salt to taste and add more seasoning and liquid if desired. Cover pot tightly with lid, and on a low flame let rice and beans cook for about 20 minutes or until grains are tender. Do not disturb the cooking process until rice is fully cooked. Fluff with a fork. This meal should be served hot with slices of beef steak tomatoes.

I recommend Infused water to go with this meal. The combination of fruits will depend on your own taste and preferences. For example: strawberry, mango, and mint.

INFUSED WATER

Simply add sliced or mashed fruits to a pitcher of clean filtered water. For herbs, such as mint, crush them to release the oils. Refrigerate for a few hours, then pour and enjoy. Change and start a fresh pitcher every 2 days.

TIPS

When cooking rice, there is a ratio of 2:1, which means for every cup of rice, the amount of liquid should be doubled. For 1 cup of rice, we need 2 cups of water.

Use stock instead of water in most dishes for the enhancement of flavors.

INFUSED

Chapter One

As the train pulled into the station at the last stop, which was my destination, I had a gut feeling that something was wrong. It was a sensation that wouldn't go away, despite the reassurance of Dragan E. Bradshaw, the attorney I'd hired. "Everything is going to be alright," was the last thing he told me. Yet there was uneasiness in the pit of my stomach, like a knot that couldn't be loosed. Symbolically, I tore to shreds what was left of my train ticket and draped my one piece of luggage across my shoulder and hurried out of the train station. On the ferry to Soy, the small town where I was born, I tried to calm down. It worked for a while, but as soon as I got off the boat, my fear returned. Suddenly, I became conscious of every nostalgic step I took, yet I gradually built the courage to press on. A work in progress, I told myself, thinking about my years of absence. It was roughly a twelve-minute walk from where I got off the ferry and then, beyond the trees, bittersweet home. It would be in plain sight, but this time things were different.

After the first six minutes of brisk walking, I smelt smoke. It was acrid smoke, quite recent but turning stale, and on an impulse, I started to run along the narrow road to this town that was so much on my mind. Something or someone on the adjacent path was running with me but was totally out of my field of vision. The loose sand by the side of the road got in my shoes, but that was a small price to pay for the freedom I was seeking. As I got closer, the stench of destruction permeated my lungs, and I started to cough. When I got to the spot that I always imagined would be the gate of the town if Soy was a gated community, I came face to face with a reality that was more frightening than anything I could ever have imagined: the town of Soy was burnt to the ground. The streets that were once my childhood playground were littered with charred remains of wood and plumbing, concrete and roofing. The library, the post office, the daycare center where I first learned the letters of the alphabet were all in a pile of rubble.

In anguish, I turned away from Soy, and with tears in my eyes, I ran straight to Truro, the neighboring town, to seek refuge. I spent two days and nights at the home of a missionary minister, Reverend Gregory Tanner. The man of God and his wife, Sister Bertha, took me in. But that wasn't all; I had collapsed on their doorstep as soon as I got there and was rushed to the emergency room for treatment. After spending the night in the hospital and being released the next day, I went back to the minister's house. I told them part of my story, and they encouraged me to rest and take it easy, but I couldn't. Neither could I return to the life I was trying to escape, and so within forty-eight hours, I was back in Soy. I walked through the ruins, trying to find answers, but the town was empty and void of life. Not even birds flew in the sky. Stained with soot and the persistent odor in the air, I stumbled my way to the remains of the house where I was born, not too far from a new Pentecostal church that was built before I left Soy. I needed to see all the evidence before I could move on.

My home was a painful, almost unrecognizable sight of

shattered glass windows, a burnt and collapsed roof, a detached porch, and a gate wrenched from its columns. The section of the front yard that was once a well-manicured rose garden was trampled and covered with debris. I couldn't go any closer; I stayed across the street and just stare in disbelief. The picture of gloom was a microcosm of what Soy had become. My childhood home, 41 Don Drummond Circle, no longer existed, and there was absolutely nothing to go back to. No matter how bright the light may have been at the end of most tunnels; the candle at the end of this one, was extinguished. If I was experiencing a terrifying dream, this might have been the point where I would wake up and find myself safely tucked in bed, like at the end of all dreams in the morning. But there was no waking up from this, and I continued to walk, hoping to make sense of the catastrophe. An atomic bomb, a meteoroid; what was it that left such destruction?

Rows and rows of houses were gone, leaving behind charred foundations that nature would come back to claim. I turned to face our neighbor's house, which still existed but only in my mind, and a child came running up to me.

The child was a little boy, and he had been hiding among four columns and a wall. He was filled with mystery and unable to speak. I could get no information of any kind from him, yet he held my hand, trembling with fear. He was not injured or hurt in any visible way, and I was puzzled as to what he was doing in this catastrophic valley. He clung to me like a piece of metal to a magnet, and I became even more confused. Looking down at him, I asked his name, but he did not respond; he just kept staring at me.

"Where do you ... live? ... Did you live?" I started to babble but got a hold of myself. The child was still glued to me, and I looked around to see if anyone else was in sight. If he had been there for any length of time, someone must have been searching for him. We stood in the spot motionless while the minutes passed and not even a fly came by. Then I came to the conclusion that he was alone in this vast, burnt out wilderness where all life on earth except for us seemed to be absent.

"Can you talk? Tell me something, anything, your name," I asked desperately. He mumbled something, which was an improvement over the last several minutes.

"Onn."

"Your name is Onn?"

"Onn," he repeated.

I walked away from Soy for the last time, with that frightened boy holding on to me. I thought about the name; if Onn was his real name, it was rather unusual. The long road stretched ahead, polluted with smoke and things carried by the wind. We moved quite slowly, finally reaching the proverbial fork in the road. It had three tines and only one was familiar, the path leading to Truro. It was a recognizable path, since the last time I had run all the way to the end, but this time was different, and I was thinking of taking a slightly different route, which might still lead to the town of refuge. The next tine of this fork led to the coast, and the other was unknown to me. It could have been a new path; I hadn't been there in a long time, and anything was possible.

Then a sudden rush of salty ocean breeze came at us from the coast, and it was as if it carried an urgent message, a call: *come*. The decision wasn't very difficult; I answered the call of Mother Nature. Didn't they say we came from water? Well, I was drawn back to it. The cool, sandy path was inviting too, and not very far down this lane, I heard a loud noise. Onn was startled and so was I, but the gigantic albatross resting on a post was far more frightened by being disturbed from an afternoon nap, from a dream perhaps. The large wings flapped thunderously, like the hammer of Thor. We saw the creature for only about thirty seconds before it disappeared into the distance, into the unknown.

We finally reached the edge of the water, where the surf was doing its usual dance of in and out, and we could actually count how long it would take for the water to land at our feet and disappear again. It had been long ago, but I almost thought it was the same spot Mia and I had gathered shells as children. It would have been mystifying if it was the same spot, because now I was trying to wash some of the soot and grime from Onn's face and feet, leaving a salty residue, but at least getting him a lot cleaner. He could barely walk, so I had been carrying him on my back. It was obvious that he was tired and needed a nap. Consequently, I looked around for a spot where he could get at least fifteen minutes of sleep. Normally, children went straight for the water when at the ocean or found some activity with the sand, but of course this was not the norm. The situation here was a tricky one, and getting to Truro before it got dark was crucial. I was in no state of mind to camp out there for the night. I had chosen this path mainly out of curiosity. Deep down, I thought it would be different, the scenery. I thought dozens of people would be camping out here; I pictured them in tents, as refugees from Soy.

A natural bundle of dried seaweed served as a comfortable mattress in the sand. We sat down, and Onn rested his head on my lap while I gazed at the ocean. I let go of my confused thoughts for a moment and went almost into a state of meditation. My eyes were closed for about two minutes, and I immediately went into a dream. I dreamed the ocean opened up just enough for me to see the fishes and some of the other creatures of the sea, but they were all snakes. Every living thing in the water was a serpent of some form or another, from the rattlesnake to the cobra. I opened my eyes, chastising myself for almost falling asleep, and yes, sleep would have been my best friend at that point, but getting to Truro was far more important.

The oceanic atmosphere was working well for me, and I was feeling better indeed. I couldn't help but wonder where I had gone wrong before my life began to unravel like an unhemmed piece of fabric. While this thought was coming to the surface of my mind, I saw something in the distance from the corner of my eye. It was a small dock, which I hadn't noticed when we first arrived. But that wasn't all; there was a boat at the dock.

In my estimation, it was about a five-minute walk with Onn. At that point, I felt like the wick of a burnt-out candle sitting in a teaspoon of wax.

I focused on the lone boat for about ten minutes, just trying to make up stories as to its identity. I could have spent all afternoon guessing, but the child woke up hungry, so it was not the time to speculate if help was within plain sight.

Moving from that comfortable spot in the sand was the hardest thing to do, and Onn immediately snapped out of his semi-nap and held on to me. Cautiously, we walked towards the dock, and there wasn't another human being anywhere as far as my eyes could behold. Seabirds, yes, but this was their home. A town destroyed by fire next to their mesmerizing domain wasn't going to prevent them from having fun and searching for food. As I got closer to the mystery boat, I started to have reservations, but Onn was almost limping now.

The boat was securely tethered to the dock by large ropes. It swayed slightly with the motion of the sea, a slow, strange dance. It was a movement that only the dancer in this case, would understand. The boat's name was printed on both sides in Greek letters: *Infused*. A copper weathervane in the form of a rooster was perched on the upper deck, a good device for someone like me with no sense of direction: the east, west, north, and south could be easily identified.

Having made it so close to a possible source of help, I didn't want to turn back. My simple short-term goal was to get back to Truro where temporary camps were set up for the refugees of Soy. We could stay in one of those camps until I could figure things out or at the mission house, where I was still welcome.

Once within proximity of the boat, I could see that it had three decks with tinted portholes. Stepping on the dock, I noticed that there were a few steps leading down to the entry deck of the vessel. Onn started to cough, and his grip on my hand tightened. Aware of the pressure of his small hand, I descended the steps with Onn in tow and stopped at the port, frozen.

Chapter Two

Still wrapped up in my need to find help, we entered the boat after a few moments of hesitation, but I couldn't see much of the interior due to the compartmentalization of its layout. There was a passageway with cabins on either side, and all the cabin doors were closed. With such a configuration, I couldn't get a clear sense of what was going on, who the owner was, or what the purpose of the boat was. I knew very well that I should have knocked before barging through the door. But once inside, it was the sound of sobbing from one of the cabins that alerted me that I was in the wrong place at the wrong time. A shadow of unease swept over me; I turned towards the exit hoping I could leave before anyone caught me trespassing. I knew I had made a terrible mistake.

The sobbing continued, and seconds later, I heard a door open. At that point, I was riveted to the spot, and so was the child behind me. A young man appeared from the cabin where the sound had come from. He seemed quite shocked to see us, and as a reflex action, he blinked then stopped short in his tracks.

If I were to guess his age I would have said he was about twenty-five, but one would definitely need his ID for proof of age. He had an angular face, and if he had been a bit taller, his head would probably have been touching the deck above. I shifted my gaze to the door he came from, but when he turned the face of his baseball cap to the back of his head, he got my full attention. Yet I looked back at the door again instead of him.

For about a minute, neither of us spoke, although I owed him an explanation; I was on his boat and not the other way around. Instead, I just kept on looking at the cabin doors along the passageway, avoiding his direct stare at the child and me. We must have been quite a sight. I hadn't looked in a mirror in days and had no desire to see one, for fear I'd go into shock. My hair could have resembled a wig of tumbleweed and my face been plastered with makeup of ashes, I wouldn't have known. Earlier, I had washed Onn's face with the sea water available, but now it was dry, and he looked as if he was wearing a mask of salt.

Finally, I thought it was my responsibility to say something, so after careful thought, I said, "I don't blame you if you call the police, but I was … was … only trying to find help … Sorry for the intrusion …"

The cabin door from which he had emerged was still ajar, and the sobbing resumed. It was the muffled cry of a female. He was about to close the door completely, but I turned around to leave, and he shifted his focus again.

"Wait a minute; I thought you said you needed help." His voice was encouraging. "And, besides, we haven't been introduced."

"Well … I …" I stammered, trying to find a reason to leave and not start a conversation.

"You don't have to explain anything now. If you're from Soy, I already know what happened." He came closer to us, only about an inch more, in a non-threatening way, and extended his hand, "I'm Zarek Stefan Cavallo. The last name Cavallo." He waited for me to reciprocate.

I shook his hand, "Gloribella Frank, and yes, I'm originally from Soy."

"Nice to meet you, Gloribella. Odd that we never met before. I was born and raised in Soy, and how big is the place? A square mile long?"

"Sorry, I don't know why. Never met every single person from there either."

"I understand. There is always the side of town unknown to us. I'm from the wrong side."

I pulled Onn forward. He was still hiding behind me. "Any chance you've seen him before?"

He looked at the boy with curiosity, then at me and shook his head. "No, never seen him before. Your son?"

I hesitated for a moment, thinking about what he had just asked. How many more times would this question arise before I could get him back to his family? I wasn't even sure of his name, and yet I felt as if I had known him all my life. The need to protect him from harm was quite resolute, and I felt as if I would go to any length, even to lie and much more. "His name is Onn, and—"

"Very interesting indeed." He made no further comment regarding my answer and changed the subject by volunteering information about himself. "Well, I just returned home after a long trip only to find out that I no longer have a home. It went up in the blast just like yours."

The sobbing in the room continued, and I looked at him directly, but he avoided my eyes. "Well, it was nice talking to you. We must go now; I've already taken up too much of your time."

"It's not what you're thinking, you know. I am not a horrible person with a boatload of prisoners."

"What?"

He smiled. "It's a joke and bad timing, plus you're leaving. To where? If you don't mind telling me. There is nothing left of Soy."

"Back to the refugee camp in Truro," I said.

"You're walking to Truro with a child who seems as if he'll pass out at any minute now?"

"He's fine; we'll be fine." The sobbing in the cabin continued and eventually turned into pleas.

"Please, please," the woman's voice begged. I took a firmer grip on the child.

"I really must go now," I said with an edge to my voice.

"That's my mother in there." He pointed.

"Your mother? What's wrong with her?"

"What do you think? She just lost her house and everything she had. But besides that, she is hungry. I'm not a very good cook. I can make some things, but everything else turns into mush. I need to find her food. I made tea a while ago, but that's not enough."

"I'm sorry about that."

"Well, here we are. All in the same boat, literally. You said you're going to Truro? Walking with that boy is not a good idea. You'll never get there before dark; that's more than two hours on foot."

I knew he was right; my plan was a disaster waiting to happen. "I have no other choice."

"I was just about to set sail when you walked in, a boat ride is about fifteen minutes to half an hour. I could give you a ride there."

I was silent for a while, thinking how free I was not so long ago. He cut through my thoughts with a convincing argument to oppose my irrationality, "I can't blame you if you refuse. I'm a total stranger, and there's the issue of trust, but there is something I wanna ask you."

"What's that?"

"Can you cook?"

"Actually, yes. I can."

"Then I'm asking you a favor. Can you make something for my mother? She'll probably eat anything at this point. There is plenty of stuff in the galley downstairs. That's the deck below."

Now I was painted into a corner. I wasn't held at gunpoint, but I didn't feel comfortable leaving anymore, and yet I still didn't feel at ease staying either. I looked him in the eye and said, "Okay," ignoring everything I had heard and read, stories about young women who were held at gunpoint and then ended up in modern-day slavery or human trafficking. Things my mother told me of a similar nature, which was also the subject of newspaper headlines, movies, and novels. They all went down the drain in a matter of seconds, and I had no explanation for it. I tried to read his expression, but it certainly didn't matter since I didn't plan to change my mind. For a brief moment, I felt as if I was returning to a life I had left behind. He looked back at me calmly, and I remembered what was said about the eyes being the gateway to the soul. Could I read this man's soul? He reached behind him and pushed open the door to the cabin from whence the cries came and said, "There she is." He pointed to a woman lying on the lower deck of a berth. She was resting in the fetal position and still sobbing.

"Mother, we have a visitor. This is Gloribella." She didn't respond or even turn around to face us. He turned to me, "Now you see. I'm not lying."

I looked at him and nodded.

"If you still don't trust me, you can stay on the beach, and when I get to Truro, I will send them to come and get you. I will tell them that you got stranded here. Someone will come. The Red Cross, perhaps."

I nodded again but wasn't sure what the agreement was. Things had gotten all complicated, and I wasn't sure how to fix anything anymore. I was tired. Tired of fixing things that eventually got broken anyway.

We left his mother's cabin and went back into the corridor. He opened another compartment door that had steps leading down to another level of the boat. It was the galley, a kitchen that looked like all the others I had seen, just smaller and more compact. It had a stove, refrigerator, dishwasher, and what seemed like countless cupboards, with the doorknobs in the shape of ancient wood-burning stoves. Then there was a small eating area with bolted-down chairs and a table. In the center of the table, there was a fruit bowl with apples and oranges.

"Take a look. I have to go back to the wheel room now and start wrapping things up here. I'll be back later," he said.

I wanted to think of something quick and easy, filling and nutritious. I saw cornmeal in a canister in one of the cabinets, and then the idea came to me. I would make cornmeal porridge, the greatest remedy for hunger, according to Nanna. I started to measure the ingredients in a bowl.

CORNMEAL PORRIDGE

½ cup cornmeal
A dash of nutmeg
A dash of cinnamon

3 tablespoons sugar
½ cup milk
3 cups water

METHOD
Mix all the dry ingredients with the water and milk. Mix well until all the lumps are dissolved. Add the mixture to a medium-sized pot and placed it on the stove. Continue to stir over medium heat, making sure there are no lumps in the porridge. Add more water and milk as the porridge thickens. Continue to stir until the right consistency is reached. Cook for fifteen minutes, then remove from flame. Add more sugar and milk according to taste.

It tasted perfect.

Zarek convinced his mother to come down to the galley to meet Onn and me. "Gloribella, this is my mom, Lottie."

"Very nice to meet you," she said.

"Thanks for having me on your boat," I responded.

"Are you sure you are not an angel in disguise?" she asked.

"I am pretty sure, ma'am."

"Then, how did you know the right time to show up?"

"Desperation, I'm sure."

"Your porridge is like medicine; I'm feeling better already. How did you learn this?"

"Something my grandmother taught me."

"Well, it's very good."

Zarek, Onn, and I also had some of the porridge. Finally, it was all gone.

The ocean, the air, and the new setting were my remedy for feeling better. It was calming, and I almost forgot where I was and what had brought me there in the first place. But it was only a temporary fix; the real problems were still very present, even though I wanted to do nothing but forget them.

"I have to go the wheel room now," Zarek announced. "Time to set sail."

Lottie was falling asleep in her chair while the little boy played with a Rubik's cube that Zarek had given to him. He was working hard to solve the puzzle by lining up all the colors, but he stayed close to me the whole time, with one eye watching everything around him. He was not just haphazardly twisting the colorful block; by the time we had left the harbor, he had nearly solved it.

We were soon in the middle of the ocean; at least that was what it seemed like as we passed other smaller islands, which were inhabited only by birds and seals or sea lions. The agitated sea was kicking up massive waves of foamy water as I searched the galley kitchen to cook another meal. I wanted to make one more dish for Lottie before we got to Truro. I saw the apples on the table and got an idea for something else. Ah! Coconut apple pancakes! I selected two of the fresh, green fruits, Granny Smith apples.

COCONUT APPLE PANCAKES

2 Granny Smith apples
¾ cup pancake mix
¼ cup unsweetened dry coconut
1 egg
Cooking spray
Water

METHOD
Prepare pancake mix according to package instructions, by adding water and egg. Mix dried coconut into the batter. Add 1 extra tablespoon of dry pancake mix to make a thicker

consistency. Core and peel apples, then slice them into disks about a ¼ of an inch thick. Place the disks in a zip-seal plastic bag and add a ½ cup dry pancake mix. Shake well until all the disks are coated. Remove them from the bag and shake off the excess pancake mix. Dip them one by one in the pancake batter and cook on griddle or frying pan in batches of 4. Cook until slightly golden brown. Remove from pan and sprinkle with confectioners sugar or pancake syrup.

When the boat docked in Truro, Zarek came down to the galley to try the coconut apple pancakes.

"These are delicious!" he said. "Never tasted anything like this before."

"Thank you."

"I need to talk to you, Gloribella." He was looking at me with a farewell face, knowing we'd never see each other again. I was sure he had a goodbye speech ready.

"Okay."

"Well, this is it," he remarked.

"I guess so."

"I'm ... sailing ... well, to Greece, in about seventy-two hours, my mom and I. You're welcome to come, Onn as well. No strings attached. We only met a short time ago, but anyone who can cook this good is pretty terrific in my book. My mom likes you and the kid quite a lot. Wait until she tastes these tarts of yours. She'll love you even more."

"They are not tarts," I corrected.

He smiled.

Chapter Three

In a humanitarian effort to help the refugees of Soy, the town of Truro had transformed some of its public buildings into camps. The churches were a big part of this effort, plus the Red Cross and other organizations all came together to help. Emergency mobile units were set up all across the town and were functioning as medical clinics, soup kitchens, and many other resources for the surviving victims of the fire. Truro was the place to be for anyone who escaped the fire in Soy.

I took Onn to one of the units just to have him checked out by the doctors, and as it turned out, he was fine, just dehydrated, as we all suspected. Strange, not many questions were asked about him that I couldn't answer.

It might have been shock, post-traumatic stress, or some other temporary mental condition, but even at that point, I didn't fully grasp the magnitude of the situation until I walked into an agency that was set up to deal with missing people. The room was solemn and overcast with grief. The busy counselors on the phones were like sponges, absorbing people's fears and frustration. Of course, there was a line, and each person had to wait his or her turn or fill out basic paperwork and drop it in a box. I chose the latter.

After leaving that depressing waiting room, I thought it was imperative that I go to the rectory to see Reverend Gregory Tanner to get some advice. Too many things had happened within the last seventy-two hours and I was overwhelmed. If I was looking for an easy answer, a quick fix and a shortcut, I was disappointed, because Reverend Tanner took me down another road. He read aloud the story of Moses from the Bible, about the baby found in a basket on the river Nile. He was about to explain something more to me, about faith and a bigger picture that I was unable to see at the moment, when we were interrupted by his secretary, who informed him that he was overdue for his next appointment. Her presence brought an abrupt end to our conversation and my visit, but the invitation to stay at his house was still open.

As I walked away from the rectory, with the boy holding my wrist, I thought about the uncertainty of the future. This was not what I had envisioned three days before when I boarded that train in Boston. I was inclined to forget why I was going to Soy in the first place, and with the current situation, I could easily erase that past. When I summed it all up, past and present, it seemed like a bad, tasteless prank that someone would pull off on the forever popular April Fools' Day.

The mission house was the minister's residence, but it was more than that. There was quite a lot that went on in that three-story brownstone with its heavily polished floors and oak furniture. Christians from across the globe often stayed there for short periods of time. It would often be their first stop before moving on to whatever mission they were undertaking. The evening I went there with Onn, I was greeted by a number of these people getting ready for their missions. They were extremely kind and friendly and were more than a shoulder to cry on. They took over caring for Onn completely when they heard of his mysterious appearance out of the ruins.

"Gloribella, I don't know your situation, but this boy might represent the phoenix in your life," one of the missionaries said. It didn't mean much at first when she said it, but then she handed me a pamphlet with a colorful picture of an unusual bird, the phoenix. The bird was being destroyed in a blazing nest. The pamphlet went on to tell the story of the phoenix rising from the ashes. Only then did it occur to me what she was actually saying. It was abstract at that point when I really needed practical answers, but I went along with it. She was only trying to help me feel better. "Your challenges will help you to become a new person," the missionary added.

The atmosphere in the house was one of friendliness and I felt that I could be as open as I wanted without the fear of judgement, yet I thought some things were better left unsaid.

Steve and Vera Umari were the Japanese couple who introduced themselves as Yin and Yang: "But that's a joke," Steve laughed as they pulled their chairs closer to mine.

"We had nothing in common five years ago when we first met," Vera chimed in.

"And then she forced me to do things, like making odd shapes out of paper! Have you ever heard of origami, Gloribella?"

"Yes, I have."

"Okay, then would you like a free lesson?"

"Can I put it on my resume?"

"Why not."

That night I had my first-ever lesson in origami, the art of folding paper into various shapes to form figures such as animals and other objects. Onn caught on much faster than I did, as he seemed to do with most things. Steve and Vera were quite pleased, and so they took him under their wings, teaching him the correct and important techniques.

As one entered the mission house, the first thing that grabbed the attention was the portrait of a lady. The artist who painted the picture successfully captured quite a lot about her in that one painting; her wit, charm, and beauty were certainly not overlooked. The lady in the portrait was Sister Bertha, and the minister referred to her as my darling wife, Sister B. She gave me a tour of her kitchen, where I would volunteer that evening as the chef. Sister Bertha didn't pick any particular menu and was very pleased with my offer and left it up to me to make the choice.

In the semi-industrial kitchen, I roamed through the pantry and refrigerator to get an idea of what to cook. I dug through the enormous refrigerator drawers and came up with red, green, and yellow peppers. Then I found string beans, and on the countertop there was a jar with asparagus in water and covered in plastic, which formed a greenhouse to preserve the vegetable. These were the basics I needed to start a very simple appetizer that would turn out to be very tasty. My plan was to prepare a three-course meal with the following appetizers.

VEGETABLE FRIES

- 3 peppers cut in strips (red, green, and yellow)
- ½ pound string beans (cleaned and stems and tips removed)
- 2 large zucchinis
- 1 bundle asparagus (about 1 pound)
- 1 tablespoon garlic powder
- 1 tablespoon black pepper
- 1 tablespoon onion powder
- 1 teaspoon sea salt
- 1 teaspoon dried thyme
- 2 cups whole wheat flour (for making batter)
- 1 cup seltzer water
- 16 ounces corn oil or enough for deep frying
- 1 cup whole wheat flour (for tossing vegetables)

METHOD

Clean and cut peppers into strips, removing seeds, stems, and unwanted parts. Clean string beans and remove stems and tips. Clean and cut zucchinis in halves and then strips of about 4 inches long, the approximate size of French fries. Clean and remove the lower parts of the asparagus, towards the root, and discard. Cut the remaining part in two halves. Combine all vegetables in a bowl and toss with whole wheat flour and allow to sit while you mix all the dry ingredients in another bowl, i.e. remaining flour, black pepper, dried thyme, onion powder, salt, and garlic powder. Whisk in ½ cup of seltzer and continue whisking until batter is formed. Add more seltzer if batter is too thick.

Remove vegetables from bowl and dust off excess flour, then dip into batter.

Add oil to a large skillet to a depth of about 3 inches, heat, and insert a deep-frying thermometer. When the thermometer reads 375°, fry vegetables in small batches until golden brown. Transfer vegetables from skillet to paper towels and serve hot with a dipping sauce if desired.

DIPPING SAUCE

1 tablespoon freshly grated ginger
1 clove garlic (grated)
½ cup orange juice
1 tablespoon teriyaki sauce
½ teaspoon fish sauce (optional)
2 tablespoons ketchup

METHOD

Combine all ingredients except ketchup in a bowl and whisk for 1 minute, then strain and discard sediments. Add ketchup and whisk for another minute.

Note: For additional dipping sauce, double or triple this recipe as required. And please make this sauce ahead of time; it will certainly reduce your stress level when trying to cook for a crowd.

Within a few minutes, those snacks were gone, and I brought out more. Since I made a lot, I kept on refilling the platters until there were no more. It was time to prepare the main course, which

I had started to prep in what I considered a very relaxed atmosphere. This main course was what I called a jerk turkey bowl.

JERK TURKEY BOWL WITH BUCKWHEAT EDAMAME SALAD

Jerk Turkey

- 3 pounds turkey parts cut into small pieces (including: wings, thighs, and necks)
- ¼ cup jerk seasoning (paste)
- 2 cloves garlic (minced)
- ½ cup green onions, or scallions, (chopped) and set aside for garnish.
- ¼ cup parsley leaves (chopped) and set aside for garnish.
- ¼ cup cold water

METHOD

Clean turkey parts in a solution of vinegar and salt, then dry with a paper towel and set aside. Then, in a large bowl, combine jerk seasoning, garlic, and water, then mix well until all the ingredients are combined. Add the turkey parts to the bowl and massage well until all the meat is coated with the seasoning. Cover the bowl and let it sit for about 15 minutes. Overnight would be better. Heat oven to 375° then arrange meat on a cooking rack, spacing them out, with a dripping tray underneath to collect the grease. Cook for 1½ hours or until meat is tender and dark brown. Drain fat from tray and collect drippings for gravy. To make a gravy to go with this dish, you need the following:

Gravy

- 1 cup vegetable stock (low sodium)
- 1 tablespoon corn starch
- 1 teaspoon jerk seasoning (paste)
- Pan drippings, collected

METHOD

Wisk corn starch, jerk seasoning and vegetable stock in a bowl then pour into a medium saucepan. Set to boil on medium flame with constant stirring. Turn flame to low and let the mixture simmer for 2 minutes. Continue stirring for another minute then add pan drippings. Let gravy cook for another minute or more while stirring, until it reaches the consistency of a glaze-like sauce. Remove from flame and pour over meat hot and cover.

To complete the meal, I made a buckwheat edamame salad, which was a healthy match for the rest of the meal.

BUCKWHEAT EDAMAME SALAD

- 2 cups buckwheat
- 1 cup edamame beans (shelled)
- 1½ cups cold water
- 2 cups low-sodium vegetable stock
- 1 tablespoon sea salt
- 1 tablespoon butter or margarine
- 1 medium red onion (chopped)
- 1 cucumber (peeled and diced)
- ¼ cup olives (chopped)
- 2 tablespoons lemon juice
- 1 cup grape tomatoes (sliced)
- ½ teaspoon Mrs. Dash® table blend seasoning
- Scallions
- Parsley

METHOD

Rinse buckwheat in a strainer under running cold tap water and remove any unwanted particles floating around. Set it to drain off excess water. Heat margarine or butter in a medium skillet and add buckwheat. Stir for about a minute to coat buckwheat with margarine and then add Mrs. Dash® table blend. Continue to stir until mixture is slightly toasted over medium heat then add vegetable stock. Cover pot and let buckwheat come to a rapid boil then turn flame to low and let it simmer. Cook for about 15 minutes until liquid is absorbed. Remove from flame and set aside.

In a small skillet put 1½ cups of water to boil, then add sea salt and edamame. Cook for about 5 minutes, drain, and set aside. In a salad bowl, combine onions, cucumber, grape tomatoes, olives, edamame, and lemon juice and toss well. Fold in buckwheat to combine with other ingredients and stir slightly.

To serve, ladle salad into soup bowls and top with turkey, spoon on the gravy, then garnish with scallions and parsley. This recipe should serve 6 people and can be doubled or tripled as the case might be.

The dessert for the evening was a mango and strawberry trifle. When making a three-course meal, prepare the dessert first since you might not have the time or energy at the end of cooking the main course.

MANGO AND STRAWBERRY TRIFLE

- 2 cups strawberries (cleaned and hulled)
- 1 angel food cake
- 2 large ripe and firm mangoes
- 1 16-ounce tub Cool Whip
- 1 cup strawberries (cleaned and hulled), reserved
- 2 tablespoons Splenda or Equal (use ½ cup sugar if preferred)
- 1 teaspoon rum (optional)
- 1 cup sugar-free strawberry jam

METHOD

Cut angel food cake into cubes of about an inch and set aside, then peel mangoes and cut the flesh away from the seeds and toss with strawberry jam and Splenda. Toss strawberries with rum. Spread a thin layer of Cool Whip at the bottom of a trifle dish, followed by a layer of angel food cake, then strawberries, then mangoes. Spread another layer of Cool Whip and repeat the layers in the same order. Finish off with Cool Whip and garnish with reserved strawberries. Set in the refrigerator to chill.

It was a delightful meal with a Thanksgiving flair. Stories were told about different things and a variety of subjects were touched upon. Since these people were missionaries, most of their experiences had some religious base. Yet each of them had his or her own unique personality. I suddenly remembered the people who were always at my mother's dinner table during Thanksgiving. The ones I remember the most were Aunt Infanta and Uncle Danny, who were loud and talked way too much. In contrast to them, there was Aunt Patience, whose name was almost symbolic to who she really was. I also remember the storytellers, the jokers, and the sleepers, who would wake in time for the over-sweet dessert that decked the tables when the main course was over.

In this present group, the cleanup was easy; I didn't have to lift a finger. It was all taken care of by the people who enjoyed the meal immensely, and within an hour, the grime and grease were gone, and the air was fragrant with the fruity aroma of pomegranate. Reverend Tanner was the first to complete his labor and joked that his years of working in a soup kitchen had finally paid off. His task of drying dishes and putting them away was finished at a record time of fifteen minutes. So with the spare time he had, he seized the opportunity to finish telling me the story of the baby Moses, who was discovered on the river Nile. I found no connection with my life and the story of Moses, but I listened. It was what ministers did: talk about Bible stories whether they have anything to do with our lives or not.

Reverend Tanner advised me to hold on to Onn for a while and not put him in the hands of strangers, meaning the government. "It would be a disaster," he warned. "The child has taken a liking to you, which is valuable and to be cherished and encouraged, considering the world we live in now. I'm sure his family will show up soon."

Reverend Tanner further remarked that if Onn was to be placed in what he called an "unjust system," he would just become a case number and an added case load to a worker who was already overloaded with similar problems, and when that case worker went home to his or her own children at the end of the day, who would Onn be left with? In what kind of people's hands would he be placed?

Those were the words that resonated in my mind long after the conversation was over. I got a few minutes to sit by myself in the humongous dining room that night, while Steve and Vera were dedicatedly passing on the craft of origami to Onn. Holding the only possession I had left, my one piece of luggage, I started to laugh. What else could I do? Feeling the soft leather, a wave of memories came rushing back to me, things I could no longer suppress but wished I could. I was going from riches to rags and not the other way around. Looking back, I thought to myself, *what was I thinking when I bought a bag for five hundred dollars when I certainly could have found a knockoff at another store for $39.99?* I opened it and ran my fingers over the contents; they were just the bare essentials I grabbed when I ran out of the house. Now I was a drifter joining the rank of countless others living on the edge. From a penthouse to taking refuge in a mission house in less than a week was quite a leap.

The morning I walked away from the man to whom I was engaged was a moment of great terror. I discovered that he was a wolf in sheep's clothing, and I was fortunate to find out before the vows of matrimony were finalized. I remembered Nick sitting at the table staring at the engagement ring I'd just returned to him. It was my final act with regards to Nick after a series of lies, deceit, and manipulation that had led to serious damage and harm. I thought my life was going somewhere when I met Nick Draiblate, a young, articulate, robust, and handsome police officer from the Boston PD, who could even fly the helicopter. I was still a graduate student, and I imagined that the future would be bright and prosperous.

After a few months of dating, we got engaged. He used one of those romantic tricks that men use to impress women into saying yes to their marriage proposals, such as putting the ring in a glove or some other unusual place. He did not have the words "marry me" written in the clouds, but it was just as clever. I was living on campus with a bunch of roommates and had just come back from a class and found a package waiting for me at the doorway of the dorm room. I picked it up and went inside, and immediately the return address caught my attention. It reads from the king of Denmark, with the coat of arms of the country and what must have been the official seal of the Danish monarchy. I was truly perplexed, so I locked the door and eagerly started to rip the package apart, revealing a beautiful box of talcum powder. The delicate fragrance was all over the room as I lifted the silver lid of the crystal box. As soon as I touched the powder puff resting on top of the enchanting scent, there was a persistent knock on the door. I stopped and walked over to see who was there. It was Nick, and he was staring at me mischievously. "Nick, what are you doing here?"

"Can I come in? And, yes, should be your answer."

I hesitated for a moment, then stepped aside and let him pass. The floor was still littered with the wrappings from the package, and the beautiful box of powder was sitting on the bed. He scanned the room, floor first, then his eyes stopped at the powder on the bed. "What's all this?" He pointed to the loosely scattered packaging.

I shrugged my shoulders in bewilderment. "Somebody sent me powder, the Danish king I assume, but since I don't walk in the circle of royalty, I think it's highly unlikely."

"I believe I can help you."

"What?"

"I can help you figure out who it came from. Remember, I am a cop." He took the powder from the bed. "Here, stick your finger in it."

I hesitated, but he insisted by gently pressing my fingers into the powder. "Move your fingers about in the box. Okay. Good, that's it," he encouraged.

Doing exactly what he instructed seemed silly and childish, but eventually, my finger struck something hard, and I pulled it up, splashing some of the powder along the way. Up came a diamond ring. He took the ring from me and went down on his knees. "Gloribella Elizabeth Frank, will you marry me?"

Before I could say yes or no, a man barged into the room, a singer and musician we had met at a concert a few weeks before.

He had his guitar and he started to serenade us with the song "Endless Love."

"Wait a minute, pal. I haven't got the answer from my lovely lady yet." The music stopped.

"Yes, I will marry you."

Two weeks later, Nick came back to my dorm room carrying a dozen red roses. "I don't want you living here anymore," he said.

"What are you talking about? Why?"

"Because I can't have my fiancée living like this. I want you to live in comfort, and I don't trust those boys who are always hanging out in the hall outside, the lustful looks in their eyes when you pass by, which drives me crazy. I don't like that."

"Okay. So where am I to live? We're not married yet."

"I have an idea."

We drove to Providence Street in downtown Boston to a high-rise building. At the front desk, we passed security and took the elevator to the fifty-seventh floor, which was the penthouse. He opened the door with one of the keys on his keychain and we went in. The sophistication and elegance took me by surprise. There were stained glass windows and doors, and museum-quality paintings and furniture, all complementary with the penthouse.

"I think you'll like it here."

"What's not to like. My only problem is that I can't afford a place like this with student loans, so it's only a fantasy for now."

"No, it's not. This place is for you."

"Mine? I'm sorry. I don't understand."

"When my uncle passed away two years ago, he left me this place in his will. It was his hope that one day I would get married and come here to live. I'm content at my parents' for now, but after we walk down the aisle, this is it, baby; this is our home sweet home."

I didn't argue; this was a step up, and not having to share a bathroom and other living space was a plus. I notified campus housing immediately and they were quite flexible. About a day later another student came over to see the room. I didn't have much to move, just my books and clothes, which Nick was more than happy to assist me with.

The penthouse was quite spacious, and there was plenty of room to spread out with just me alone there. Nick visited quite often, and it seemed like he wanted that more than anything else. Then, about a month after I was settled in, he came over and told me he had a terrible disagreement with his parents. He'd said some terrible things to them that he wished he could take back but couldn't. He wanted to know if it was okay for him to move into one of the guest bedrooms until we were married. He said he would be of no distraction between me and my studies whatsoever, knowing how important they were. More importantly, nobody needed to know that he was living there; the last thing he wanted was for people to start talking or to cause problems with my family. Well, the apartment was his for the time being, until we were joined in holy matrimony. It didn't feel right saying no, especially with the terms he offered.

It was my final year in graduate school, and soon after, we could set a date for our wedding. If that wasn't the perfect arrangement for an unmarried couple in these modern times, I wouldn't know what else was. Having Nick close by would also give me the opportunity to know him better before we took the next step. We lived under the same roof, with no strings attached, and he was true to his word; he never tried to change the rules in that respect.

The reaction from my friends varied. Some thought it was cool and others didn't care one way or the other. But a handful of people thought Nick was doing that to keep an eye on me and to use it as a strategy to control, so I had to remind them that we were engaged and it really didn't matter at that point. My very close friend, Luke, stayed neutral and had nothing negative to say. "Whatever makes you happy, I'm all for it," was his comment.

Strangely, after a while, Luke began to complain that Nick really didn't like him and was trying to set him up. Suddenly, he was being constantly harassed by the police. Sometimes he would be stopped twice in one day for some form of moving violation. Luke said they were all invalid. He would go all the way to court, and luckily for him, the judge would dismiss the charges. Luke firmly believed that Nick was behind them all, and it was because of his close friendship with me and my fiancé's insecurity.

Eventually, I graduated and got my master's degree. I landed a job as an executive chef at a downtown restaurant in Boston. It wasn't exactly what I went to school for, but it paid well. I was working with food on another level until I found something that related directly to the science of food and its preparation. The Belly of the Pig, as the restaurant was called, was quite popular in the Boston area and was highly publicized. Reviews were good and the owner was very pleased with his success.

When I wasn't busy in the restaurant, I was in the prep kitchen crafting and creating new recipes.

From my personal cookbook, I developed the following recipes:

BEEF PUMPKIN SOUP

- 3 cups kabocha pumpkin (diced)
- 2 quarts low-sodium beef broth
- 1½ pounds beef with bones (for soup)
- 1 16-ounce package frozen vegetables (corn, peas, carrots, etc.)
- 2 stalks scallions
- 1 stalk celery (diced)
- 1 medium turnip (diced)
- 2 sprigs fresh thyme
- 2 cloves garlic
- 1 cube low-sodium beef bullion
- 1 small green pepper (seeded and clean)

METHOD

In a large stock pot, pour in beef broth and bring to rapid boil then add beef and continue to boil for 10 minutes; then bring boil down to simmer for 45 minutes. Add mixed vegetables, celery, turnips, pumpkin, garlic, and beef bouillon cube. Cook for another 30 minutes with occasional stirring and checking for flavor. Lightly pound scallions on a piece of aluminum foil and add to soup, along with fresh thyme and green pepper. Cook for another 10 minutes with occasional stirring and checking for flavor. Flavor can be enhanced with beef bouillon and salt-free beef seasonings. Ladle soup into bowls. Serves 6 people.

Another favorite at the Belly of the Pig was:

SWEET POTATO AND SALMON CAKES

- 1 16-ounce can salmon (use fresh salmon if available)
- 2 medium sweet potatoes
- ½ cup finely chopped onion
- ½ teaspoon black pepper
- ½ cup minced red pepper
- ¼ cup fresh cilantro (chopped)
- ½ teaspoon lime zest
- 2 tablespoons fresh lime juice
- ¼ cup cornmeal
- ¼ teaspoon sea salt
- 1 cup whole wheat flour
- Oil for frying

METHOD

Peel and cut sweet potatoes, and then steam until tender. Place potatoes in a bowl and sprinkle sea salt to taste and mash with a potato masher. Open salmon and drain; reserve liquid and remove bones. Mix cornmeal, flour, and salt in a separate bowl and set aside. In the potato bowl, add onion, black pepper, red pepper, cilantro, lime zest, and lime juice, and then mix with a wooden spoon until all ingredients are combined. If the mixture is dry and needs more liquid, add a few drops of the liquid reserved from the salmon. When the right consistency is reached, begin to form cakes using an ice cream scoop to measure each one. Coat each cake in the flour and cornmeal mixture and fry in a skillet with oil until golden brown. Serve hot with tartar sauce.

Tip: Tartar sauce is really mayonnaise and sweet relish mixed together. Mix ¼ cup mayonnaise with a tablespoon sweet relish and you get your tartar sauce.

Another favorite at the restaurant was:

PORK AND BEANS CROQUETTES

For this recipe, fresh pork is used, but if canned pork is available and will make your life much easier, go for it.

- 3 pounds fresh pork shoulder (with bone in)
- 1 tablespoon sea salt
- 1 tablespoon black pepper
- 1 16-ounce can Bush's baked beans
- 1 cup whole wheat flour
- 1 tablespoon vegetable oil (for searing pork)
- 1 tablespoon garlic powder
- Lettuce leaves
- 5 garlic cloves
- Oil for frying

METHOD

Season pork by rubbing with salt, pepper, and garlic powder, then use a small knife to poke holes all around the meat and stuff with cloves of garlic. In a heated skillet, sear pork on all sides in vegetable oil until golden brown. Transfer to a slow cooker along with all the juice it produces, then remove drippings from skillet and transfer to slow cooker as well. Set cooker on low and cook for about 8 hours. Allow meat to cool in the slow cooker then transfer to a platter and use a fork to pull the meat from the bone. Discard all the fat but reserve some of the skin without any fat. Combine lean meat and skin in a bowl using about 3 cups. Add baked beans plus sauce in can. Mix with a spoon while adding flour a little at a time until it reaches the consistency of a moist dough. Form croquettes and deep fry in a skillet. Transfer to paper towels and serve on leaves of lettuce or as lettuce wraps.

Then there was the tuna cucumber boats everybody loved:

TUNA CUCUMBER BOATS

4 medium cucumbers
1 5-ounce package garlic and herb spreadable cheese
2 8-ounce cans of tuna in oil
1 medium onion (chopped)
2 tablespoons freshly chopped parsley
1 tablespoon lemon juice

METHOD
Wash and peel cucumbers, leaving some of the skin, then cut length-wise into the shape of a boat. Use a spoon to gently scoop out the seeds—be careful not to damage the boat shape you've created. Drain oil from tuna and flake with a fork in a bowl, then add cheese, onion, parsley, and lemon juice. Mix well with a fork and fill each cucumber boat with the mixture. Arrange on a platter and serve cold with your choice of raw vegetables or by themselves.

Another dish on the menu at the Belly of the Pig is Kabocha pumpkin salad for people who didn't eat potatoes.

KABOCHA PUMPKIN SALAD

3 pounds kabocha pumpkin (peeled, seeded, and cut into ½-inch cubes)
1 package ranch dressing
¼ cup Greek yogurt
¼ cup Hormel bacon bits
1 medium onion (chopped)
1 tablespoon Mrs. Dash® table blend seasoning
3 hard-boiled eggs (chopped)
1 stalk celery (minced)

METHOD
Steam pumpkin cubes in a steamer until cooked but not too soft or mushy. Allow some firmness in the texture. Transfer

from steamer to a salad bowl and add onion and celery while pumpkin is still hot, then put aside to cool. Add the remaining ingredients to the bowl and gently fold them all together. Do not overmix. Set in a refrigerator to chill and serve cold.

HOW TO ACHIEVE PERFECTLY COOKED HARD BOILED EGGS

Set oven to 325° then place eggs on a rack and bake for 30 minutes. Remove from oven and plunge into cold water to cool down. Peel and use for your salads or other dishes.

Turkey was one of the few dishes on the menu at the Belly of the Pig that we made only a few times a year. At Thanksgiving, of course, it was quite popular, but for people who made a special reservation way ahead of time, it would always be available. For the seasoning of the bird I choose the brining method.

POULTRY BRINING

1 cup sugar
1 cup kosher salt
1 gallon water
5 cloves garlic

2 bay leaves
1 tablespoon allspice
1 sprig thyme

METHOD

Combine 1 cup of sugar and 1 cup of kosher salt in a large pot and add 1 gallon of water. Bring to a boil on medium heat, stirring constantly until sugar and salt are dissolved, then continue to boil for another 1–2 minutes. Turn off heat and remove from stove. Add 5 garlic cloves, 2 bay leaves, 1 tablespoon allspice, and 1 sprig of thyme. The seasoning and spice you add to the brine will depend on your own taste and liking. Taste brine to determine flavor and add more seasoning if needed. Let the brine cool completely and pour into a container large enough to fit a 20-pound turkey.

PREPARING AND ROASTING THE TURKEY

Clean turkey in vinegar, salt, and water, removing giblets and taking care not to contaminate surrounding area. Dry bird with paper towels and make incisions all over the turkey before immersing it in container with brine. Make sure it is completely covered with the liquid before putting it in a refrigerator for 4 hours or overnight.

Set oven to 450° and remove turkey from brine. Rinse under cold water and pat dry with a paper towel then tie legs together and wings close to the body of the bird with cooking twine to ensure even roasting of the meat. Line a large roasting pan with carrots, celery, potatoes, onions, and garlic, plus turkey giblets, along with 2 cups of water. Place turkey in roasting pan over a rack to allow dripping. Roast at 450° uncovered for 30 minutes then lower temperature to 325° and cover loosely with aluminum foil. Roasting time will depend on the size of your bird, which you will find on the package. Check on turkey every half an hour and baste with juices from pan with a baster when necessary. Monitor color of the bird and add water to the pan if juices get too low. Check the internal temperature of the bird with a digital thermometer until it reads between 170°–180°F. Remove turkey from the oven and let it rest covered for 30 minutes before carving.

MAKING THE GRAVY

Collect pan drippings with vegetables and giblet that are at the bottom of the roasting pan and discard of as much of the fat as possible. Place them all in a blender with low-sodium stock and blend until it reaches the consistency of a sauce then pour into a saucepan. Over a low flame stir the mixture until it is boiling. At this stage, your gravy is quite easy to burn so keep a watchful eye and stir constantly until it all comes together. Taste and add dry seasonings if necessary.

For that meal, I served a pickled cucumber salad and buckwheat black bean muffins.

PICKLED CUCUMBER SALAD

4 cucumbers (cleaned, peeled, seeded, and diced)
1 red onion (chopped)
½ cup parsley (chopped)
1 teaspoon freshly grated ginger
1 cup fresh orange juice
1 tablespoon olive oil
1 jalapeno pepper (seeded and chopped)
1 tablespoon fresh dill (chopped)
½ teaspoon sea salt

METHOD

Add cucumbers to a large salad bowl. In a mixing bowl, combine all the other ingredients and whisk together until dressing is well mixed. Combine dressing with cucumbers in salad bowl. Cover with plastic wrap and place in refrigerator for an hour.

BUCKWHEAT AND BLACK BEAN MUFFINS

1 16-ounce can black beans (drained and mashed with a potato masher)
2 tablespoons flax seed
1 cup buckwheat
1 cup extra sharp cheddar cheese
1 onion (minced)
1 cup low-sodium chicken stock
1 cup extra sharp cheddar cheese (for topping)
1 clove garlic (minced)
1 teaspoon butter or margarine

METHOD

In a small pot combine chicken stock, garlic, and butter or margarine, and bring to a boil. In the meantime, rinse buckwheat in a strainer under cold running water for 1–2 minutes and shake off excess water. Upon boiling, add the buckwheat to the pot and stir. Then let it boil rapidly for a minute before covering with the lid and lowering the flame. Cook buckwheat for 15-20 minutes or until grains are tender. Remove from stove and set aside. Combine extra sharp cheddar cheese, minced onions, black beans, buckwheat, flax seeds, and mix them all together. Be careful not to overmix, but mix just enough to combine all the ingredients. Spoon the mixture into a muffin pan sprayed with cooking spray and top with reserved extra sharp cheddar cheese. Bake at 350° for 15 minutes or until golden brown.

RUM AND RAISIN BANANA MANGO CREAM PIE

1 cup white rum
1 cup golden raisins
4 ripe bananas
2 ripe mangoes
1 16-ounce tub Cool Whip (divide into halves)
2 cups banana pudding
1 Graham cracker pie crust

METHOD

Soak raisins in rum overnight in an airtight container and keep pie crust in refrigerator. Peel mangoes and cut flesh away from seeds. Dice flesh of mangoes and strain raisins from rum. Cut bananas into thin slices, then in a food processor pulse raisins and mangoes for only a few seconds to achieve a rough chop. To assemble the pie, fold half the Cool Whip with mangoes and raisins. Similarly, fold bananas with banana pudding. Layer pie shell with alternating layers of mangoes, raisins, and Cool Whip, along with bananas and banana pudding, ending with the latter. Top the pie with the other half of the Cool Whip. Place the pie on a cake dish with a cover and set in a refrigerator for 2 hours.

EGGPLANT MOZZARELLA SANDWICHES

2 large eggplants
1 teaspoon kosher salt
2 cups whole wheat flour
3 eggs (beaten)
2 cups seasoned breadcrumbs
¼ cup parmesan cheese
2 pounds fresh mozzarella
Vegetable oil for frying
4 beefsteak tomatoes
½ cup shredded basil

METHOD

Peel eggplants and slice into circular disks of about ⅛ of an inch thick, then sprinkle with salt, wrap in paper towels, and place under heavy weight to absorb some of the moisture. Let eggplant sit under the weight for about an hour. Set up dredging stations with three shallow bowls. In the first bowl put flour, followed by eggs, then breadcrumbs and parmesan cheese. Dredge eggplant in flour, shaking off the excess, then in the egg, followed by the breadcrumbs and parmesan mixture. Place them on a rack while slicing mozzarella cheese and tomatoes. Heat enough oil in a skillet and fry in batches. Remove from oil and place on paper towels. Make your sandwiches after the frying of each batch by placing cheese, tomato, and basil on eggplant slice. Keep sandwiches warm in oven. This can be an open or closed sandwich.

RED KIDNEY BEANS AND PORK BELLY STEW

- 2 cups red kidney beans (rinse and soak overnight)
- 2 pounds pork belly
- 2 large cloves garlic
- 1 quart low-sodium vegetable stock
- 1 tablespoon vegetable oil
- 1 teaspoon black pepper
- 2 stalks scallions (for garnishing)
- 2 cups basmati rice
- 1 tablespoon margarine
- 1 tablespoon dried thyme
- 4 cups hot water
- Salt

METHOD

Trim as much fat possible from the pork belly and cut into small pieces. Season with salt and pepper. In a skillet that has a lid, fry pork in vegetable oil in until golden brown then remove from pot and set on paper towels. Drain all the fat, leaving the glaze at the bottom of the skillet. Drain kidney beans from water and add beans to skillet, along with vegetable stock, pork belly, garlic, and thyme. Bring pot to a rapid boil and boil for 10 minutes, stirring often, then let it simmer covered for an hour or until beans and meat are tender. Constantly stir the pot as the beans start to break down and thicken the pot. Add more seasonings along the way, such as garlic and thyme as needed.

Turn the flames off when the right consistency is reached, which should be a thick stew.

BASMATI RICE

In a medium pot, melt margarine and add basmati rice. Toast rice in margarine for about a minute, using a wooden spoon, coating all the rice with the margarine, then add hot water and bring pot to rapid boil, and boil for 1 minute. On a low flame, cover pot tightly and let rice steam for 15 minutes. Fluff with a fork. Serve kidney beans and pork belly over basmati rice; garnish with scallions.

I introduced them to ginger beer, which was very simple to make. Ginger beer was a non-alcoholic drink that went very well with the hardy pork belly stew and rice.

GINGER BEER

1 pound fresh ginger
2 cups granulated sugar

1 quart water
Club soda or seltzer

METHOD
Clean ginger then lightly pound with a mallet to loosen juice. Combine water and sugar in a larger pot and stir until sugar is dissolved. Add the ginger to the solution and boil on medium heat, stirring occasionally until liquid boils down to a simple syrup. Turn the flame off and remove from heat. Let the syrup cool down, then strain and pour syrup into a pitcher. Add seltzer or club soda. Serve over ice.

A Note about Ginger: The rhizome ginger derives from a family of spices known as zingiberaceae, and its use dates back to early civilization. In China it was in use as far back as the sixth century BC. Research on the use of ginger is ongoing, and in some findings, it is noted that the spice contains chemicals that work against the viruses of the common cold. Other substances in ginger are known to relieve nausea due to morning sickness in pregnant women. It is a travel sickness remedy, as well as a medicine for the suppression of coughing. As a general use, ginger is used for settling of the stomach.

Due to the conflict of schedules and being constantly busy, there were times when I didn't see Nick for days. It seemed like I had suddenly immersed myself in the world of overworked people with only two weeks of vacation every year. I was beginning to think that if that was my life pattern until I was sixty-five, I wouldn't even have time to bare children. I knew Nick was coming home because he would always leave the bed unmade, but I didn't see him. My sister advised me to enjoy the freedom of being unmarried while it lasted, because once it was over, it was over. I took whatever Nick told me about his schedule to be true; the job of a police officer wasn't easy, and their patrol hours were not definite and they could be called in at any time. His friends would come over some weekends, and I would cook a few of the recipes I just described above for them, including a twenty-pound turkey.

We were about to set a wedding date as soon as Nick's parents got back from France. They had bought a business there and sometimes would be gone for months. He did not want them to miss our wedding, and so we hoped that was the final delay. During this long engagement, Luke got arrested and charged with having illegal firearm that was used in a robbery. I was mortified, and so was everyone who knew Luke. He was not that type of a person; he did not believe in using guns and would never own one lawfully, much less illegally. They were trying to pin the robbery on Luke since the robber was never caught. This was all a mystery to everyone: how did this all land on Luke?

I asked Nick if he could do anything for Luke, talk to someone, the officers involved in the case, perhaps put in a good word for the guy, something positive on his behalf, keeping in mind he wasn't a criminal. Nick assured me he would do his best but couldn't promise anything.

A few days later, he came back saying the case against Luke wasn't from his precinct and he didn't know the cops involved in the arrest. They were new, trying to earn brownie points, and weren't going to let it go. My heart sank when I got the bad news; it was terribly depressing. The sad thing was that Luke was convinced that Nick had something to do with it. So I confronted Nick there and then. "Luke thinks you are behind the whole thing. Is it true?"

"What! No! I can't believe he would even think of something like that. Why? Does he hate me that much?"

"Well, it's actually the other way around. Luke doesn't think you like him."

Nick made a face and used his fingers to draw quotation marks when he placed emphasis on some words. "Even if I didn't like the guy because he is supposedly too close to my girlfriend, I would just tell him to back off. Setting him up wouldn't be my style. The question is, do you believe that?"

"No, I don't. There has to be some mistake somewhere, some other explanation for this whole mess with Luke. I feel better knowing you're not involved, and I'm going to hire him a lawyer."

"Well, that's what friends are for. I would do the same for any of my buddies if I thought they were innocent."

I went out the same day and had a consultation with Dragan E. Bradshaw. He was the type of lawyer who could get a court order to exhume bodies if necessary. Dragan would leave no stone unturned whenever he got going on a case. He wasn't cheap either. I gave the deposit he asked for, and he assured me that if Luke spent a single night in jail, he would give me every penny back.

Luke and I met when we were high school seniors working on the class yearbook. We did other projects in school, including newspaper articles, fundraising for the new gymnasium, and the time we worked on that difficult science project for biology. The assignment was to find a parasitic creature, observe it, and from our observation, write a paper. It was a difficult task, but with the help of the Audubon Society we were able to locate a cuckoo bird, and from then on the assignment got better. We had a good working relationship and were very good friends, but that was as far as it ever went. We were never interested in each other romantically and had never crossed that boundary. When we got older, other people came into our lives and our friendship remained the same. Whatever other people saw from the outside came purely from their minds.

Common Cuckoo-fledgling (Cuculus canorus)

Chapter Four

I snapped myself from the past and ran my hand through the one expensive bag I was left with. I tried to figure out the contents and why I'd chosen the things I had in it and why I left other things behind. There certainly wasn't much in the line of makeup for sure, except for the bare necessities. My recipe book was very much present and intact. It contained hundreds of recipes and menus that I had worked on over the years. I selected a few that I had perfected and would prepare for the missionaries next time. One of my personal favorites was tostones with scallion cream sauce. Tostones was the Spanish name for fried green plantains.

FRIED GREEN PLANTAINS

4 green plantains
½ cup peanut oil
1 cup low-fat sour cream

½ cup low-fat Greek yogurt
2 stalks scallions
Sea salt

METHOD

Peel plantains by slicing through the skin lengthwise on both sides of the plantains, then gently lift the skin off with your fingers. Cut the plantains into diagonal pieces about ¼ of an inch thick and soak in salted water for 5 minutes. Remove plantains from the brine and pat dry with paper towels. Heat oil and fry plantains for 2 minutes on both sides then transfer to paper towels and press to flatten with a plantain press or tostonera. Fry plantains in batches and be careful not to overcrowd pot when frying. Fry a second time, and for the second frying return pressed plantains to hot oil in batches. Fry until plantains are crispy and golden brown. Return to fresh paper towels and lightly sprinkle with sea salt.

Scallion Cream Sauce Dip
(Prepare this sauce dip ahead of time)

Chop scallions using only the green leafy top. Mix sour cream and Greek yogurt in a bowl then add scallions and a pinch of sea salt and whisk it all together. Serve this cream as a dip for the plantains.

Reverend Tanner had given me a new copy of the Holy Bible, the King James Version. I felt it was the one he liked the best. He left a bookmark at Exodus 2, the story of Moses, for me to further explore. The quietness of the room and the soft glow of the light took me back to Dragan E. Bradshaw's office. After I wrote Dragan the check, he jumped on the case immediately to set Luke free.

Dragan went on the phone and was trying to arrange for a preliminary hearing. If the case against Luke was weak, Dragan said he could get the judge to dismiss the whole thing without even going to trial. That was the kind of confidence this attorney had.

I met with Dragan and Luke in another meeting shortly after to get some more clarification and get a clearer picture of what happened. From Luke's own account, he was driving down his street a few blocks away from his house when he was stopped by two police officers and was motioned to pull over. The first thing they said was that he was speeding and was way over the speed limit for that zone. Next they ordered him out of the car, and one of the officers had him up against a fence doing the routine pat-down while the other was in his car searching. Luke said he almost passed out from shock when the announcement came that they found the gun in his glove compartment. Dragan said there was a mystery: the semiautomatic pistol was wiped clean of fingerprints but was inside Luke's car. How was that possible? The only other person who had driven his car was his cousin, about a year before. To get more clarity, Dragan asked Luke if it was possible that the gun could have been hidden there before the cops stopped him. Luke said that would be totally impossible; he hated guns and none of his friends carried them.

Dragan already had a file on each of the two cops; apparently, their entire life story, which he didn't share. But there was also a third file, and that one belonged to Nick. Dragan held up Nick's file and showed me the photograph on the front. "Is this your fiancé, Nick Draiblate?"

"Yes, that's him."

Dragan wrinkled his brow slightly as he glanced at Nick's file, but his expression quickly returned to normal. It was hardly noticeable, but I caught it. He held up the two photographs of the other officers and asked Luke if these were the men who arrested him. Luke recognized them immediately, and Dragan asked if I had ever seen them before. I studied the pictures carefully, and as much I was hoping I could pass them off as perfect strangers, there was something familiar about them. "I think I have seen them before."

Dragan looked at me with new interest, as if I had just entered the room and he had never seen me before. "Are you sure?"

"Yes, but I just can't remember where."

Dragan launched into a series of questions similar to those

a hypnotist would probably ask. His voice was calm and encouraging. "Take your time and consider if it was in your home, at a party, or on the street that you saw them. The quicker we are able to place them, the faster I can put the facts together and wrap this case up." He handed me a color photograph of the two officers.

I went home somewhat scared and extremely jumpy that day. I was grateful Nick wasn't there, and that night I went to work. The hustle and bustle at the Belly of the Pig was a blessing in disguise. The food tickets kept coming at a rate of about a dozen per minute, and I had no time to think of anything else. Hungry and unsatisfied customers in a restaurant weren't something to be taken lightly, and I kept that idea at the front of my mind while the pots bubbled and skillets sizzled. One of the most popular dishes that night was spinach and feta cheese lasagna rolls in green pea sauce.

SPINACH AND FETA CHEESE LASAGNA ROLLS

2 16-ounce packages frozen spinach (thawed)	1 small onion (diced)
	2 cloves garlic (minced)
	½ cup ricotta cheese
1 box wavy lasagna noodles	2 cups mozzarella cheese (reserve half for topping)
4 ounces feta cheese	
1 pound ground lamb	Salt and pepper

Green Pea Sauce

2 cups green peas (frozen peas are more readily available)	1 medium onion (chopped)
	¼ cup parmesan cheese
3 cups low-sodium vegetable stock	1 teaspoon salt-free garlic and herb seasoning
	3 cloves garlic (grated)

METHOD

For green pea sauce, bring vegetable stock to boil in a medium pot then add green peas. Cook peas for about 7 minutes. Then remove from flame and add all the other ingredients to the pot and stir well. With the use of an immersion blender, blend all the ingredients until they form a sauce. Set sauce aside.

Squeeze water from spinach in a towel or cheese cloth and set aside. Put lasagna noodles to boil according to package instructions. Remove noodles from the pot and drain well, then lay flat on wax paper or aluminum foil to prevent them from sticking. Brown lamb in a skillet after combining onion, garlic, salt, and pepper. Drain fat and set aside. In the same skillet combine ricotta cheese, feta cheese, and spinach, and cook for 5 minutes, stirring constantly. Turn off flame and add lamb and mozzarella cheese to the skillet, then stir to combine all the ingredients. Add about 2 tablespoons of the spinach mixture to each lasagna piece and roll each one individually. Ladle a few spoonfuls of the green pea sauce into a casserole pan and spread it along the bottom of the pan. Arrange the rolls neatly in the pan and cover with the green pea sauce. Top the dish with the remaining mozzarella cheese and bake at 375° for 30 minutes. Broil on low for about 5 minutes to get a beautiful golden crust. Make sure to keep an eye on the dish while broiling. Remove from oven and let it rest for 15 minutes before serving.

Pork was in much demand that night too, and why not? The place was called the Belly of the Pig. Many of the customers were looking at the pulled pork and plantains on the menu.

PULLED PORK AND PLANTAINS

1 teaspoon allspice (powder)

1 pork shoulder (about 3 pounds)

1 tablespoon black pepper

1 teaspoon sea salt

2 stalks scallions

8 cloves garlic
1 teaspoon onion powder
1 teaspoon dry thyme
2 cups apple cider vinegar
4 green plantains
1 tablespoon of vegetable oil
1 cup of low-sodium beef stock

METHOD

Clean pork using apple cider vinegar and paper towels to pat dry. Combine dry seasoning except black pepper to form a rub. Use a pointed knife to cut deep incisions in the pork and stuff with garlic cloves. Massage the pork with the dry rub seasoning mix and let it sit for 15 minutes in the refrigerator uncovered. Remove pork from refrigerator and bring it to room temperature. Brown pork on all sides in a large skillet, then drain fat and transfer to a slow cooker with pan drippings. Sprinkle with black pepper and add 1 cup of low-sodium beef stock to the slow cooker, cover, and cook on low for 8 hours. Set to boil a pot of salted water. Add 1 tablespoon of vegetable oil. Cut plantains into quarters with skin on and cook until plantains are tender and skins start to fall apart. Remove plantains from pot and peel skin away. Remove pork from slow cooker and reserve juices. Remove as much fat from pork as possible and shred with a fork. Mash plantains with a potato ricer and moisten with reserved juices from the slow cooker. Serve shredded pork hot over plantains, with a drizzle of tzatziki sauce and garnish with green scallions.

It was also a night for sauces, and one of our chefs, who was an expert in making them, made tzatziki sauce.

TZATZIKI SAUCE

1 clove garlic (grated)
Pinch of salt
1 teaspoon lemon juice
1 seedless cucumber (grated)
1 8-ounce container of Greek yogurt
1 teaspoon fresh dill

METHOD

Mince dill as fine as possible and extract water from the cucumber through a strainer. Discard the water and combine all the ingredients in a mixing bowl. Mix well, cover bowl, and place in a refrigerator for 2 hours. Your sauce is ready to serve and must remain refrigerated. Tzatziki sauce can last for over a week in the refrigerator.

In keeping with the theme of sauces, when a customer ordered crispy fried tilapia, it was quite fitting that some choice of sauces should be offered, and a caper sauce was chosen.

CAPER SAUCE

1 tablespoon butter
1 tablespoon whole wheat flour
1 cup milk
1 tablespoon chopped capers
1 teaspoon caper juice (vinegar in which capers were soaked)

METHOD

Melt the butter in a saucepan and gradually whisk in flour. Add milk little by little with constant stirring until the thickness of a sauce is achieved. Add capers and vinegar, stir, and remove from flame.

CRISPY FRIED TILAPIA

4 tilapia fillets
¼ cup whole wheat flour
¼ cup cornmeal
Salt
Zest of 1 lemon
2 tablespoons butter or margarine
¼ cup corn oil

METHOD

Mix flour, cornmeal, salt, and zest of lemon in a bowl. Dredge tilapia in flour mixture then shake off excess flour. Heat oil and butter in a skillet and fry fish until crispy and golden brown. Serve hot with caper sauce.

This dish was also served with a platter of glazed carrots.

GLAZED CARROTS

4 medium carrots (peeled)
1 teaspoon margarine
1 teaspoon olive oil

1 tablespoon ketchup
1 cup low-sodium chicken stock

METHOD
In a skillet, melt margarine in olive oil, and then add carrots. Sauté the carrots in the oil and margarine on high heat until they are lightly browned, then add ketchup and cook for another minute. Adjust heat as needed. Gradually add the chicken stock until glaze is formed and carrots are tender.

Chapter Five

I kept the pictures of the two police officers in my bag, studying their faces daily. A whole long week passed by and there was no breakthrough in remembering where I saw them. My relationship with Nick didn't change, and I wished I could find a way to clear Luke of the crime and also Nick of the halo of suspicion shining above his head.

The Badger was a social networking site very similar to all the popular ones on the Internet. The only difference was that the members were primarily police officers and other members of the armed forces. Ninety-five percent of the people who joined were in that category. The few people who weren't were in some way connected to the men and women of law enforcement. Nick showed me the site when we first got involved. It seemed he wanted to prove to me that he had nothing to hide and we could trust each other. He encouraged me to join the site, which was another way for us to communicate and leave each other silly messages and posts. Using a fictitious name was okay, Nick said, so he picked one out for me. The Red Vixen was my screen name, and for my profile picture I wore a red wig and other accessories to go with the redness. This was totally for him, and so we created this persona only he recognized and who was quite fulfilling to this fantasy he had. The Red Vixen could only talk to Nick on this site, but surely attracted a lot of attention once I was signed on, but I ignored them all. Nick had 772 friends and I had only one, him. It really didn't matter to me because it was his fantasy and not mine.

The members posted pictures, vented, blogged, and all the beauty and ugliness in human beings came out as usual. I wrote things on Nick's wall and he bragged to his friends about me in the very same space, and so I eagerly went to his site sometimes to see what he was up to and what he was venting about. He had just started to do a lot more overtime than usual, filling in here and there for friends who were out sick or on vacation, but had promised to cut all of that once we got married. All this overtime would be spent with me he said.

It was a slow night at work about a week after the meeting with Dragan and Luke, and on breaks from updating recipes, I went to my webpage on Badger. There was no note from Nick, so I went to his page, and there wasn't much activity there either. I wasn't surprised; where would he find time? The poor guy was busy fighting crime. Next I clicked on his friends and just started to randomly scroll through the list. I stopped at the familiar ones I knew well then moved on. Most of these friends he had met at the police academy, others he worked with, and some requested his friendship through other mutual friends. I couldn't tell who was who in each particular case, but he knew them all on some level.

I continued through the list, and suddenly, I froze at a particular face, lingering in disbelief and terror. I move on down the list of friends and stopped at another familiar and frightening face. In despair, I must have touched the wrong key, because the computer screen blanked out and the page was gone for a moment, and I eventually found myself at a search engine. I held on to the edge of the chair as if to balance myself, and I heard people in the restaurant talking but didn't know who they were. I felt as if I was on another planet, or my mind was playing tricks. brought myself back to the restaurant where I was working and the computer before me. The two men I'd just looked at on Nick's page were the police officers who arrested Luke. They were the two officers Dragan wanted me to remember. I closed the page and shut the computer down then rushed to the bathroom. I closed the door and just stayed there for a few moments while my forehead felt as if it was resting on a hot plate. A cold, damp towel helped. My eyes happened to focus on the time: my watch said 9:07. I knew I had to get in touch with Dragan, as was our agreement.

I retrieved Dragan's business card and dialed his cell number. After several rings, I got his voicemail and left a detailed message and asked him to call me back as soon as he received it. After that, I tried calling Luke. He answered and there was a lot of noise in the background, and I knew he was in a bar, probably doing what most people do when their lives are spinning out of control. They drink. "Hey, Glor, what's going on?"

"Luke, could you come by the restaurant. We need to talk and I need to show you something."

"Sorry, Glor, I'm in enough trouble as it is. Nick sent me a very powerful message to keep my distance. He wants my head on a platter."

"Yes, and I want to fix that problem, so please get yourself over here. I'm trying to sort things out. And if you haven't eaten yet, I can make some fish and chips."

"I had it all figured out a long time ago, but with the odds stacked up against me, what chance do I have?"

"Luke, listen to me. Can you drive? Should I come and get you?"

He babbled on for another couple of seconds while I listened. Then he said, "I'll be there."

"Okay then, I'll start the fryer."

I hung up the phone on the wall, and when it rang a few minutes later, it was Dragan on the line. I was standing in front of a fryer of bubbling hot oil; I was dropping in cutlets of snapper and watching them float to the bottom of the frying machine. "Gloribella?" he started out after I made the formal greeting, "Belly of the Pig, may I help?"

"Dragan Bradshaw here."

"Hope you're not in pajamas by now, Dragan."

"No, no, not at all. Actually, I'm just leaving the office. We've been working on a difficult case with a colleague of mine. What's up?" I pictured him putting his papers together with the cell phone glued to his ear, six feet tall with a receding hairline, and moving very light on his feet with the perfect weight for his body size. His appeal, along with other qualities in his personality, fit his career exceedingly well. The moment I met Dragan, there was very little hesitation in putting Luke's case in his hands, and it was that charisma that made him so successful. His confidence made him totally trustworthy. That was my first impression of him, and that was still the mental image I held when I was on the other end of the line with him.

"Dragan, could you stop by the restaurant; Luke is on his way here as well." I knew that was how he worked both formally and informally or else I would never have asked.

"Well ... yes, of course."

While I stood by the fryer, I thought about Nick. The emotions of disappointment, betrayal, and anger came and went just like the bubbles in the frying oil.

Dragan arrived at the restaurant before Luke did. I wasn't surprised, and after a few minutes, I wondered if Luke would ever show up at all. The Belly of the Pig was still quite scanty when I sat down with Dragan in an isolated booth. If I was the owner, I would just close the place and send the staff home, but Zachary, the owner, needed to collect every last penny.

I introduced Dragan to the menu that we invested a lot of time over the years perfecting, giving him a brief summary of what some of the dishes consisted of, since he wanted to know. If I was to guess his age, I would have said he was somewhere around thirty-eight to early forties and was definitely the marrying type. The single light beam over the booth showed his gold wedding band as he leafed through the menu folder. When he was all done, all he wanted was a glass of carrot juice. Before I could ask why, he apologetically explained that his wife went through the trouble of making him chicken kabocha dumplings with anchovy caper dip and he dared not go home to tell her that he had already eaten. As a result, he had been practically having only liquids all day. He assured me that he would return to the Belly of the Pig pretty soon, bringing his friends as new customers. Now I understood why he remained so slim and trim; he was highly disciplined. Instead of a glass, Jasmina brought him a whole pitcher of carrot juice made from carrots, almond milk, sugar, and nutmeg.

As Dragan was about to pour the juice in a glass, Luke walked in. Jasmina brought the fish and chips, and Luke dove in immediately. We then launched into what must have been one of the most difficult conversations I have ever had. I had come to terms with my suspicion that Nick might definitely have had something to do with Luke's trouble. I showed them Nick's social networking page and the two cops as his friends. We explored the possibility of what could have happened, and then Dragan assured Luke that he would make sure he walked as a free man. He drove the point home when he showed us a video that was sent to him. It was captured on a kid's cell phone camera at the time of the incident. The boy was passing at the precise moment when Luke was stopped, and while one of the cops had Luke up against a fence searching him, the other was busy in his car. The kid took a close up, and when the video went into slow motion, we saw exactly how the cop planted the gun in the glove compartment.

Dragan explained that he had gone into the neighborhood and interviewed over fifty people, and at least five saw the incident, but none was as comprehensive as the twelve-year-old boy with the cell phone camera.

One of the last things Dragan said to me before walking through the door. "Gloribella, I'm not in your shoes, but if I was, I would have some tough questions for the one I was going to marry."

At 12:30 a.m., when the restaurant closed, I couldn't go

home. I wasn't ready to face Nick. I was too angry and acting as if all was well would be unbearable. I walked over to the Quality Inn and spent the rest of the night there. When I got home at 8:45 a.m., he was out, which gave me even more time to put my thoughts together. My first impulse was to search Nick's room, but I had no idea what I would be looking for. I passed the door several times and couldn't go in, since part of me thought it was wrong. I knew I wasn't going in there to put his laundry away as I often did. My determination to play this sleuth, and for a good cause, was crowded with doubts and fear, but eventually, despite the uncanny feeling, I did go in. The bed was unmade, as usual, which had become a joke between us. "I will remember to make the bed when I am sharing it with someone other than just me," was Nick's common excuse. Another burst of doubts and regrets entered my mind because I knew that once I started this there was no turning back. The life we had had before would never be the same.

Next to the bed, a door opened into a large walk-in closet. Nick had lots of things that were still not unpacked, and the closet itself was like a never-ending tunnel of darkness. It took two bulbs to illuminate the space. The first section of the closet, closest to the entrance, was where all the clothes were kept. They were neatly hung on hangers of polished wood. Ties and shoes had their own little section further back. Some shoes were still in boxes, just like the day they came from the store. Farther back in the closet it was dark, and that's where the second bulb would have come in handy, but it was burnt out and never replaced. I tried the light switch a couple of times just to make sure the light mechanism wasn't playing tricks on me, but yes, the bulb was really blown. I searched for a flashlight and found one that gave me enough light to see the stack of things back there. The not-unpacked things in the darkness were mainly suitcases piled on top of each other. There was a total of four.

Nothing was unusual about the suitcases, and it would take time to go through all of them. I turned off the flashlight and walked away. My lack of determination to turn the closet upside down might have been the result of guilt, but I also had a strange feeling that someone was watching me in the semidarkness of the space. There were moments when I felt the steady gaze of invisible eyes, perhaps the lens of a camera, which would have been impossible to detect considering the way the storage area was constructed.

I went to the kitchen to make some tea, which I figured would calm my nerves. As the water began to boil, I became conscious of the whistling of the kettle. It was like the eerie call of a creature I couldn't identify. Shutting off the stove, I could see the heavy puffs of steam emitting from the kettle and turning into vapors that vanished in the far corner of the kitchen.

While the teabag steeped, I checked my messages and voicemails. There was a voicemail from Nick that I didn't know about. It was recorded at about 11:00 p.m., while I was still at the restaurant. Nick was saying that he was stuck at work with a double shift and couldn't come home. He said I should meet him for brunch at the Honey Pot, a local diner close by.

I called him back right away and he picked up after two rings. "Hi, Nick, I just saw your message."

"It's okay, baby. I haven't had time to look at my phone either. Had a helluva night. I'll tell you about it later. Is the Honey Pot okay?"

"Yeah."

"What time?"

"Eleven-thirty is good."

"Okay, sweets, looking forward to it."

The Honey Pot was within walking distance, so I had a whole hour to torture myself with guilt. After the cup of tea, I was actually feeling better, and I thought of some mindless task to keep myself busy before I faced Nick.

I turned on the robotic vacuum cleaner and watched it glide across the floor. Room to room it went, under tables and chairs and back into the open. It was doing a thorough job of cleaning the house. Did I do a complete job in searching Nick's room to uncover the truth behind this crisis? This might be the only chance I would ever get. While I was there talking to myself, the robotic cleaner went around me and continued with its business of cleaning. I went straight back to Nick's room, and standing close to the bed, I looked at everything that was within view and all neatly in place. There was nothing questionable, not a single object, written note, or anything that could implicate him in any wrongdoing as far as I could see.

While I was there contemplating, the robotic cleaner entered the room. It sensed that I was standing there and went around me and under the bed. It stayed there for a couple of minutes, humming, and then came out from another side of the bed. I was inspired and energized by the artificial house cleaner and went straight for the walk-in closet.

My curiosity was aroused when I gazed at the large suitcases at the far back of the closet, and I wouldn't be satisfied until I knew what was in them. I went back to the dark corner, and with the aid of the flashlight, I managed to get the first suitcase flat on the floor. I unzipped the huge thing, and there was no big surprise. It was neatly packed with sweaters. Many of them were still unworn, with their tags and labels in place. The garments were fragranced with some sort of cologne or delicate soap and emitted a very masculine scent. After looking through the first suitcase, I quickly moved to the next, and it turned out to be just more clothes and personal items not yet opened. I fixed everything in pretty much the same order I found them and moved on to the next suitcase, the third one. By then I had started to question again why I was doing this and what was I hoping to find. More importantly, how would I start this conversation with Nick? It was a discussion that couldn't be postponed, considering the new information at hand and the likelihood that he could be involved with Luke's arrest. The need for honesty between us was as important as water was crucial for the sustaining of life. The lies, secrets, and half-truths were taking their toll and becoming a barrier in the communication we once had. I almost injured my back lifting the third suitcase and was wondering how heavy books could

INFUSED   57

be when packed together. Nick had previously told me that he had lots of books on various subjects, but I had never seen the entire stack. I assumed they were still packed somewhere or at his parents' house. Normally, people would pack books into boxes, but Nick was in a hurry to move, so a suitcase was probably his best choice for his books.

When I opened the suitcase, I jumped backed in horror; the suitcase was packed with guns of various descriptions. The fourth and last suitcase was the same, guns and ammunition neatly packed in rows. My suspicion that there was more to Nick than I previously thought was confirmed. As I quickly put the suitcases back in the order I found them, panic set in, but even in that state of mind I realized I would need proof of what I had seen. I ran for my camera and took as many pictures as I could of the entire scene, including the contents of the suitcases. By then, my mind was going wild, my thinking was askew, and I was running about the apartment grabbing the most important things I owned and shoving them into a bag. Then I went out the door, slamming it behind me.

Before I meet Nick at the Honey Pot, I stopped downtown at the bank and dropped off some of the stuff I grabbed, at the safety deposit box I had previously rented.

I was about a minute late and Nick was already seated. I could see the tired look on his face from the lack of sleep, and a certain degree of vulnerability. There were two inner voices in my head as I looked at him; one was telling me to go easy on him and the other reminded me of the idiom "a wolf in sheep's clothing." Had I not hired the right lawyer, the probability of Luke going to prison would have been much higher.

Nick stood up and pulled out a chair next to him. "I already ordered your favorite, hope you don't mind. Earl Grey with two teaspoons of honey; just as sweet as you are."

The true mark of a sociopath, I thought to myself, and the charm would have work if I didn't know the truth. "Hi, Nick, thanks." The inner voices came back, and the soft one was saying, be polite, you'll get through this, just don't succumb;

yet at the same time, my face was on fire with fury as I took the seat he offered me.

"I didn't want to scare you in the voicemail," he began, "but it was a night of living hell. My partner got shot right in front of me. So between the hospital and all the reports I had to write, I'm lucky to be sitting here next to you and not in an asylum."

If he was suspicious of what I had discovered and this was a plot to disarm me, it surely wasn't going to work. "I am sorry; I didn't know it was that bad."

"Yeah …" He rambled on. "Well, here I am unloading all my misery on you without asking about you."

"Well, the nightmares just won't go away, will they?"

"Nightmares? Nightmares of what?"

"Of Luke going to prison."

Nick became silent for a moment, removing his cap and scratching his head. "Well, if it's just for the gun in his possession, he might not do any time because of his clean record, but let's say he did commit a crime with the gun … well … we don't know. The law can be quite arbitrary. We just have to leave it up to the judge and his lawyer. G., a crime is a crime, and there are consequences."

"You see, that's the problem. Luke did not commit a crime. The only crime he committed was having me as a friend, and I feel awful about it."

"Why do you say that? Oh … well, I got it … but that's his opinion. I can't change his belief, but I have nothing to do with his problems."

"Nick, this is more than an opinion and a belief. He has good reasons to think you are involved."

"Yeah? How so?"

"Well, for starters, the two officers who are on the case, you claim you didn't know them, but you are friends with them on Badger. They posted on your wall before and after the arrest."

"Yes, G., friends in the social media, but not in actual life. There is a difference. I'm sure you are aware of that."

"You told me you didn't know them."

"I don't!" he insisted. "G., why this questioning? You don't trust me? We are about to get married."

"Nick, you have got to come clean with me about everything if we are getting married. There can't be any secrets."

"But there are no secrets," he protested.

"No secrets? But we are sharing an apartment with two suitcases of guns and ammunition, enough to start an army, and you are saying there are no secrets?" He opened his mouth to say something, but for once he couldn't think fast enough. I took the ring off and placed it on the table in front of him. He stared at it and closed his eyes then opened them again. As he did so, beads of tears were forming at the corners of his eyes. "I don't think we are ready for a lifelong commitment." I pointed to the ring on the table as a reference to the commitment I was talking about. I couldn't avoid noticing how beautiful it was, even more dazzling than the day it was fished from the box of talcum powder. "I am leaving now, Nick. I can't do this." I walked away without saying anything more and did not wait for his reaction.

As I walked through the city, I heard bells tolling from a nearby church. It was either announcing the midday hour or making a mockery of the wedding I thought I could have had. I went to see Dragan and told him what just had happened. I left the chip from the camera with him of the closet pictures. "Go!" he said. "Go someplace far and clear your head. I'll take care of the rest. I'm very sorry about this mess, but everything is going to be alright."

I did a few more things before I headed for Soy. I called my boss, Zachary, to tell him that there had been an emergency and I needed to take off for a while, no further explanation other than I was heading for my birthplace. All he said was to keep him posted and he'd call Paul, the replacement chef. Zachary had two executive chefs, Allison and me, and we alternated between the night and day shifts. He made enough money to keep Paul on a retainer's fee so Allison and I could have breaks, since Zachary no longer came to the restaurant. He ran the business from home. All correspondence was done over the telephone and the Internet and an occasional meeting at his apartment after midnight. He hadn't been in public since his bariatric condition worsened. He went from 160 to 500 pounds after his divorce and became a recluse. We could not help Zachary until he was ready to help himself and we always hoped he didn't die before he was ready to make that decision.

When I hung up the phone with Zachary, I thought to myself, *Who I am kidding; I can never go back, not ever.* Even at that point, I felt as if I couldn't be honest with him for a couple of reasons. First, I was thinking that I'd failed him and all that he taught me about the business went down the drain. Second, I didn't want to tell him exactly what had happened or why the sudden departure, quitting the job on the spot without any notice. I just couldn't think of any quick, believable story off the top of my mind.

I knew Nick wasn't going to give up that easily. As soon as he pulled himself together and devised another plan, he would seek revenge and come after me. The guns in the house weren't something he wanted me to know about, and I shuddered as I wondered why he was keeping them or who he was holding them for.

Chapter Six

For the remainder of that night in the mission house, my mind went in and out of the past, and sleep was very sporadic. The next morning, I met Reverend Tanner in the kitchen having coffee and reading the newspaper. He showed me the gifts he had for all his missionary house guests: coffee mugs. I made breakfast for the group, breakfast quiche in mugs.

QUICHE IN MUGS

1 egg
½ cup milk
2 tablespoons cheddar cheese (grated)
¼ cup bacon bits
1 slice whole wheat bread (crumbled)
1 pinch Mrs. Dash® table blend salt free seasoning

METHOD
Spray coffee mug with non-stick cooking spray and add crumbled bread. Beat egg and milk in a bowl, then whisk in bacon bits

and Mrs. Dash® table blend seasoning. Pour mixture on bread in mug and top with cheddar cheese. Cook in microwave oven for 1 minute uncovered. Carefully remove the hot mug from the microwave and let it cool for another minute. This recipe can be refrigerated overnight and cooked in the morning.

Then I took Onn for a walk around Truro to where people from Soy were still hanging out and trying to make sense of their lives and the rebuilding process that was to come. I went from shop to shop, hoping someone would recognize the boy, but it wasn't happening. I thought about the renewing of my own life and wondered how I could help Onn, but the mystery of him was yet to be solved. I estimated his age to be about ten, taking into account his physical build, but I could have been wrong. Onn didn't say much; he preferred action, and every now and then he would surprise me with something new. Reverend Tanner took a picture of him and asked me if he could publish it in the local papers in Truro and the surrounding towns of Cape Cod. Anyone who knew of him would more than likely to come forward.

It was about 12:30 p.m. when I took Onn out for lunch. I made a quick dash to the restroom while I waited for the food, and I happened to glanced in the mirror. My complexion was pale and I had probably dropped ten pounds. Our lunch order was fish and chips to go, so I led us quickly out of the restaurant after seeing what I looked like. I truly didn't want to be around people if I could help it. Most of all I needed time to reflect and think about what I should do next.

The boardwalk where all the boats were lined up was the perfect place to sit and have lunch. Opening up the brown paper bag, the aroma of the meal was overpowering and just as good as the way we made it at the Belly of the Pig. Our dish was:

FISH AND BAKED SWEET POTATO CHIPS

2 pounds cat fish fillets or tilapia fillets
1 cup whole wheat flour
¼ cup wheat germ
1 tablespoon black pepper
1 envelope Maggi fish seasoning
2 cups buttermilk
Oil for frying
2 pounds sweet potatoes (about 3 medium potatoes)
1 tablespoon olive oil
Sea salt

METHOD

Soak fish in buttermilk for an hour, and while fish is soaking, clean and peel potatoes. Cut potatoes into wedges and coat with olive oil. Heat oven to 400° and spray baking sheet with non-stick cooking spray. Arrange potato wedges on tray about ½ an inch apart and bake until tender and golden brown. Combine whole wheat flour along with all other dry ingredients in a shallow bowl then pat fish dry with a paper towel. Cut fish in pieces about 3 inches long, then coat well in flour mixture. Set fish on a wire rack and heat oil in a suitable skillet and fry fish on both sides in batches until golden brown. Remove fish from skillet and place on another wire rack. Remove potatoes from oven and serve hot with fish.

My mother was the first person who taught me to make fish and chips, just before she became seriously religious later in her adult life. My mother worked as a waitress when she wasn't in the theatre or doing auditions. At one of these waitress jobs, she met a young woman with whom she developed a friendship. For several months, the woman invited her to visit the Pentecostal church, and each time she refused. When we were small children my parents were devout Catholics. They never missed a single communion. After one visit to the Pentecostal church, the lives of my family members were changed forever. My mom was baptized that same night and came home speaking in tongues. By the end of the week, in my mother's mind, we were all heathens and would go to hell if we did not follow her lead. Of course, she couldn't get my father to agree or any of my siblings to go to church with her. We were all rebellious teenagers doing our own stuff with no time for church.

After my college graduation, my mom threw me the most lavish party one could have imagined. She went as far as to invite friends from my childhood, people I hadn't seen in many years. At the helm of this party were her new friends from the Pentecostal church, her present inner circle. Then my mom did something that was totally unexpected and out of character. Just before the party was over, she introduced me to a man who was about twice my age, the assistant pastor in the church. He had great manners, was quite polite, and would certainly be a good catch for most women on the prowl for a husband.

We talked for a few minutes, and then I returned to the other guests. At the end of the night, when the party was over, he said, "Great meeting you, Gloribella. Sister Frank was right. You are every bit as beautiful as she said. Hope we can have lunch sometime soon." Only then did I realized what my mom had done: she was matching me up with this man. I didn't realize how serious she was until the next day when she pulled me aside to talk. She was wearing a permanent ear-to-ear smile and occasionally she giggled like a schoolgirl hungry for gossip from her best friend. The scary part of the whole thing was, my mother was never that kind of a parent. She was very strict and quite particular with everything we did, from dressing to our choice of friends, and she made it quite clear, "I am your mother, not your friend."

Excitedly, Mom said to me, "So what do you think about him?"

"About who, Mom?"

"Alex, of course, Reverend Mulroney, you silly girl!"

I shrugged my shoulders, not quite sure how to respond seeing the eagerness in her expression. "He has all the qualities of a minister and he is quite polite."

"Gloribella, let me put it to you this way, he's crazy about you."

"Mom, how could he be? We've only met once and he knows nothing about me."

"Sweetheart, men don't necessarily have to know anything about you at first sight. The attraction is there and that's all that matters for now. It is the first impression that he'll remember."

"Mom, I don't know about this. You should have at least given me the heads up before we were introduced."

"There wasn't enough time and I didn't know he would be smitten so quickly. Another thing is, the young girls in the church are already battling and competing for his attention. Sooner or later, one of them will catch his eye."

"Mom, has this man ever been married? He's over forty, isn't he?"

"As a matter of fact, he was at around the age of nineteen. A terrible mistake, he told me. He was way too young, and within a matter of months, he was separated, and ultimately, he was divorced from this girl. Gloribella, take the advice of a silly old goat of a mother and marry Alex when he asks you."

"But how do you know these things, Mom? This man is practically a stranger."

"I made it my business to find out what is important. Alex is a man of God and he respects women. He adored his mother, and that in itself is a plus. I want what is best for you, Gloribella. You are beautiful, smart, educated; you would make the perfect wife for Reverend Mulroney. I have seen the others who are going after him and they are not even worthy to walk in your shoes."

"Mom, you have esteemed me very high, and I love you too, but I do have flaws."

"Who doesn't, child? Your heavenly father sees every one of them, and through prayer, you will overcome all the shortcomings and have beautiful children for Alex. I can already picture them, my grandchildren. And, my love, pay no attention to those other guys who are lusting after you. I can already tell they are all wrapped in expensive packaging, but that's all there is to it. Alex is the real deal."

Needless to say, I didn't marry Alex, and I never went on a date with him, since I didn't want to lead him on. The glowing picture of him that my mother painted was probably true, but I didn't want to find out. There was no way I was going to marry a man my mother handpicked for me, especially one I wasn't attracted to.

Not very long after the incident, Mom became very cold towards me, and eventually we stopped speaking to each other. She became so indignant that I was forced to leave home. I saw a side of her that I never knew existed. I moved to Boston and stayed in touch with only my dad. I visited him on his birthdays and on Father's Day every year. I never came closer to Soy than Truro to meet him.

I learned that after a while my father caved in and went to the Pentecostal church with Mom. I knew his heart wasn't in it; he did it only to please her and to get some peace at home. Dad kept himself busy with his job as a piano tuner, driving from town to town as the occupation demanded.

Following up on Alex, he did get married to a woman in the church, and from the union they had one child, but then she disappeared with her child shortly after. According to my sister Mia, I might have dodged a bullet.

When my father started to get ill and just before he passed away, my mother reached out to me for the first time in several years. Nick and I drove up from Boston to the Pentecostal church where my family was worshiping. Then something happened in the service that I didn't quite understand. The people suddenly came up to Nick, laid their hands on him, and started to pray. It was all unintelligible because they were quite loud, speaking all at the same time, and half of it was in tongues. Nick, of course, was embarrassed when I asked him later what was wrong with him. Whatever it was, the whole church was ignited and quite stirred. He didn't respond and I dropped the subject and moved on.

As I went in and out of reminiscence, visiting the past and trying to determine how to move forward, Onn and I finished the lunch of fish and chips. The kid went back to the solving of his Rubik's cube. This was probably the third time he solved the puzzle since it was given to him. The big question on my mind was, where was my mother? Did something tragic happen to her? As far as the officials knew, there were no fatalities that they could verify at that point. People were missing, yes, but there was no supporting evidence that they had perished in the fire. It was a daytime explosion, and therefore not many people were home. There were injuries, and those people were being treated at a local hospital.

I went back to the mission house during the late afternoon and was asked to make dinner for the visiting missionaries, so I went through the pantry and came up with a dish that could serve a dozen or so people. The meal was curried beef with mushroom and celery rice.

CURRIED BEEF

- 3 pounds chuck steak (cut into cubes)
- ¼ cup vegetable oil
- ½ teaspoon sea salt
- 2 stalks scallions
- 1 large onion (chopped)
- 2 tablespoons curry powder (more or less depending on how strong you want curry to be)
- 2 teaspoons grated ginger
- 2 cups low-sodium beef stock
- 3 fresh okra (minced)
- 4 cloves garlic (crushed)
- ¼ teaspoon ground thyme
- 1 cup butternut squash (cubed)

METHOD

Clean beef with apple cider vinegar and dry with paper towels, then season with salt, curry, ground thyme, crushed garlic, ginger, and onion. Let meat sit for an hour. Heat oil in a skillet then remove meat from seasoning and scrape off all pieces of seasoning sticking to the meat. Brown the beef cubes in batches until golden brown.

Drain fat and return meat to the skillet along with seasoning that was scraped off. Add butternut squash and minced okra along with low-sodium beef stock. Bring pot to a rapid boil for 5 minutes then cover and let it simmer for an hour, stirring occasionally. Remove pot from flame and add chopped scallions.

MUSHROOM CELERY RICE

2 cups rice	2 cups celery (chopped)
4 cups low-sodium vegetable stock	4 cups mushrooms (chopped)
1 tablespoon margarine	2 tablespoons avocado oil

METHOD

Cook rice in vegetable stock according to the 2:1 liquid to rice ratio. On a medium heat, brown and cook mushrooms in a skillet with margarine. When mushrooms are brown and the liquid has evaporated, remove from skillet. Heat avocado oil in the same skillet and cook celery for about 5 minutes. Fluff rice with a fork and transfer to a serving bowl, then fold in mushrooms and celery. Serve hot with beef curry.

After having the curried beef, the missionaries were quite blown away by the dish and wanted to know more about other curry dishes, so I shared the following with them. Most, if not all meats, can be curried, so using the same recipe for curried beef, or beef curry as some people call it, they just needed to substitute the meat. Goat and lamb made great curries. Same for poultry: chicken, turkey, duck, etc. Pork could make an excellent curry, and with all meats, including some bone added additional flavor. They could be removed before the dish was served. When using poultry in your curry it might be necessary to reduce the cooking time by about 15 minutes, and dark meat was always better for curry. Sister Bertha wanted to make a dish of split peas curry, so this was the recipe that I gave her:

SPLIT PEA CURRY

1¼ cups yellow split peas
1 quart chicken stock
4 cloves garlic
1 onion (chopped)
2 tablespoons curry powder (more or less depending on how strong you wanted your curry to be)

1 tablespoon grated ginger
¼ teaspoon ground thyme
1 tablespoon margarine
2 stalk scallions
2 okras (minced)

METHOD

Wash split peas, then search through and remove any hidden particles among the grains. In another suitable pot, sauté onion, garlic, okra, and ginger in margarine for 3 minutes then add split peas. With continuous stirring of the mixture for another minute, add curry powder and thyme until split peas are slightly toasted. Add the chicken stock and bring the pot to a rapid boil for a minute then turn the flame to low. Stir constantly until grains begins to dissolve and the curry thickens. If the curry becomes too thick, add more chicken stock and seasoning to the pot. Serve hot over rice and garnish with scallions.

I woke up the next morning to the aroma of bacon and coffee, and as I approached the kitchen, I could hear chatter and laughter. The missionaries were already making breakfast with Steve and Vera as the main cooks. They urged me to help myself to coffee and to the large platter of eggs, toast, sausages, and bacon. It was the final day of their stay in the mission house, and Vera and Steve wanted to do something special for everyone before their departure. A contact list was drafted as we ate and drank, and the list was passed around. When it was completed, Reverend Tanner made copies and handed them out. It was sort of a bitter-sweet moment because, despite the unity we shared at the time, in a few hours, it would all be over, and some of us would be on our way to other parts of the earth.

Onn sat with us at the table, but his mind was totally on the new paper art he picked up from Steve and Vera. He glanced eagerly every now and then at his stack of origami paper, which he had been meticulously transforming into objects. He was just waiting for the moment when he could start working on them again.

Zorro was such a catchy and appropriate name for an artist such as the one at the table with us. I didn't quite get his life story or what his role would be on the mission field. He was charismatic and could grab one's attention just with a simple comment, such as, "The buttons on your shirt, I've seen them before." His paintings were beautiful, especially the one he did of Cambridge College where he was a student.

Then there was the couple from Iran whose mission was to teach Arabic at a school in Boston, and at the far end of the table, facing me, was the quietest one in the room, Hortense, a young woman who seemed to have travelled all over the world doing missionary work, from Canada to New Deli. All she said was that she missed her cat and that a friend was taking care of it in Christchurch, New Zealand, where she resides. "Gloribella," she said to me, "will you send me a few of your recipes? Your food is very good."

"As soon as I sit before a computer again, I will send you the recipes."

"Where is your computer?"

"In a vault."

That ended the conversation between us, but she looked at me as if she had just read my thoughts and knew everything that was going on in my life.

The minister instructed us to form a circle and he prayed, after which his wife and eldest daughter sang a duet, and then the scripture about the mission of the *seventy-two* was read. The next half an hour or so was basically a church service with the sacraments of the Holy Communion and the washing of feet. At certain intervals I felt quite out of place not being a missionary in the true sense of the word. I wasn't even a regular churchgoer.

When the missionaries were gone and all the rooms were empty, it didn't feel right staying there anymore without a mission of my own. Obviously, there were things for me to do, so I revisited my contact list of all my relatives and friends who could possibly know of the whereabouts of my mother, picking up where I left off the last time in the search for Mom. Everyone I spoke to was just as concerned, disturbed, and eager to know what had happened to her. My brothers, Sam and Owen, were beside themselves with worry, and my sister Pilar was clueless and holding on to her faith, but Mia had an idea. "Mom had started to date again."

"Any mention as to who the lucky guy is?"

"No. I don't think she is ready to bring him to the family as yet. He is quite wealthy from what I understand."

"Sounds like Mom." I remembered that when she was frustrated with Dad she would always say if she could do it again, she would definitely find a rich man.

"I'm sorry, Gloribella, I don't even know the man's name. I didn't think it was any of my business or even important at the time."

"Do you think she is with him now?"

"Quite possibly, but I'm not sure."

"How long did you know about this, Mia?"

"Only a week before the fire. I thought you knew ..."

"Mia, I'm the last person Mom would tell about her personal life. You know that."

"Yeah ... but stranger things have happened."

My mother was trained in theatre and always blamed us for her not making it big and going on to Hollywood. Apparently, this new person in her life started out as a fan of her shows at the local theatre, but none of this tale could be confirmed. As far as we knew, this might only be a myth.

After I got off the phone with my sister, I made a quick preliminary plan of what I was going to do when I left the mission house that day. Going back to Boston was off the list because I could never see Nick again. I thought about settling in another small town close to Truro until the matter with Onn was sorted out.

Back in the streets of Truro, I look around for a real estate agency, hoping I could talk to an agent who might point me in the right direction of what I was looking for. Then I saw a young woman staring down at the sidewalk as if she had just lost something. As she scanned the street corner, she checked her bag and pockets. I knew she must have lost something, a ring, perhaps an earring. It had to be something small the way she was looking. Unconsciously, I looked down myself to see if I could be of any help in locating the missing object, having no clue as to what it might be. We both looked up at the same time, and after a few seconds, our eyes met. We recognized each other immediately. "Lauren! What are you doing here, and more importantly, what did you lose?"

"Oh, my God! Gloribella! The home economics teacher? How many years has it been?"

"Many, many."

She looked at Onn holding on to me, "Oh ... your son? So cute."

I paused, deciding what to say to avoid the awkward questions, but looking at her, I could see that she had changed her hair color to a sort of maroon red with a purple tint, so there would be at least one other thing to talk about. I turned to Onn. "Did you hear? She said you were cute. Say thank you." He looked up at Lauren, nodded, and smiled.

It seemed so long ago when I taught home economics briefly at Holy Cross Middle School in Soy. Lauren was the substitute teacher for special ed. Although I thought she would be better as a gossip columnist, she was a good teacher and had a knack for the profession. We worked collaboratively on an article and would sometimes hang out after work. After I left Holy Cross, and subsequently Soy, I lost contact with Lauren, like with so many other people over the years. The fire in Soy had drawn many folks back to check on their families, and Lauren was among the many. Her family got out safely.

Well, we both had some time to spare that morning, so we

walked around Truro for a long time catching up on the latest gossip and sharing things in our lives. Lauren had moved away from the area long ago, to Cambridge, Massachusetts, and was recently married and expecting her first child. I clued her in on the situation with Onn, but she was shocked when she found out that I had no idea as to where my mother was. "Oh ... my God! I'm so sorry. I hope Miss Estella is okay!"

"Well ... we're holding up, and my sister Pilar is praying, we all are."

My sister Pilar became a nun shortly after she left college. It sent a shockwave through our family, and my mother almost had a stroke when Pilar made the announcement. But the first time I saw her in her religious garb, her habit, I knew she was happy and content. Her personality had never changed. Articulate, confident, and ready to take charge of situations, that was Pilar. We met her at the airport, coming from Rome, and I almost wanted to be a nun myself. She was dressed in blue and white and wore a cross of shining silver. She was tall and almost like a model for the Vatican walking down the runway.

"Onn is so attached to you. I would never have thought he wasn't your son. I am a practical person, but I would be inclined to believe this is an omen of some sort, a good one, though. I hope my baby will grow up to love me just as much as this little boy loves you."

"I'm sure your baby will love you even more; it's the natural order of things."

"There are no guarantees, are there? Pregnancy alone carries a million and one risks."

"Something tells me you'll be fine, Lauren." She didn't respond to my affirmation.

"How long are you staying in Truro, Gloribella?"

"I wish I had the answer, but that would depend on a lot of things."

"I only asked because I'm signing up with a volunteer group at one of the refugee camps. Would you like to stop by? I know your hands are already full, but who knows what you might discover."

I wasn't quite sure why I agreed, considering that would totally alter my plan of going to the real estate agency I had been searching for.

The campsite we arrived at was an old warehouse about the size of a football field not far from the waterfront. A Red Cross van was parked outside next to the Porter Potty Johns. Inside the camp folding beds, sleeping bags, and cots were everywhere. After passing through the sleeping quarters, we entered a kitchen set up to feed the hungry. As soon as we entered the space, a man in a chef's uniform approached us. "I am Avery. Are you the new volunteers?"

My plan for the day didn't include volunteering for anything, because mentally and emotionally I wasn't up to it. But for the last few days, I'd been trying very hard to keep my mind active, and a diversion such as volunteering might be just the thing for me. There was also something about the urgency in the man's voice that had a lot to do with why I said, "Yes, we are the new volunteers."

"I need to leave soon, but don't worry, you are not alone. Others will be joining you as well," the chef said. Well, it must have been quite a relief for him, because Lauren and I jumped right in as soon as we fitted our aprons on. I looked around the kitchen and saw several boxes of cauliflower, and Avery saw when I looked at them. "And there are even more to come. I'm not sure what we'll do with so many of them."

"Pizzas," I said

He looked at me, and I could tell he had questions but not enough time to ask them. "What a great idea! But just how will you do that?"

"The pizza crust, we can make a healthy crust from cauliflower."

"Wow! I'll let you be in charge of that then."

Lauren and I got a seven-minute tour and introduction, after which we were immersed in the kitchen, and I started on the pizzas. The basic recipe for these pizzas is as follows:

CAULIFLOWER CRUST PIZZA

1 head cauliflower
1¼ cups mozzarella cheese
¼ cup parmesan cheese
1 egg (beaten)
1 tablespoon salt-free Italian seasoning
1 8-ounce package pepperoni
½ cup marinara sauce

METHOD

Cut florets from cauliflower and chop florets in a food processor until they reach the consistency of course corn meal. Pour into a microwavable dish and cover with plastic wrap. Poke holes in the plastic wrap and microwave for 3 minutes. Remove from microwave and let cool. Squeeze cauliflower in a kitchen towel to remove all the liquid and return to bowl. Add ¼ cup mozzarella cheese, parmesan cheese, egg, and Italian seasoning. Mix all the ingredients and form into a dough. Press the dough into a flat, thin pizza crust. Spray baking sheet and dust with flower then bake pizza crust for 15 minutes at 400° then remove from oven and cool. After cooling, add marinara sauce, followed by 1 cup mozzarella cheese, then topped with pepperoni and bake for 20 minutes at 400°.

Onn stayed in the kitchen with me the whole time, and I kept him occupied by having him help me top the pizzas with pepperoni. He was of great help. As I watched his small hands move, I was even more curious about him, about how much he probably knew but wasn't sharing.

After a while, I stepped outside to take a breath of fresh air, and I found myself pacing because it had just dawned on me what my next step should be. I quickly went back in to check on the baking of the pizzas, after which they were served to the guests. They were a big hit, and long after they were devoured, people came looking for more. Then I realized that my volunteer time in the refugee camp was over and I must move on.

I took my apron off and motioned to Lauren. "I better be going now."

"Time slips away when we are having fun. So, will we ever see each other again?"

"We will, and we'll stay in touch. If it wasn't for stooping down looking for ... what were you looking for anyway? That's what got my attention."

"My wedding and engagement rings. I took them off this morning when I washed my hair and didn't put them back on. I left them in the bathroom. Then I dropped a coin, and for a moment I thought it was one of my rings, but I am pretty sure they are in the bathroom where I left them."

"Well, if you need a godmother for the baby, I'm available, and you have my email address."

"And those recipes that we talked about, I'll be looking forward to trying them."

"They'll be coming to you soon, I promise."

Onn gripped my hand as we left the refugee camp. Spontaneously, he said, "Bye, Lauren!"

Lauren looked at me in amazement and then at Onn. "Bye, cutie, it was nice spending time with you today."

He repeated her words as we walked away, passing people heading for the camp that we were just leaving. The smell of sea water mixed with the aromas from restaurants was unforgettable and could never be captured with words. Within the last couple of hours, I had had some time to read the passage from the Bible that Reverend Tanner had given me to look at. A child, Moses, had been found by a stranger, but then ended up being raised by his own family. I really didn't have time to ponder much on that since my entire life had suddenly unraveled, and I was thinking about how to put it back together in a practical way and wondering if I could find out what my purpose was.

The pizza-making process was relaxing and also a time for some reflection, and I imagined that my life could be in danger; I didn't know it. Considering my confrontation with Nick, a man I thought I knew but had no clue who he really was, it was not a bad idea to just vanish without a trace. If he and his cronies decided to come after me, Soy would be the first stop. Then finding out that Soy was gone, Truro and the surrounding area would be next. So, yes, I decided to vanish without a trace.

I stopped on the sidewalk for a moment, just long enough for Onn to notice. "Where are you going?" he said. He surprised me.

"To the boat, honey."

"The boat?" he repeated.

"Yes, the boat."

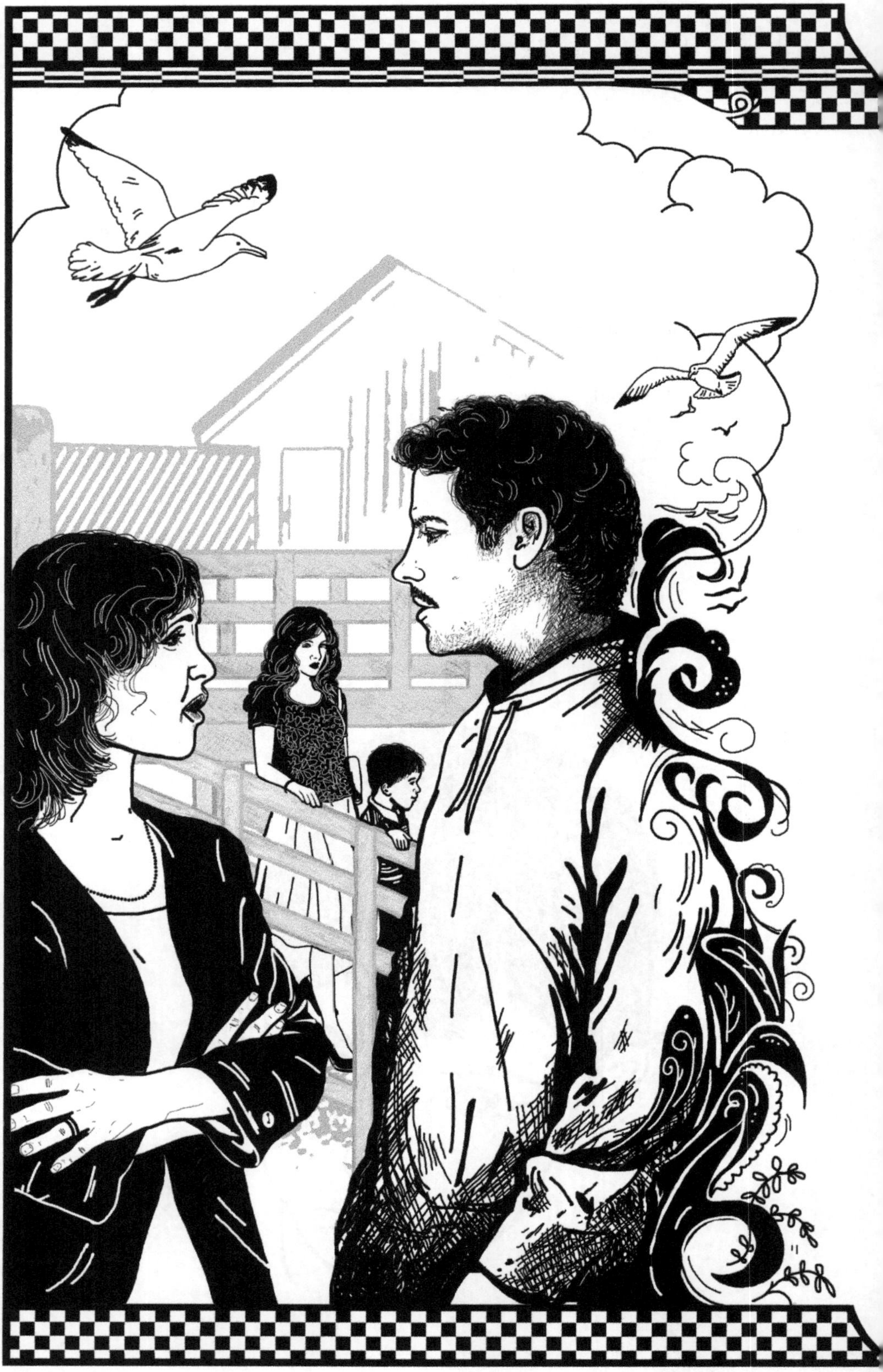

Chapter Seven

It was about fifteen minutes short of the seventy-two hours that Zarek said he would wait before setting sail for Greece. As far as I could see, his boat, *Infused*, was still in the dock. When I got closer but was still at a distance, I spotted him on the upper deck before he saw me, or at least I thought so.

Access to the boat from the boardwalk was via a set of narrow wooden steps. By the time we got there, Zarek was no longer on the deck. Onn and I took the first few steps down and were about to venture farther when I heard a conversation between Lottie and Zarek. I stopped in my tracks and held Onn back.

"Glad you made it back on time, Ma. Didn't want to sail without you."

"Yes, Son, but what about the girl … Gloribella? Is she here?"

"Mother, we talk about this before. Don't get your hopes up about Gloribella. We are only strangers to her, and she doesn't trust us."

"Yes, I know, and she reminds me so much of your sister."

"Ma, she does not. Danielle is nothing like Gloribella, and don't forget how selfish your daughter is."

"Zarek! Stop that now! I won't have you speak about your sister like that."

"Okay, Ma, this is not the time to argue, but my sister must have heard about the fire by now, and we've been waiting a few days for her to call or show up. Where is our precious Danielle?"

The conversation trailed off as they walked away, deeper into the boat. I waited a few minutes for them to finish the conversation before I entered. Zarek was sitting on a stool on the lower deck when we walked in. He was distracted and didn't seem to notice our presence. He took a cell phone from his pocket, looked at it, got up from the stool, and turned in our direction. He looked at me, astonished, and was almost short for words. "Oh, you are here. I was about to set sail. Never thought I would see you again."

"Well, you thought wrong."

"Your cabin ... well, the one you stayed in the last time is clean. I'm going up top to close things off and get ready to set sail. See you in a few minutes." He shook my hand and walked past me towards the entrance. I realized the matter of trust hadn't been resolved between us, and there was very little I could do about that.

"Where is your mom?" I called out as he moved away swiftly.

"In her cabin, about to take a nap." He answered over his shoulder.

I went to the compartment door and entered the accommodation that was provided for Onn and me. The boy immediately went to the upper level of the berth, where he could look through the scuttle. I sat on the small chair and wondered what the next chapter in my life was going to be like. While I was lost in thoughts and Onn was back to sorting through his stack of origami papers, I heard a knock on the door, just a slight tap. I opened it and it was Zarek.

"Hi, is everything okay?" he asked.

"Fine so far."

"I was wondering if you wanted to join me in the wheel room. I should show you how this boat works, just in case you have to take over from me. You may as well be my first mate."

"Great! Me sailing a boat," I sort of laughed to myself. I turn to Onn, "Do you want to stay here, honey, or come to the front of the boat with us?"

"Stay here," he said.

"Okay, I'll come back and check on you in a few minutes. I have more drawing books just in case you need an additional one."

Onn nodded and I walked with Zarek to the wheel room, where all the controls for this huge thing were. "How are you?" He asked.

"Good," I lied.

"Any luck finding your family?"

"Nope, but it's just my mother. The rest of my family is fine. How about your folks, are they okay?"

"Yes, everyone is fine, and I don't remember if I told you that my dad had passed away a few years ago. My immediate family now is just my sister and Mom."

"And your sister, where is she now?"

"Not anywhere close by here, that's for sure. Probably in Boston. We can never keep tabs on Danielle. But tell me about your situation; it sounds more pressing."

"Well, I met some nice people while I was staying at a mission house, and Reverend Tanner was quite helpful, but I haven't been able to get any information on Onn."

"Okay, well ... you're here. Never thought I'd see you again."

After my first five minutes of conversation with Zarek, I realized that I was avoiding details about my life prior to the day I arrived in Soy, and he had picked up on it. I did the same thing in the mission house, and the people there thought I was living in Soy at the time of the fire. I was trying to wipe my memory clean of the years I spent with Nick. I knew that sooner or later his name would be all over the news, and I was glad that I wouldn't be in his life when it all happened.

Zarek knew that my thoughts were far away when our conversation paused, and he kept the silence while my mind roamed. Then he woke me up by saying, "I'm not a cook by any means, but I made you something ... Well, I thought ... just in case you came back, I would impress you with something unique."

"What did you make?"

"A caviar. Previously, I called it a vegetarian caviar, but many people say if fish is in it, then it's not vegetarian. What do you think?"

"Difficult to say. There are people who call themselves vegetarian and still eat fish. I am sure it would be disappointing to the person who came up with the concept of vegetarianism if we misuse the idea."

"Well to avoid confusion and conflict, I just call it Zarek's caviar."

"Wow! That's special. I am looking forward to it. Where did the recipe come from?"

"Well, it's a long story that I don't want to get into right now, but it's from the mother of a friend who I saw recently, and I'm almost sure that I followed this recipe correctly, down to the last detail."

"Okay, go ahead, impress me."

"It needs to warm up a bit. This is not cold caviar; it's the warm version."

"Very well, I'll wait."

We walked to the galley kitchen where Zarek retrieved the caviar from the refrigerator. It was stored in a small pot, which he placed on the stove. With a click of the knob, the blue flame appeared like magic and went to low. Within a few minutes, the warm caviar was ready and served with plantain chips. It was surely delicious and addictive. He explained to me how it was made. This caviar, according to Zarek, was made from a Caribbean fruit called ackee, which had a long history and originally came from Africa. This fruit was paired with salted cod, the perfect marriage; and was canned for export with no change in the flavor or texture from being preserved.

ACKEE AND CODFISH

(Zarek's caviar)

1 16-ounce can ackee
8 ounces salted codfish fillets (already deboned package)
1 onion (minced)
1 plumb tomato (minced)
1 stalk scallion (chopped)
¼ cup red bell pepper (minced)
1 tablespoon black pepper
½ cup avocado oil (grapeseed, vegetable, or corn oil can also be used)
1 bag garlic plantain chips

METHOD

Rinse the salt from the fish in cold water and soak for 4 hours, changing the water a few times. Discard the salted water and pour boiling water over the fish. Let it sit for 3 minutes then strain. Drain the fish on paper towels to remove excess liquid, then coarsely shred with a fork, and set aside. Drain ackee from brine and set aside. In a large skillet, heat oil and sauté onion and bell pepper for 2 minutes. Add half the black pepper to the skillet and continue to cook the mixture. Add the codfish and tomato then cook for another minute. Fold in ackee and the remaining black pepper followed by the scallion. Stir and cover the skillet for 2 minutes then turn off the flame. Let it cool and serve warm with garlic plantain chips.

"There are some details that you need to know about our trip to Greece," he said.

"Okay, I think I am a fast learner."

"We are not going all the way on this boat, only part of the journey after we set sail. Before midnight, we will transfer to a submarine."

"A submarine, wow! Why?"

"It's faster and safer."

"Who owns the submarine?"

"Well, mainly my family ... we manufacture infused oils. We are situated on an island called Patmos; hence our company is called the Oils of Patmos. So my job really is to promote the company, which involves a lot of travelling."

"So, what happens when we go to Patmos?"

"I usually stay a couple of days, sometimes up to two weeks, then set sail again with more oils to wherever needs them, my very own Triangular Trade Route. When my mother was in Soy, I would visit her for a couple of days then return to Greece. But as you can see, this trip is different."

"That is a great job if you ask me. You are never tied down in any one place, no time to get bored with that one. So how do I fit in?"

He looked at me and smiled, then turned his head away shyly. "Don't worry about it; you'll fit in perfectly. You're a natural, Gloribella; you fit in anywhere."

While I thought it was the perfect answer, a tiny speck of doubt entered my mind, and I badly wanted to get past it. It was amazing how quickly he read my thoughts, and before that element of uncertainty got any bigger, he clarified his statement. "What I mean is, you're into food, you're a chef, and my company makes infused oils ... That is a perfect match. As you already know, infused oils are a great enhancement in certain dishes. My uncle ... I can convince him to hire you as a consultant for Oils of Patmos ... Well, that's if you agree." And like a footnote with further explanation, he showed me a small brochure of the products the company produced. With his presentation and personality, if I was a potential customer, he would definitely have made the sale.

"How did you get started in the infused oil business?"

"My grandfather started it years ago, then handed it down to my dad and uncles, and here I am many years later trying to keep the business afloat by trying to recruit interesting people like you to join us."

"Interesting? Do you think I'm interesting?"

"Yes, from the little that I know and have observed, but I would love to know what you think about us."

"Well, you and your family must be quite smart to be successful and to keep a business going in a tough economy such as Greece."

"Does that mean you are willing to take this journey with me into the unknown?"

"Uncertainty seems to be the norm for me these days."

He looked at me questioningly. "What do you mean?"

"Coming home to find your town burnt to the ground was definitely unexpected."

"I lost my home too, and I'm sorry about yours, but the only thing I can tell you that's comforting is that going to Greece will be totally okay with my family. They are the coolest people in this world."

The operation of a boat was new to me; all the gadgets and computer controls lit up as the engine started. Zarek gave me a crash course, which I hoped I would never have to put into action, and yet it would be something unusual to put on my resume just to see how potential employers would react. So when I finally learned the rules of the sea, at least some of them, we sailed out of Truro.

We were heading for another port when I asked him what Patmos was like. "To say the place is beautiful wouldn't do justice to the island because lots of places fit that description. Patmos is mesmerizing. My grandfather was mesmerized the very first time he saw the place."

"Why mesmerized?"

"Have you ever been to Greece?"

"No."

"What about pictures of the place, on TV, books, or anything else?"

"Yes, of course, the Parthenon, how could anyone miss that?"

"Well, that's in Athens. Patmos is a different story. And, by the way, everything about Greece begins with a story in

Greek mythology, and those stories always involve the gods and goddesses."

"That much I know."

"Are you familiar with any of them?"

"Yes, a few, like Apollo and Aphrodite."

"Very good! That's a nice background for your first lesson about Patmos; well, according to the myth, the island originally rested at the bottom of the sea. It was visible to some people, and the gods and goddesses of course. Artemis saw it first, shining at the bottom of the sea like a precious piece of a jewel. It appeared to her when Selene dragged her moon chariot across the sky."

"That I didn't know."

"If I could rewrite the myth, I would call it 'Destiny.'"

"'Destiny'?"

"Yeah."

"Why 'Destiny'?"

"Well, the goddess Artemis didn't come looking for Patmos; she saw it while visiting the temple on Mt. Latmos, nearby, so that was a coincidence. What if she didn't meet Selene? There would be no light. The rest of the myth states that Selene was constantly asking Artemis to raise the island from the sea, and eventually she convinced her. As to why Artemis was reluctant, I don't know. However, she wasn't powerful enough to undertake such a task, so she went to her brother, Apollo, but he wasn't able to do it alone either; more help was required. He went to Zeus, and the god raised the island from the sea. Helios dried it and made Patmos habitable for man and beast.

"One more thing I want to point out, and that's the family connection. Artemis was the sister of Apollo, and they were both the children of Zeus. Now, an island that was supposedly founded in such an extraordinary way has to be something special. Wouldn't you say so?"

"Most definitely."

"Well, that's all I have for now. When you get to Patmos, go to the library and learn more about the myth. Finally, once you make a connection with the island people, they will treat you like their own family. It's one big family affair once you get settled in."

"It sounds fantastic."

"My mom will be staying there from now on ... Well, the house burnt down, and there is nowhere else for her to go at the moment."

The conversation was cut short when we pulled into another harbor. "This is where we transfer to the submarine," he told me.

"Do you operate the submarine as well?"

"Yes, but not alone. That's a much bigger operation with a crew of experienced engineers, but no chef."

"No chef? So how does everyone eat?"

"Everyone sort of fends for himself and herself, but we would be honored if you would nourish us with a few of your dishes."

"I'll try my best."

I went to check on Onn in the cabin. He was quite happy to show me what he had been doing for the last several minutes. He did quite an extensive drawing on a large sheet of paper Lauren had given him. The picture was quite clear and the logic was easy to follow, which sort of shocked me. It was of a little boy running on a path that very much resembled the one I took when running to Truro; only, the boy was running in the opposite direction. My suspicion was that the little boy was him, and looking at the drawing further, it was confirmed. He had written a name as the boy got closer to burning Soy. He wrote the name Johnno. "That was very good." I said to him. "Is that your name?"

"Yes." He nodded.

"Is that the name you want me to call you now and always?"

He nodded again.

"Johnno, we are moving from the boat to a submarine now. Make sure you have all your stuff, okay?" He nodded in agreement once more. This new information about the boy could have been helpful in Truro, but now the plan was to put all of that on hold and step out into the unknown.

Onn was now Johnno. I met Zarek and Lottie on the

boardwalk. Lottie ran to hug me. "I just found out a minute or so ago that you were here. I was taking a nap on the boat. I'm so happy that you decided to join us on the journey to Greece. We have more in common than you really know."

Turning to Johnno, she said, "And you, young man, you've put on a couple of inches within the last few days." She pinched his cheeks.

Zarek cut in, "We've got to go. We have to stay on schedule."

Chapter Eight

The horseshoe-shaped harbor wrapped tightly around the edge of the island like a parasite sticking to its host. It was alive and flowing with marine activities ranging from simple to complicated, but other things were happening too. The people I observed were totally absorbed with what was important to them, and others around were just mere shadows as far as they were concerned. If I was recording this in a diary, this was my observation: a mother bent down to tie her child's shoelace, a man in a sailor's uniform hurried towards a waiting boat, a photographer took a picture, men worked on the sails of a boat, and in the near distance of the sea, a yacht approached the harbor. Anxious passengers awaited the expensive boat, and one man even got a close-up look at it through his pair of binoculars.

Zarek informed me that we were still in New England as Johnno bent down to pick up a toy soldier he found on the ground. The last thing of interest that I observed before boarding the submarine was an egret, a great egret. From its boldness, I thought it either lived there on the waterfront or was a frequent visitor to the place. The creature seemed to stare at me accusingly with stern, jewel-like eyes, then it proudly displayed its beautiful plumage as a sort of insult and moved on. If the photographer nearby was looking for a meaningful moment to capture, he'd missed his chance.

The setting sun transformed the horizon and clouds into gold, reminding me of the Greek myth about King Midas and the golden touch. It was said that when the wish to turn things into gold was granted by Dionysus, everything the king touched turned into gold, even his own daughter.

I thought about the submarine for just a few minutes before I entered its domain, and I realized that I really didn't know what to expect. I imagined it as a machine with a stomach, much like a shark travelling below the dark surface of the water. I kept that image in my mind for a long time.

The submarine was at the right end of the boardwalk, and its entire body was under water except for the conning tower, which was the entryway to the submerged craft. Zarek took me on a tour of the submarine even before I met the crew. The machine and engine rooms were endless networks of wires and cables of various sizes. It was impossible to memorize the names of all the parts, and after trying a few, I gave up and accepted my limitations, grateful that I hadn't taken up engineering as a career.

The submarine had a crew that was almost impossible to believe was real. They were something very much like a storybook tale. The men were all vertically challenged, with heights of four feet and under; I could hardly believe my eyes. A woman of average height hovered over them as if she was the guardian of their souls. She introduced herself as Agatha R. B. Cross. At first, I was not quite clear as to what her role was on the submarine, and my guess was that it wasn't clear to her either. She gave the men stern looks of warning, as if they were wasting time just by being polite to me, a stranger. But despite her, they were great people with beautiful hearts and souls.

This time Johnno had his own cabin next to mine. "It's not a long trip," Zarek said to me. "By the time you realize it, we'll be in Greece. And the woman, Agatha R. B. Cross, pay no attention to her. She'll try her best to boss you around, but don't let her. Don't even be polite to her for the sake of being polite."

"Who is she anyway?"

"A leech that doesn't know when to let go, that's what she is, and if it was up to me, those tentacles would have been cut a long time ago."

"And the rest of the crew, why are they all … ?" He finished the sentence for me without addressing the stature of the people.

"Because nowhere else would hire them. They are all victims of discrimination. They are brilliant men, as you will later see. They are masters of sea navigation but couldn't find jobs."

"Wow! Amazingly interesting."

Zarek then showed me the miniature kitchen, which was like another machine room in itself, but this was one with which I was familiar. I made a quick decision to do just casseroles and pies. They were simple meals, easy to serve and store. I set to work and lost track of time preparing the following.

SWEET POTATO HAM CASSEROLE

- 7 medium sweet potatoes
- 1 8-ounce can cream of celery
- 1 cup cheddar cheese (shredded)
- 1 cup Swiss cheese (shredded)
- ¾ cup sour cream
- ¼ cup onion (chopped)
- 2 tablespoons avocado oil
- 2 cups cooked ham (diced)

TOPPING INGREDIENTS

- 1½ cups wheat germ
- ¼ cup melted margarine

METHOD

Heat oven to 400°. Clean and scrub potatoes with a brush under cold running water, pat them dry, and cut into 1-inch cubes. Toss potatoes and onions in avocado oil and place on a baking sheet. Bake potatoes for about 30 minutes, until golden brown.

Combine potatoes and onions with cheese, cream of celery, sour cream, and cooked ham. Stir mixture and transfer to greased baking dish. In a small bowl stir together topping ingredients and spread evenly over casserole. Bake at 350° for 35–40 minutes or until casserole browns and is crisp at the edge.

SAUSAGE AND BLACK BEAN CASSEROLE

1 package semi-frozen Italian sweet sausage
2 16-ounce cans low-sodium black beans
1 onion (chopped)
4 cloves garlic (minced)
½ teaspoon black pepper
1 cup grated cheddar cheese
Fresh parsley

METHOD
Use a sharp knife to cut along the length of the sausage then carefully remove the contents from the casing. In a non-stick skillet, mash the sausage with a potato masher while it's being cook. Drain as much fat as necessary during and after the cooking process, reserving some to cook onions. Remove sausage, and in the same skillet cook onions and garlic for 5 minutes. Drain black beans and reserve some of the liquid from the can. Combine all the ingredients except the cheese and parsley in a mixing bowl. Mix well, and if the consistency is too thick, add some of the reserve liquid from the can. Transfer mixture to a non-stick baking dish of appropriate size and top with the cheese. Bake at 350° for 30 minutes or until cheese turns golden brown and casserole bubbles crisp at the edges. Garnish with ribbons of parsley. Serve with slices of fresh tomatoes.

GREEK MACARONI AND CHEESE

1½ cups whole wheat elbow macaroni
1 cup feta cheese
1 ½ cups Havarti dill cheese
1 tablespoon fresh mint (chopped)

¼ teaspoon fresh dill
1 cup fat-free milk
2 tablespoons whole wheat flour

1 tablespoon margarine
Salt and pepper

METHOD

Cook macaroni according to package instructions, strain, and reserve some of the cooking water. In a suitable saucepan, melt margarine over low flame and stir in flour. Stir constantly until flour is cooked in the margarine. Gradually add the milk to the skillet and continue to stir until the mixture thickens and forms a sauce, or roux. Add more milk if necessary. Add salt and pepper according to your own taste then stir in cheese, both Havarti dill and feta. Mix well until all the cheese is melted then stir in macaroni and dill. Transfer to a greased baking dish and bake for 30 minutes at 375°, then garnish with the mint.

BEEF PUMPKIN SAVORY PIE

1 pound ground beef
1 teaspoon Mrs. Dash® table blend salt-free seasoning
¼ cup black olives
¼ cup green olives
1 cup pickled vegetable
1 roasted pepper

2 cloves garlic (grated)
1 tablespoon dried parsley
1 frozen pie crust
2 cups cheddar cheese (divided)
4 cups kabocha pumpkin (cooked and crushed)

METHOD

Season ground beef with Mrs. Dash® table blend and brown in a hot skillet, then drain fat and set aside. Bake pie crust for 15 minutes at 375°, cool, and set aside. Combine all ingredients except ground beef, cheese, and pumpkin in a food processor and coarsely chop the ingredients. Remove from food processor to a mixing bowl, then add 1 cup of the cheddar cheese and mix the ingredients all together. Transfer the mixture to the pie crust and cover with the crushed pumpkin. Top with the other cup of cheese and bake at 350° for 30 minutes or until top is golden brown.

Although it was the impression that there were no cooks on board, someone did a splendid and thoughtful job of stocking the pantry. Despite the casseroles that I put a lot of thought and energy into, I thought my job would be incomplete if I did not include dessert, and that was where my lemon carrot cake came in handy. In stock, there were a variety of boxed cake mixes, and among them there was a lemon flavored cake.

LEMON CARROT CAKE

1 box lemon cake mix	4 medium carrots (to make 1 cup carrot juice as a substitute for water)
Zest of 1 lemon	
½ cup vegetable oil	
3 eggs	
	1½ cups water
	2 tablespoons grated carrot

METHOD

To make the carrot juice, clean and chop carrots then add to a blender. Add 1½ cups of water and blend. Remove from blender and strain. For the cake, follow package instruction and substitute 1 cup carrot juice for water, then add grated carrot and lemon zest. Bake according to instructions.

The crew on the submarine came out to eat in pairs and small groups as soon as someone else could take over their responsibilities. I didn't see much of Lottie, but I knew she was spending a lot of time with Johnno, a child with the mind of a sponge, who would make any teacher happy. She was a teacher by profession and exactly what he needed, a stabilizing force during what had to be a shattering phase in his early life. For one reason or another, I discovered that Lottie avoided all contact with Agatha R. B. Cross. They never spoke or looked each other in the eye, which I thought was odd. I didn't know their history but I could sense some form of uneasiness between the two.

At some point during the journey, probably the fourth day on the submarine, Agatha came to the kitchen. I guessed it was to satisfy her curiosity as to who I really was since there was no introduction. "So, I heard you're heading for the big house, eh?" I knew what she meant, but I feigned ignorance at first.

Eventually, I said, "Yes, I guess I am."

"Oh, I see," she said disdainfully. Looking me over from the feet up, she added, "I used to be just as pretty as you, long flashing hair, perky breasts, and small waist. I even used to be a chef too." Before I could respond to her comment, she walked away.

Zarek came in shortly after he saw Agatha leaving. "So, what was she saying? What did she want?"

"She wanted to know if I was heading for the big house, whatever that is, and the rest of it was some strange compliment."

"Well, where you are going is none of her business, and none of her compliments are genuine."

"Okay, you don't seem very fond of her."

"Like I said, she's not genuine, and a couple of times she has insulted friends of mine."

"She seems to be lonely and obviously carrying some heavy burden."

"Well, she should see a psychiatrist, and we can't help her with that."

"Is it that bad?"

"Believe me, it is, but that's her problem ..." He paused thoughtfully before carefully saying, "Take a break from the kitchen. Would you like to see my cabin?"

"Yes, of course, I would be honored."

He laughed, "Very funny."

Zarek's cabin was down the hall from the kitchen, and of course it was slightly larger, with a wider berth and more storage, but everything else was the basic set-up.

"Nice, very nice, you deserve it." I sat at the edge of the berth looking at the white navy uniform hanging on a rack. "Is there any vital information that I need to know about this trip?"

"Like what?"

"Like why a submarine and not a regular ship?"

He laughed again. "I guess at some point my family might have had money to burn. Just kidding, only my uncle could answer that, but I guess its extra income."

"Any other passengers on board besides us?"

"No others for this trip, but sometimes we do have passengers. Frequent travelers too, some people who are afraid of air planes and even honeymooners. We charge a cheaper fare; as I said, my uncle can tell you all about it if you are interested."

"So how far away are we from Greece now?"

"Not very far the last time I checked. We've been on the seas for four days now. Are you okay with this?"

"It's quite a different experience."

"Yes, of course. Anything new with Onn?"

"I never got a chance to tell you, but just before we set sail, he told me that his name is Johnno."

"Really! Wow! That's cool, Johnno, quite an unusual name; another form of John, isn't it?"

"I haven't had any time to research the name, but it seems logical."

We talked for a long time about Johnno and the possibility of many things regarding the mystery surrounding the boy. Finally, he said to me, "Can I ask you a personal question?"

"It depends on how personal it is."

"No ... no! I'm not trying to get forward or anything like that; just trying to get to know each other a little better."

"Okay, what's the question?"

"Do you have a boyfriend?"

"Well, according to a former roommate of mine that would be highly personal, but since we are practically strangers, I don't see a problem. The answer is no. I just broke off an engagement and I gave the ring back."

"Are you serious? Why?"

"It was never meant to be."

"How did you know it wasn't meant to be?"

"Well, stuff happened, and it was better finding out now than five years down the road."

"What did you find out?"

"That we weren't right for each other."

"How long were you with this guy?"

"Five years."

"Wow! Sorry. For some people that's a lifetime to be with another person. No wonder you look a little shaken up. Did you catch him cheating?"

"Sometimes I wish I did. What made you ask that?"

"Because about half of all breakups are the result of cheating."

"Are you speaking from experience?"

"No, I'm not. I just have a lot of friends who have been through it, and I also know how some girls think. The moment suspicion enters the mind, it's over."

"Who told you that? There is always proof of cheating long before a relationship ends."

"Not always; it happened to my best friend. His girl left him on the assumption that he was unfaithful to her, when in fact he wasn't."

"He's your best friend; you'd believe anything he tells you."

"So you think I am gullible...?"

"No, but friends stick up for friends."

"This is not one size fits all. My friend happens to be a decent person. He would never cheat on the woman he loved; neither would I."

There was a pause between us, and I couldn't think of what to say next, but finally I managed to say, "So now that my life is an open book, what about you?"

"What about me?"

"Do you have a girlfriend or are you seeing anyone?"

He hesitated, "... Yeah ... yes."

"A girlfriend?"

"Yeah."

"Okay, so, where is she?"

"She is in school now, at Cambridge College in Massachusetts, trying to get her MBA."

"That's great since you're already a businessman, good match."

"I'm not quite sure what she wants to do. She keeps changing her mind about careers."

"That's not so unusual. When you're in school, the choices and opportunities are unlimited. I started out teaching."

"Really, what did you teach?"

"I taught home economics at a middle school for about a year."

"I didn't know that."

"Then after teaching, I went back to school, and following that, I worked as a chef. Now, here I am. So what I'm really trying to say is that it is not unusual for young people to be undecided with career choices."

Zarek became melancholically silent for a moment, and then he said, "Well, I hope she makes the right choice, because there is a huge loan to pay back. I don't want to be in debt for the rest of my life."

"I think she will make the right choice."

"Like you deciding not to marry your ex?"

"It wasn't as simple as that. There was a lot of turmoil that drove me to that decision." I was glad he didn't ask me to explain any of it at that precise moment, because I would be totally cornered.

Instead, he started to spill his guts. "I always dreamed of having a family like the one I grew up in, with my dad and mom, my sister, Danielle, and I. Now I'm not sure if I'll ever have that. Here I am, almost 27, with an ambitious girlfriend who may or might not want the same things. I am just a simple, normal guy, not looking for fancy cars and things like that."

"Why might she not want those things?"

"I can't fully explain it. You would have to know her to understand what I am talking about."

His insecurity, honesty, and vulnerability took me totally by surprise. I wasn't expecting that from someone the likes of him, with his perfectly tanned body and the looks of a model. I felt the need to restore his pride, although I really didn't know him that well. "I have never met your girlfriend, but based on what you've said, that's the dream of any average person."

He smiled but did not respond verbally.

"So, your sister, Danielle, what is she like?"

"Smart, she is very smart. She was evaluated as a gifted child when she was quite young, and all her years in school, she was at the top of her class, always getting As. She did extremely well in college, but after she graduated from Brown University, she never did much with her degree. She took odd jobs here and there, sometimes as a clerk or waitress. Most of the time she would rather chase after guys who aren't interested in her. My mom finds it very disappointing, but never really admits to that, and the rest of the family doesn't care one way or another. So there you go; that's the overall picture of Danielle for now, until she proves us wrong."

Zarek and I talked for another half an hour, and he was diplomatically trying to find out why I broke off the engagement with Nick, but I couldn't discuss it with him. Zarek was a very sweet guy who I had known for less than a week. I wasn't ready to tell him that my ex-fiancé was an alleged criminal. I didn't think it was a wise thing to do at all.

Physically and mentally, I became totally exhausted, and Zarek sensed it. Some of what I was saying wasn't making sense anymore. "I'll walk you back to your cabin. You seem exhausted, and we are close to Greece. Get some sleep."

GREECE

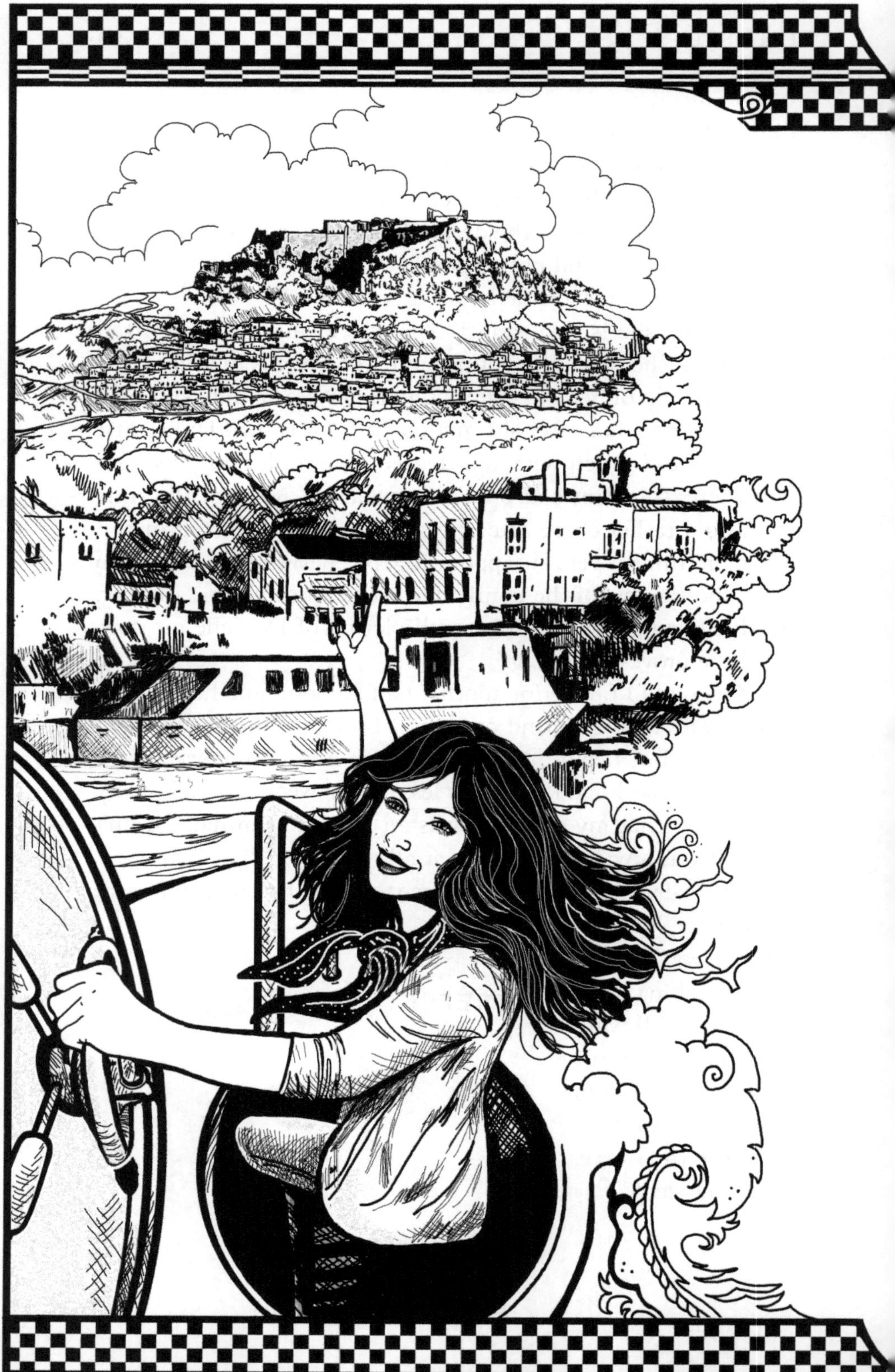

Chapter Nine

I woke up to find that all the lights in the submarine had turned red, with no knowledge why or for how long I had slept. Mustafa, who was the captain, came to me to explain the docking procedures of the submarine. It was then that I realized we were in Patmos Harbor. He was the perfect gentleman and knowledgeable of all things relating to the sea. Before returning to his duties on the submarine, he thanked me for all the wonderful casserole dishes I prepared on board. "I hadn't eaten like this in a long time and was beginning to feel spoiled. But, anyway, have a wonderful stay in Greece and hope to see you again."

"You're welcome, Mustafa. The pleasure is mine."

I had no prior knowledge of what Patmos looked like. I had never even seen it on a postcard, and I had no time to do any inquiry about the place. However, the name was popular in Mom's Pentecostal church because it was where the apostle John wrote the book of Revelation. In a nutshell, I didn't know what to expect. As I was climbing up the ladder-like steps of the submarine, I felt a tingle of excitement that I hadn't felt in a long time, and then, like the unveiling of a piece of artwork, an extravagant painting, I saw Patmos. From the harbor, I looked above and saw a dazzling maze of whiteness. They were houses. Then I noticed something else sitting almost on top of the houses like a crown, an amazing edifice that looked like a medieval castle, contrasting with the houses of white. Later, I found it was the Monastery of Saint John the Divine. All I could say was, "Wow!"

"I told you so," Zarek remarked, smiling.

A private car picked us up and drove us through the streets of the small capital, Chora, and the experience felt like I was in a dream, like I was still in that submarine underwater dreaming. It became clear that I wasn't dreaming when Zarek's voice blared into my consciousness while he patted me on the shoulder. "We can come back later if you would like."

"How long have you been coming here?" I asked.

"Since I was a boy, for summer holidays and sometimes family gatherings. Most of my cousins got married here."

"I can see why. The place is blissful and perfect for weddings."

We were driven to a house, actually a mansion, within the cluster of other homes, and were greeted in the main hall after our presence was made known by a doorbell that chimed the Westminster Quarters. Zarek's aunt and uncle, Temp and Joshua appeared from different doorways. "Desirae, my love, I'm so happy to finally meet you," Aunt Temp said in a caring and affectionate manner, throwing her arms around me. "You're even more dashing than Zarek described. Did you change your hair color?" She must have seen the expression of shock on my face because she pulled away as if a high voltage of electricity just passed through her body.

Lottie quickly cleared up the misunderstanding. "No, no, Temp, this is not Desirae. This is Gloribella, a friend of ours. Desirae is still in the States."

"Oh … I'm so sorry … I just thought … Well, welcome, Gloribella, we are so happy to meet you. I'm getting old. I forget things easily."

"It's okay, Aunt Temp," Zarek said. "I thought I'd shown you a picture of Desirae, but I realized I didn't. She promised she'll be here as soon as she can take off from school."

The man of the house, Uncle Joshua, kept quiet during the episode of mistaken identity but laughed hysterically as if he knew all along that I was not Desirae. "Welcome, my dear. Now you're a friend of the family as well. Hope you will like it on this side of the world." He kissed me on the cheek. "When was the last time you guys ate a Greek dish?" He looked at Johnno. "And you, young man, I bet you have a hardy appetite for some lamb pilaf. Luckily, Philippa is in the kitchen right now working on it."

Joshua was a robust man of about forty-five; he had a striking resemblance to Zarek, being the younger brother of Zarek's deceased father, Jonah. The death of his father left Zarek with some unaddressed emotions which he refused to talk about.

Before we entered the kitchen to feast on Philippa's Greek-style lamb pilaf, Zarek took me aside. "I want to apologize for the mix-up with you and Desirae. As you can already see, my family has a dramatic streak."

"No need for an apology. They are very nice people. I'm also tickled at the idea that they would think I am as lovely as your girlfriend."

The expression on his face changed to serious. "Stop, you're a traffic jammer and you know it, and that's why I can't understand how that guy let you get away. He really didn't know how lucky he was."

"Well, I'll take that as a compliment then."

The kitchen we entered, led by Uncle Joshua, was certainly a chef's dream, and I could see that this family had a flair for elegant living. The testimony to that was the sprawling and tasteful space that the heart of the home occupied. It was a representation of two worlds, the old and the contemporary. Equipment and utensils from both eras were prominently displayed and in use as well. While the stainless-steel refrigerator held its dominant spot in the kitchen, an ancient smoking device for curing meat was also present. A high-powered food processor was on a modern counter top, but in a corner, next to an old chair, was a large, three-foot mortar and pestle carved out of wood.

"Philippa, are you ready for us?" Uncle Joshua asked, interrupting my mental assessment of the kitchen.

"Yes, sir, it is all done."

"Grab a plate, everyone. Its buffet-style today."

The aroma coming from the chafing dish was somewhat addictive, and when the Greek lamb pilaf was finally revealed, I was at the point of salivating like Pavlov's dogs. I helped Johnno get his food and then sat next to him, taking on the role of a parent, making sure he was up-to-date with table manners. The lamb pilaf was absolutely perfect and delicious. It was a well-cooked meal, and if I was asked to rate it on a scale of one to ten, my rating would probably exceed that number immensely.

The group at the table was catching up with family matters and concerns but at the same time keeping me in the conversation and making me feel welcome. They politely explained who the people they talked about were, until Aunt Temp couldn't help bringing up the subject of the fire in Soy. "It must have been rough for you guys. It's still difficult for me living so far away to comprehend. I just can't. Gloribella, do you have any idea what could have happened to your mother? Lottie was telling me that she's missing."

"Yes, and we are keeping our hopes up. It is likely that she's with friends. My mom started a completely new life after my father died. I've never even met some of her new friends. Hard to keep up with her these days, so that's my hope."

Aunt Temp sighed, "Dear God, that's my hope too. Did everyone agree that the fire was caused by a faulty gas line that runs underground?"

"Yes, it was finally accepted by everyone."

"Which brings me to another subject I was thinking about, Gloribella," Uncle Joshua said. "My nephew told me that you're a food technologist. I could really use your help in our operation here in Patmos. I would love to hear about what you do."

After an informal interview, I was offered a research position with the Oils of Patmos, right there at the kitchen table over the lamb pilaf and a drink they called watermelon delight. I got the recipe later.

WATERMELON DELIGHT

2 cups watermelon	3 cups seedless red grapes
2 cups cantaloupes	9 cups ginger ale
2 cups honeydew melon	Alcohol (optional)

METHOD

In a blender, combine fruits and blend, then pour into a pitcher, add ginger ale, and stir. Chill and serve cold or over ice. (Do not overfill the blender; blend in batches. Please note that some blenders require liquid when blending, so in this case, use some of the ginger ale.)

The interesting thing about the job was that I didn't even need to stay in Greece. I could do my research anywhere, thanks to computers and modern technology. I had one more person to thank, Zarek. It wasn't quite clear why he was doing this for me, pulling strings left and right, but if there was an ulterior motive, I wasn't that type of a girl. For a moment, I was lost in thoughts, and I wasn't sure what to think anymore. It was as if reality kept shifting and I was always at the border of what was real and what wasn't. But regardless, I thought I needed to verbally thank Zarek for the escape to something that was different at a time when I needed it.

Everyone had left the table except for me, and I wasn't even sure when they exited. Even Johnno was gone with someone, probably Lottie. I couldn't remember. Zarek's uncle had given me something to read after I accepted his job: the new employee package. I guess that's where some of my concentration was. I had a pen and was filling out the blanks on the white pages and then I got to a box on the last page where I should write a biographical sketch of myself. That caught me by surprise, and I paused for a long time, thinking of what I could write about myself that would be of interest to this potential new employer.

Philippa came to clear the table, and it was as if her presence woke me up. I offered to help, but she refused my assistance. "That won't be necessary, miss. You've come a long way from America and you look really tired. I will show you to your room. Just give me a minute." Philippa was a beautiful Guyanese-Indian woman. She was elegantly dressed in a yellow, floral sari with matching headdress, even when cooking.

I didn't protest when she came back a minute or two later to escort me to my room, which was the size of my cousin's studio apartment in New York City. It was some type of a master bedroom with its own bath and dressing room. Vibrant colors were everywhere, in contrast to the white outside of the house and all the others like it. The four-poster bed, with canopy curtains in the room seemed as if it was built-in, and facing this sleeping chamber was a flat-screen television set mounted on the wall. I focused on the picture tube, as my dad called it, for a while, trying to remember the last time I actually sat down to enjoy a television show or movie. Turning back to the bed, I noticed that the bed clothes were all matching blue satin. Once more, I thought of how fortunate I was; it was almost too good to be true. Philippa was about to pull away the first layer of satin like she was a chamber maid, but I stopped her. From my understanding, she was their personal chef, not their maid or mine. All her jewelry seemed to be of fine gold, from bracelets to rings and a necklace. As she reached for the sheet, I noticed the bracelet on her right hand; it was a coiled serpent with bright ruby eyes. I knew it had some Hindu meaning, but my thoughts were too fragmented to concentrate on anything like that.

Long after Philippa had left the room, I realized I was still standing up clutching my new job description and everything I needed to know about the Oils of Patmos and the formulas for its continued success. The thin curtains stirred as a slight breeze oozed through the window, revealing a partial view and daring me to walk over and take a look. I was delayed only for a moment to glance at a rotary phone on the night table. It was only a replica of an original.

The breathtaking view took me by surprise, and I felt as if I had forever become part of a historical picture. I gazed at Patmos Harbor and the surrounding island until the rotary phone rang and took my attention away from the Patmos that the apostle John might have gazed at hundreds of times. The classical ring was so loud and the only way for it to stop was to pick up the receiver. "Hi, this is Gloribella."

The voice at the other end said, "And this is Zarek, calling from my cell phone. If you're not exhausted, I'm wondering if you would like to walk a bit. You must be curious about this place, and I might even buy you an ice cream cone."

"Sounds like some sort of a bribe."

"I hope it works."

"It does because I happen to like ice cream. One more thing, at the risk of sounding irresponsible, do you know where Johnno is?"

"Don't worry; he is with my mother. She has assumed the role of his private tutor, babysitter and so on.. Remember, she has no grandchildren as of yet."

"Okay then; see you in a bit."

We took an ancient road from the house. It dated back several centuries, to the same time as the center of town. It was sort of surreal when I thought of what had led up to all this. I wanted to ask Zarek straight up why he was so kind to me, but I couldn't. It was too great a moment to ruin with cynicism. I was still wondering what other people would think. "Would your girlfriend approve of you walking with me like this?"

"Hell no, she's not all that open-minded. I wish she was, though; it would complement her beauty."

I decided not to comment; although, it was an answer to a direct question I had asked, and that left the door wide open for him to return to an old subject we had talked about before: someone I would rather forget about, Nick.

"What about your ex? I didn't get his name."

"Nick."

"Would he approve of us walking like this?"

He struck a nerve and I flashed back to the times I hung out with Luke while Nick decided to stay home and watch television, saying it was okay to go out and have fun with my friends, male or female. Little did I know what was going through his mind, eventually leading up to me ending up in Patmos.

"He would say it was okay, but I couldn't be sure if he was being genuine."

"You see, that's the difference. Desirae would absolutely disapprove. She does not believe that a man and a woman can be friends with no strings attached."

"Well, of course, we all know that's not true."

"Certainly not," he said.

"It's all about beliefs, reasons to trust and not to trust, and most importantly, it depends on one's personality."

He was silent for a moment as if he was thinking about the right thing to say.

We continued down the hill, bathing in the beauty and tranquility of the moment in total silence.

Then I broke the silence. "Why don't I treat you to the ice cream cone?"

"Nah, that's one of my traditional rules. The man buys the ice cream even when the lady is just a friend."

We walked a long way down the hill until we got to a tavern in Hora Square. In Greek tavern is a *taverna*. Zarek's Greek was beyond average, so he was able to translate for me the various flavors of ice cream on display. In a few seconds, he gave me a list of all that they had available, and in the end, I choose vanilla.

It might have been the setting or the air we breathed or Patmos itself, but never before had a vanilla ice cream cone tasted that wonderful to me. Sitting at the alfresco, or outdoor, tables of the *taverna*, we licked the dripping loveliness with delight. It seemed very much like we were ten years old once more. I was careful to prevent even one drip from going to waste.

"So what it's like to work for your uncle?"

"He is much better to work for than strangers. Just don't piss him off."

"What?"

"Just kidding; he's a cool guy, not one of those unapproachable bigwigs at all, and if I make a mistake, he'll work with me to correct it in a professional way. That's what I like about him. Your new job with him is the best, though."

I was about to answer when a strange-looking woman caught our attention. She was walking in our direction from a distance. Her hairstyle looked very much like Medusa's without the actual serpents.

Zarek grabbed hold of my arm just enough to get my attention. "Let's go!" he said. The urgency in his tone warned me not to hesitate. We dashed inside the crowded *taverna* and exited through a side door.

"What on earth was that all about?"

"That was the mad woman of Chora, Elsada Welch. I have no time or patience for her today."

"A mad woman?"

"A woman from America with lots of money and time on her hands. She talks about Greek mythology as if the myths were true. She even has some ongoing reading/study group in her home."

"Sounds like she is really dedicated to this hobby. Is it sort of a conflict with the theme on in the island? The symbolism of Christianity is really strong here. The islanders, do they mind that she … ?"

"No, not at all. She keeps it under the heading of classical literature, as she taught it as a professor back in America. She has also helped people a lot here, especially these days when nobody has money anymore."

"So is it only the obsession with Greek mythology makes her the mad woman of Chora or … ?"

"Did you see the way she was dressed?"

"Yeah, sort of. You didn't give me much time to observe, but I saw the hair."

"I was trying to save us. What gets me the most is, if she holds you in a conversation, you can never get away, even when you try to end it."

"I understand. Sort of annoying."

He laughed, "She claims to have psychic powers too."

"Okay, I get the picture, she's not a normal person."

Being on a small island and staying in a village as closely knit as Chora, I knew it wouldn't be the last time I would see or hear of Elsada Welch.

For the next two weeks, exploring Chora alone became less and less challenging, once I became familiar with the layout of the village. During those priceless and exploratory days, I stumbled upon the old flagstone road that emptied into Skala. The Hellenistic path seemed so ancient and Biblical that I almost imagined I would encounter some prophet of old strolling by. Then I would probably ask him to help me figure out Johnno, a predicament I had temporarily placed at the back of my mind.

Instead of Moses or Elijah, a middle-aged monk barreled into view. His religious garb of black and gold added another layer of mystique to the scenery. He might have been travelling from Skala and presently headed for the monastery. The holy man slowed down when he was a few feet away from me on the opposite side of the road. He studied me carefully and probably made some quick assessment, then he smiled politely and continued on his journey up the hill. He must have known right away that I didn't speak a single word of Greek; just a lone tourist just strolling by.

Chapter Ten

The Oils of Patmos was in the heart of Skala, the main hub of the island and where most of the trade and commerce took place. Each time I looked at the small seaport town, I traveled far back in my mind, searching for comparisons, but I always came up blank. And then I came to the conclusion there were no comparisons. This place was in a class by itself, and I still wondered how I had come there.

One of those times, when I returned to what was real, I was sitting in an office no bigger than a cubicle. In the adjoining office, I heard Zarek's uncle talking business on the phone. An encyclopedia of herbs and plants was open in front of me and I was at the table of contents page. Research was what I was about to start, and one of my inspirations was in the room in front of me on top of a filing cabinet. It was an indoor plant sucking water from a roundish glass bowl. The roots of the plant grew through rocks, forming a mass of tangled growth in the bowl. A solitary fish swam in the bowl and was constantly feeding on the algae among the roots of the plant.

This office, and Patmos in general, had become my new reality in a nutshell. It was a fragile foundation because I didn't ever know what to expect next. I worked with the tools that were presented to me. Many of them were God-given, while some were man-made, and I gratefully used them to the best of my ability. Uncle Joshua gave me a laptop for research, and I nervously gaze at it every few minutes, remembering what had happened the last time I looked at a computer. My own personal computer was locked away in a bank's vault in Boston.

It took all the courage I could muster to start this super-speed machine and get it running, and once it was in operation, I worked for about an hour on the research project I had started. Before shutting down the computer and moving on to something else, I checked my email. The first one I opened was from Hortense, who I'd met in the mission house. She'd arrived safely in Christchurch, New Zealand. She wrote the following:

```
Dear Gloribella, I often thought about you and
the little boy, and it was very nice meeting
you, etc. Please send me the following recipe.
```

The first one she mentioned was Scotch bonnet curry goat wrap.

SCOTCH BONNET CURRY GOAT WRAP

- 1 quart low sodium vegetable stock
- 3 pounds goat meat (cut in small pieces)
- 2 tablespoons curry powder
- 1 tablespoon garlic powder

- ¼ Scotch bonnet (Scotch bonnet pepper is a very hot pepper, so be cautious)
- 1 tablespoon onion powder
- 1 onion (chopped)
- 4 cloves garlic (smashed)
- ¼ tablespoon sea salt

2 bay leaves
1 tablespoon grated ginger
¼ green pepper (chopped)
1 tablespoon dried thyme
4 stalks scallions
2 tablespoons avocado oil
1 package rice paper

METHOD

Remove most of the fat from the meat and rinse meat in vinegar and water. Drain and pat dry with paper towel. Season goat meat with dry seasonings such as curry powder, onion and garlic powders, sea salt, and dried thyme. Let the meat sit for 2 hours. Add avocado oil to a hot skillet and brown meat on high heat. It takes about 5–10 minutes working in batches. Return all meat to the skillet and add vegetable stock along with ginger, onion, green pepper, garlic cloves, bay leaves, and Scotch bonnet pepper. Cover with the lid and let the goat simmer for 2–3 hours. Cooking time will depend on the tenderness of the meat and how much heat the pot retains. The meat will fall off the bones when done.

PREPARING WRAPS

Select a large cutting board and follow directions on the rice paper wrap. Dip rice paper wrap in warm water and lay flat on board. Place 2 heaping tablespoons of boneless meat in the middle of the rice paper and quickly fold each end from left and right then top and bottom, forming a wrap. Garnish with scallions. Wraps can be eaten as-is or steamed.

POPCORN TURKEY

2 pounds turkey breast (cut into ½-inch cubes)
1 tablespoon black pepper
1 package Goya Sazón
1 teaspoon Mrs. Dash® table blend seasoning
1 teaspoon onion powder
1 teaspoon garlic powder
1 cup whole wheat flour
Avocado oil

METHOD

Use avocado or vegetable oil for frying or (any oil that does not smoke when heated).

Combine all the dry ingredients in a large mixing bowl and mix well. Toss turkey cubes into bowl mixture and let it sit for 5 minutes. Remove turkey cubes to a strainer and shake off the excess flour. Heat enough oil in a skillet until the temperature of the oil reads 335° on a deep-frying thermometer. Drop turkey cubes into hot oil in small batches and cook until golden brown. Remove from pot when cooked and transfer to a wire rack over a baking sheet. If popcorn needs more cooking, place the tray in an oven set at 400° for 5 minutes. Serve hot with your favorite chips, vegetable, and hot sauce.

TURKEY TERIYAKI AND CILANTRO RICE

- 4 skinless boneless turkey thighs (ask butcher to remove bones if that is convenient)
- ¼ cup low-sodium teriyaki sauce
- 1 tablespoon rice wine vinegar
- 1 tablespoon low-sodium soy sauce
- 1 tablespoon grated ginger
- 2 cloves garlic (grated)
- 1 onion (grated)
- 1 teaspoon sesame seeds

METHOD

Clean, remove fat, and cut thighs into small bite-size pieces. Mix all ingredients in the form of a marinade and pour in a zip seal plastic bag, then add turkey. Seal the bag, letting out the air, then gently massage the meat in the bag. Let it sit in the refrigerator for 2 hours; overnight would be ideal. Drain marinade and pat the turkey dry with paper towels. Store marinade in the refrigerator. In a cast iron skillet, heat avocado oil and sauté meat for 10 minutes on medium heat, then transfer skillet to a 400° oven. Strain marinade over a tea strainer or cheese cloth and pour into a small saucepan and cook for 7 minutes. Add a few teaspoons of water if necessary until it turns to sauce. Cook turkey in oven for another 20 minutes or until the turkey becomes dark brown. Add sauce from the stovetop to the meat in the oven as needed. Serve over cilantro rice.

CILANTRO RICE

1 cup rice
1 teaspoon margarine

2 cups low-sodium chicken stock
¼ cup cilantro (chopped)

METHOD

In a small pot, cook rice according to 2:1 ratio. Melt margarine in pot and add rice. Coat rice in the margarine for 2 minutes by constantly stirring, then add chicken stock and bring rice to a rapid boil. Cover pot tightly and turn flame to low. Cook for 20 minutes, then cut flame and let the rice sit for 5 minutes. Fluff with a fork then combine cilantro with rice in a serving bowl.

MUSTARD MACKEREL AND BANANA

2 salted mackerels (deboned)
¼ cup yellow mustard
1 red onion (chopped)
1 plum tomato (diced)
2 stalk scallions (chopped)

1 teaspoon black pepper
¼ green pepper (chopped)
¼ cup avocado oil
6 green bananas

METHOD

Mackerel

Rinse and soak mackerel in cold water over night. Drain and re-soak in boiling water for 15 minutes; drain again and re-check for bones, then set aside. Heat oil in a skillet then sauté onions and scallions, add mustard, then mackerel. Cook the mackerel for a minute before adding black pepper, green pepper, and plum tomato. Fold all the ingredients together and cover the skillet. Cook for 3 minutes stirring occasionally. (Fresh mackerel fillets can be used instead of salted mackerel. If fresh mackerel is used, then skip the soaking procedure and go straight to cooking. Salt to your own taste.)

Green Bananas

Set a pot of water to boil and salt generously. Remove the tips of the bananas, and with the skin on, place them in the boiling water. Add a tablespoon of vegetable oil to the pot and let the bananas cook for 15 to 20 minutes. The skin will crack when they are ready. Drain water and carefully remove skins with a fork. Serve hot with mustard mackerel.

SALMON BURGERS

This recipe would be perfect for leftover salmon.
- 1 pound cooked salmon (canned salmon can also be used)
- ½ cup onion (chopped)
- 1 egg (beaten)
- ½ cup green pepper (finely chopped)
- ½ cup whole wheat bread crumbs
- 1 teaspoon lemon zest
- 1 tablespoon lemon juice
- ½ teaspoon cilantro (chopped)
- ¼ teaspoon black pepper
- 2 tablespoons clam juice
- Avocado oil

METHOD

Flake salmon in a bowl and combine all the ingredients with the salmon. Mix well and form into burgers, about 4 or 5. Fry in a skillet on both sides until golden brown. If canned salmon is used, substitute liquid from the can for clam juice.

Dressing

- 1 cup orange juice
- 1 tablespoon lime juice and zest of 1 lime
- ¼ cup cilantro (chopped)
- ¼ cup olive oil
- 4 garlic cloves (minced)

Combine all ingredients in a mason jar and shake well. Serve burgers with slices of beef steak tomatoes, dressing, and your favorite condiments, on bun or separately.

GRILLED ZUCCHINI BROWN RICE

2 large zucchinis
2 tablespoons avocado oil
2 tablespoons basil pesto sauce
4 cloves garlic
1 package Uncle Ben's brown rice (2 cups)
4 cups low-sodium chicken stock (hot)
1 tablespoon margarine or butter

METHOD

Melt margarine in pot and add garlic. Lightly cook garlic in margarine and be careful not to burn the garlic. Add rice and coat with garlic and margarine for about a minute, then add chicken stock. Stir once and bring to a rapid boil then reduce heat to low and cover pot. Let the rice cook for about 30 minutes until grains are tender and all the liquid has been absorbed.

Whisk avocado oil and pesto in a large bowl. Clean and dry zucchini then cut into strips of 2½ inches long; add to bowl of pesto mixture. Let zucchini sit in marinade for 15 minutes to half an hour. Grill zucchini in a grilling basket. Serve in bowls over brown rice. Great for vegetarians.

COLUMBUS DAY HASH

¾ pound pancetta (cut in ¼-inch cubes)
5 cloves garlic (minced)
1 onion (diced)
3 turnips (peeled and diced)
3 carrots (diced)
1 sweet potato (peeled and diced)
2 beets (peeled and diced)
12 Brussels sprouts
1 cup celery (chopped)
Chopped parsley
Pepper

METHOD
Set oven to 400°, and in the meantime, in a large heated cast iron skillet, cook pancetta until golden brown then remove and set aside. In the same hot skillet, using the fat from the pancetta, cook carrots for 3 minutes, then add the remaining vegetables except parsley. Cook vegetables for 5 minutes stirring constantly. Add pancetta and pepper then transfer to hot oven and cook until all vegetables are equally tender. Remove from oven, garnish with parsley, and serve hot as a side dish.

ROASTED CAULIFLOWER STUFFING

1 head cauliflower (cut into florets)
½ cup parmesan cheese
1 teaspoon garlic powder
1 tablespoon olive oil

METHOD
In a food processor, pulse cauliflower until it resembles coarse cornmeal. Transfer to a microwave-safe dish and cover with plastic wrap. Microwave for 4 minutes. Remove and cool. Squeeze and remove water through a kitchen towel. Transfer to a mixing bowl and add the other ingredients. Transfer to a non-stick baking sheet and bake for 20 minutes at 400°. Remove from oven and serve as a side dish instead of potatoes or as a stuffing.

On that same day, I sent recipes out to Nora Muir, another friend I met at the mission house, and she wanted the following:

BEAN AND PEPPER STUFFED BELL PEPPERS

8 bell peppers (cleaned, seeded, and deveined)
1 16-ounce can refried beans
1½ cups low-fat sour cream
1 cup salsa
4 stalks scallions (chopped)

3 tablespoons reduced-fat cream cheese
1 jalapeno pepper (seeded and finely chopped)
2 tablespoons chopped chipotle pepper in adobe sauce
1 teaspoon ground cumin
½ teaspoon chili powder
1 cup Monterey Jack cheese

METHOD

Set a large lobster pot of salted water to boil. Carefully immerse the peppers to be stuffed in the boiling water and blanch peppers for 3 minutes. Remove from water, drain, and cool. In a large bowl combine all the ingredients except Monterey Jack cheese. Thoroughly mix the ingredients and fill each pepper. Spray a large roasting pan with non-stick spray and transfer peppers to pan. Top with Monterey Jack cheese and bake uncovered at 350° for 25 minutes until peppers are golden brown and bubbly.

ALMOND MANGO BARS

½ cup semi-frozen almond butter (cubed)
2½ cups almond flower
¼ cup Splenda
½ cup cold butter (cubed)
½ teaspoon salt
1 medium mango (peeled and chopped)
½ cup sugar-free orange marmalade
6 eggs
1 teaspoon lemon zest
1 cup flaked coconut

METHOD

Place almond butter, 2 cups almond flour, Splenda, 2 eggs and salt in a food processor, then process until blended. Add butter and pulse until mixture is crumbly. Press mixture into an ungreased baking pan and bake for 15–20 minutes at 350°. In a clean food processor, add mango and sugar-free orange marmalade; process until smooth. Add the remaining almond flour and process until combined. Add eggs and lemon zest and process to combine all the mixture. Pour over crust in pan and sprinkle with coconut.

Bake for about 30 minutes or until golden brown around the edges. Cool on a rack and cut into bars. Refrigerate leftovers.

ROASTED SWEET POTATO SALAD WITH BACON

2 pounds small sweet potatoes (quartered)
¼ cup olive oil
1 cup vinegar
1 cup kosher salt
1½ quarts cold water
½ teaspoon pepper (divided)
4 ounces cream cheese (softened)
½ cup sour cream

1 teaspoon Mrs. Dash® table blend salt-free seasoning
½ teaspoon garlic powder
2 cups roasted kernel corn
½ cup finely chopped red onion
½ cup red pepper (finely chopped)
½ cup real bacon bits

METHOD

Combine salt, vinegar, and water in a large bowl, and stir until all salt is dissolved, then add potatoes. Let potatoes sit in solution for 1 hour. Remove potatoes from brine, dry with paper towels, then toss with oil and ¼ teaspoon pepper, then place on a non-stick baking sheet and bake at 400° for 40 mins, or until tender. Move the potatoes around on the sheet while roasting, giving them all equal amount of heat. Set potatoes aside. In a large bowl, combine cream cheese and sour cream and beat with a hand mixer until smooth. Add Mrs. Dash® table blend and garlic powder, along with bacon bits. Remove mixer and fold in corn, onion, and red pepper. Fold in potatoes and let salad sit in the refrigerator for 30 minutes. Serve cold.

GRAPEFRUIT BUBBLES

3 cups fresh grapefruit juice
3 cups diet ginger ale

2 cups seltzer
Ice cubes

METHOD

In a large pitcher, add generous amounts of ice cubes. Pour grapefruit juice then add ginger ale and seltzer; stir and serve.

JICAMA CARROT SALAD

1 jicama (shredded)
1 Granny Smith apple (diced)
1 cup shredded carrots
2 tablespoons orange juice
½ cup golden raisins
½ cup mayonnaise (low fat)

METHOD

In a large salad bowl, combine all the ingredients. Chill and serve with your favorite poultry: fried chicken, for example.

ORANGE CRAN-APPLE SPLASH

2 cups orange juice
1 cup cranberry juice
2 cups apple juice
1 cup seltzer
Ice cubes

METHOD

In a pitcher with ice cubes pour all the ingredients over the ice cubes and stir slightly. Remember, recipe can be doubled and a splash of alcohol can be added.

Nora and I had a fun discussion about how onions made her cry, but she wanted a good recipe for pickled onions, so this was what I came up with:

PICKLED RED ONIONS

1 large red onion (thinly sliced)
¼ cup lime juice
¼ cup red wine vinegar
1 teaspoon kosher salt
1½ tablespoons cilantro (chopped) (optional)

METHOD

In a small bowl, whisk lime juice, red wine vinegar, salt, and cilantro until salt is dissolved. Fold in onions and chill for at least 4 hours. Stir occasionally while chilling.

GRILLED SNOW PEAS BUCKWHEAT AND SALMON BOWL

½ pound snow peas (grilled)
1 cup buckwheat
1 16-ounce can salmon
1 shallot (chopped)
1 clove garlic (chopped)
3 hardboiled eggs (chopped)
1 tablespoon avocado oil
1 teaspoon margarine
¾ cup water
¼ cup liquid from salmon
2 cups mixed greens
1 cup parsley (chopped)
¼ cup scallions (chopped)
1 cup toasted crumbled seaweed

METHOD

Open can of salmon, drain, and reserve liquid. Remove skin and bones and discard; flake salmon and set aside. Rinse buckwheat through a fine strainer under cold running water and set aside to drain excess water. In a heated skillet, add margarine, then sauté shallot and garlic for 2 minutes. Combine water and liquid from the salmon (a total combination of 1 cup) to the skillet, stir, then add buckwheat. Bring the pot to rapid boil then turn the flame to low and let the buckwheat cook for 15–20 minutes covered. Remove from heat and set aside to cool. In a large bowl, combine buckwheat, grilled snow peas, eggs, and mixed greens. Fold in salmon, scallions, and drizzle avocado oil, then garnish with seaweed and parsley. Serve in bowls.

*Please note that seaweed already comes in packages pre-toast. All you need to do is crumble.

PEACH AND MANGO DELIGHT

16 ounces freshly blended peach juice
16 ounces freshly blended mango juice
1 tablespoon lemon juice
2 cups club soda

METHOD

Pour mango juice into ice-cube tray and freeze into solid cubes. Mix peach juice and lemon juice in pitcher, then stir in club soda. Remove frozen mango from ice-cube tray and put into another pitcher. Pour in peach juice mixture. Lightly stir and serve.

PARTY BACON SANDWICHES

1¼ cups real bacon bits
¼ cup celery (finely chopped)
¼ cup sweet relish
1 tablespoon bacon mayonnaise
4 ounces whipped cream cheese
1 loaf of cocktail bread
½ cup parsley (chopped)
1 tablespoon pimento

METHOD

Combine all the ingredients except parsley, pimento, and bread in a bowl. Mix well and chill. Spread bacon mixture over each slice of bread and top with parsley and pimento.

Apart from sending out recipes, I was faced with the unpleasant task of writing to Zachary to tell him that I had resigned from my executive chef position at the Belly of the Fig. I did not want to give the poor guy the false hope that I would be coming back because I wouldn't.

I had an opportunity to visit a few of the museums in Patmos that day, and it was quite an event. Although there are major differences, the drawings, paintings, and carvings were pretty much the same as I'd seen in museums around the world. They carried a common theme: ancient human beings, their fears and struggles, hopes and dreams. Demons and evil spirits, as interpreted, were a huge concern at a time when there were no scientific explanations.

On the way back to the house, a few of the local people tried to engage me in conversation, but the language barrier turned what could have been a meaningful event into frustration. I realized how badly I needed to learn Greek if I was to make friends or have any worthwhile connections with the people who live on Patmos.

Philippa was cooking up a storm when I got inside the house. Meats of various kinds were laid out on a cutting board and she was picking out spices from a rack. She paused with a jar in her hand when I entered the kitchen. It was great that we were finally on a first-name basis. Conversations had become a lot easier. "Hi, Gloribella."

"Philippa, the place smells wonderful! What's your secret?"

"Well, let's put it this way: you can take the girl out of Guyana, but you can't take Guyana out of her."

"Very well put. How did you manage with the Greek? I understand you speak some without any struggle."

"I struggled for a long time, especially in culinary school, but when I came to Patmos, I got better at it."

"How so, and why better in Patmos?"

"I met a woman who ran free classes and had a natural gift for teaching. When I tell you she is good, she's really good. So I took the opportunity and it paid off."

"Really!"

"Yes, and she still offers them. If you would like, I could hook you up with her whenever you have some time to spare."

"Are you kidding me? I will make time. So, what are you cooking now?"

"Pepper pot. We're having a special visitor."

"Oh, okay ... well, not anyone I would know anyway. I'm still trying to find my way around here."

"As a matter of fact, you might know her. Its Zarek's girlfriend, Desirae."

I was sort of shocked when she said that, since I had spoken to Zarek only yesterday and he made no mention of her coming to Patmos. "I know of her, but there was never any mention of her visiting Greece."

"I never met her either, but she'd heard of my pepper pot, obviously, from Zarek."

"Well, from the ingredients you have here, it sounds like a tasty dish."

"Thanks, and if you have time, you can stay and watch how it is prepared."

"Philippa, I appreciate this very much. Not many chefs would share a secret such as this."

While she cooked, we talked a little about the history of Guyanese pepper pot.

PEPPER POT

(Most combinations of meats can work in this dish.)

- 2 pounds chuck steak or brisket (cut in 1-inch cubes)
- ½ pound corned beef or pork
- 2 pig trotters (i.e., pig's feet)
- 2 pounds of oxtail
- Black pepper
- 1 cup cassareep
- 1 red bell pepper (chopped)
- 1 1-inch piece orange peel
- 1 cinnamon stick (about an inch long)
- 3 head cloves
- 2 quarts low-sodium beef stock
- Salt to taste
- Vegetable or grapeseed oil for searing meat

METHOD

Clean meat with water and vinegar, then dry with paper towels, then season with black pepper. In a small pot add enough beef stock to cover pig trotters, or feet, and cook until half tender.

Remove from pot and set aside. In a suitable pot with a lid, heat oil and sear meat in batches. Drain excess oil and return meat to pot. Add pig trotters and other ingredients and let the meat simmer until tender. Adjust flavor, salt if necessary. The cooking time is about an hour. Serve hot with bread, rice, or another staple.

Chapter Eleven

There were too many adjectives to describe Desirae's physical beauty, about a paragraph's worth, and as I glanced at her from time to time, she reminded me of a Greek goddess, the immortal being etched on the delicate china that adorned the dining table from which we feasted on Philippa's pepper pot. In Guyana, the meal was traditionally served with bread, but that night we had basmati rice, which was a perfect match with the pepper pot. But not even such a fine, delicious meal could take the attention away from Desirae. Her aura announced charm and seduction, and she told a story about her grandmother, who gave her the name Desirae Gardenia, but for some reason or the other Gardenia did not appear on her birth certificate; she added it later. Her Cambridge College education was quite apparent in the way she talked about politics and the Greek economy.

Every now and then Zarek and the others at the table glanced at me hopefully, looking for some input on some of Desirae's ideas and knowledge about almost everything, but I kept a low profile. She plainly wanted to shine for her audience, and I let her, and by all means, she should as the future-daughter-in-law in their family.

Finally, she spoke to me directly. "Gloribella, I heard that you are a chef and a food technologist. "Did you help to prepare any of this?"

She knew very well that I didn't. "No, none at all. It's all the hard work of Philippa."

"Oh. So, where did you go to school?"

"I did my graduate work at MIT."

"Wow! What a small world."

The conversation continued as she leaned her interest towards me, almost ignoring everyone else at the table, until Philippa came to announce that her desserts were ready and waiting on us.

DATES AND RUM BARS

1 cup dates (pitted and chopped)	1 cup slivered almonds
	⅓ cup white rum
2 cups unsweetened granola	1 tablespoon vanilla
	½ cup figs (chopped)

METHOD
In a food processor, add all the ingredients and pulse. On a baking sheet lined with parchment paper, spread the mixture evenly and refrigerate for an hour. Cut into bars and serve.

Being busy with my new role at Oils of Patmos, I rarely saw Zarek or Desirae, but I knew they were on a tour of the island. Every morning I would be up at seven to make breakfast for Johnno before Philippa came to the kitchen. Some of his favorites were toast, pancakes, and sandwiches cut out into various shapes using cookie cutters. He was very much into shapes and funny faces, and I found cookie cutters at a shop in Skala to help with that endeavor.

ORIGAMI PANCAKES

1 cup pancake mix	Favorite fruits for topping and shape enhancement, such as raisins and bananas
1 cup milk	
1 egg (slightly beaten)	
	Pancake syrup

METHOD

In a medium bowl, add milk and egg to pancake mix and stir until batter is moist, or follow package instructions. In the meantime, heat griddle or skillet. For each pancake, pour ¼ cup of batter onto skillet. Cook until bubbles form on the surface and edges become dry; turn pancakes and cook for 2 more minutes or until cake becomes golden brown. Use cookie cutters to make desired shapes and decorate with fruits, syrup, and jellies.

Johnno would make the shapes himself if he was up to it.

ORIGAMI FRENCH TOAST

6 white or whole wheat bread slices	¼ teaspoon salt
2 eggs	2 tablespoons butter or margarine
½ cup milk	Orange marmalade

METHOD

Use cookie cutter to cut bread in the shapes you desire. (Save trimmings for bread crumbs, etc.) Whisk egg, milk, and salt. (Do not overbeat.) Dip bread shapes into egg mixture, making sure they are well coated on both sides. Heat butter in a large skillet and add bread. Cook on both sides until golden brown and crispy. Remove toast to paper towels. Serve with orange marmalade or any other jellies or jam you prefer. Maple syrup is also great with French toast.

After breakfast, Johnno's day started with home school led by Lottie. I joined in before I went to my daily assignments. The research took me all over Patmos and I met many people. It was quite a challenge getting hold of a local farmer who was a cultivator of capers and a lot more to his credit. He cancelled several appointments within a two week period.

When I did catch up with him, I had to take Philippa with me to help with the translation. Orion's farm was in a stony valley not far from a pasture where a small herd of cattle grazed. We got there when the sun was still overhead and the trees cast irregular shadows on the green grass. The prevailing peacefulness was only interrupted a few times from the blaring horns of ships in the bay of Skala. Orion was quite busy, so our visit was tightly scheduled, and he was only available for half an hour, his lunch break.

We had lunch with him, small Greek sandwiches made from thin slices of lamb, cucumber, tomatoes, and tzatziki sauce, along with mint lemonade cocktail. Then while we watched a small video about growing capers, we had baklavas and coffee. Orion spoke some English, and with the help of Philippa when he switched over to Greek without warning, I was able to understand him. It was officially my first business meeting with a native of the island.

Orion didn't just farm. His availability was pretty much tied up with his trade as a plumber, and from what Philippa told me, he was quite reliable and was in great demand in Skala and around all of Patmos. However, growing capers was his first love, and it was not just a business; it was also a hobby. Orion took great care in making the video himself with captions in both Greek and English. Off screen he explained to us how he got into the business of capers with a brief history of the land. When he bought the property, the caper bushes were already growing wild, and he realized the value of the farm. Unknown to the seller, he knew the capers alone could help pay off the loan he took out from the bank, so he expanded the farming of the bush and launched a marketing campaign. Orion's fiancée,

Lindsey, was from England. She helped with the capers when he wasn't around, but he made all the business decisions.

Philippa admitted that she had totally forgotten about these flavorful flower buds used around the world in so many cuisines. The short video was quite helpful and informative, and showed a recipe of how it was used in chicken piccata. For starters, growing capers from seeds was very difficult and complicated. So without patience and time, bypassing that idea and purchasing a jar at the grocery was by far a much better choice. Capers came from one of those plants whose versatility lent it to multiple uses. Like the coconut palm, every part was useful, and nothing went to waste. The delight of capers as an addition to many cuisines was only one version of the story. Those who made medicines from the plants had seen another side of the caper, benefits such as the boosting of liver function, the curing of gout, and a long list of other healing properties. In a conversation, later, Lindsey explained that one of their regular customers was the local florist. That was something else I never thought about.

The appointment with Orion ended with a contract and him agreeing to provide us with loads of the marvelous Capparis spinosa, or caper bush, on a regular basis. Philippa looked at her watch, and it was almost 2:00 p.m. She had one more appointment before heading back to the house to start dinner, and that interested me right away, since everything on the island had some element of antiquity and was a vehicle of learning. I was especially curious since she was taking me on the appointment, which meant it wasn't private at all. I didn't ask any questions; I just followed her lead after we bid goodbye to Orion and Lindsey. We followed the old country road along the valley in the opposite direction from which we came. We didn't get very far from the valley when Orion drove up in his truck and stopped at our feet. "I have room for two," he announced in English, mainly for my benefit. "Where can I drop you ladies off?"

Needless to say, the destination Philippa gave was totally beyond my comprehension. I just stared at her and nodded.

Orion's truck was packed with tools for his trade, along with shelves and hooks stacked with plumbing supplies. And, yes, as I looked around at them, they were all Greek to me.

It wasn't long before we were out of the vicinity of the peaceful valley and into the maze of dazzling white houses in the village of Chora. Then, in his friendly way, Orion pointed out a few houses where he did plumbing work on a regular basis.

The island of Patmos never ceased to amaze me, and I was trying to absorb it all both mentally and with a small camera I carried around constantly. Surprisingly, we stumbled upon another landmark sight. Orion stopped as instructed by Philippa, and we looked out at an astounding structure with columns looking very much like the Parthenon. Architecturally, it was one of the white mansions on the hill, just a bit different. The arched double doors of iron and glass stood like sentinels instructed to guard with their lives. Under the unfading shadows of the Monastery of Saint John the Divine, Orion bid us goodbye while Philippa dialed her cell phone.

A tiny speck of curiosity crossed my mind when she spoke in Greek on the phone. She whispered to me after covering the mouthpiece, "The language teacher. I booked an appointment for you." A buzzer rang and she pushed one of the arch doors. I was stunned at what I saw next. Instead of stepping into a foyer or hall as expected, like Disneyland, a movie set, or an illustration from a book of fairytales was the best way to describe what I saw. The outer walls and tall columns that reminded me of the Parthenon were only a façade and cover for what was inside. We were at the entrance of a garden with a walkway in the middle, and tall trees rose to the top with their branches intertwining loosely and untamed. The walkway leading to the house at the far end of the garden was about sixty yards long. The green, velvety lawn stretched itself out to the front porch of the house with not a single blade of grass out of place.

The two-story house was partly hidden behind the trees, and its whiteness was somewhat altered by the shadows of the trees.

"Well, this is quite an attraction," I remarked, and before

I could say more, or Philippa had a chance to respond, Elsada Welch, the same woman described as the mad woman of Chora, came out to greet us. In my mind's eye, I could see Zarek pulling me away as we made a run from the double doors.

Philippa was calm and confident, but of course, she had learned Greek from Elsada Welch. She was living proof that it could happen. Consequently, within those short few moments, much of Philippa's tranquility rubbed off on me.

The exchange of greeting between us was brief, and it was obvious that the mad woman, according to Zarek, had important things to do. "Welcome, my dear. Come on in. Philippa told me of your interest in the Greek Language." We followed her down a pathway of cobblestone as sunlight embroidered its way through the trees.

The entry hall on the first floor was a theatre with a stage behind thick curtains of purple velvet. Men and women were scurrying about in costumes, softly muttering to themselves. Elsada disappeared into the house theatre, and I turn to Philippa. "What on earth is this? Why are we in a theatre?"

"It's the way she teaches. She makes learning fun and exciting, especially a new language as intimidating as Greek."

"And she does all of that for free?"

"Yes, all for the love of teaching Greek, but she does not advertise."

"Wow," I kept my voice down and resisted the temptation to mention Zarek's theory about Elsada's insanity. It was an idea that I began to seriously question; as the thought entered my mind, she emerged from a doorway wearing a slightly different outfit.

"Let me properly introduce myself to you," she said to me. "I am Professor Elsada Welch, the literary geek around here, but believe me, my dear, it's for a good cause. It's no fun not speaking the language here."

I extended my hand. "Gloribella Frank. It's a pleasure meeting you."

"Any experience in the Greek language before, Gloribella, or the culture or food?"

"I have very limited exposure to most things here; some foods, yes, and I discover more and more every single day I'm here."

"Well, you're very lucky; a fresh start is good. I don't have food today but perhaps next time, yet what you are about to experience will make you forget about food for a while. In just a few moments we'll be performing *Eros and Psyche* in Greek. The actors are all students of mine, both past and present. My hope is that you'll be part of this group in the near future. It's not difficult once you immerse yourself in the experience."

I nodded pleasantly, knowing very well I would never find time for that, and she handed me the script in Greek with the English translation written under each line of the play.

"This is your first handout. Just sit and enjoy the play and feel free to ask any questions later. I'll be happy to answer them for you."

Elsada left us and the curtain went up a few minutes later. A narrator came on stage and gave an introduction to the play, and after every couple of scenes, he would come back to narrate, especially at scenes where imagination was crucial to the understanding of the story. I followed my English translation, looking back and forth from it to the Greek. All the scenes were acted out on stage, and so this was *Eros and Psyche* in a nutshell:

The king and queen of an unnamed kingdom had a daughter who was the most beautiful creature ever to be born. Her name was Psyche, meaning "the soul." She was so beautiful that people from every walk of life went to see her and showered her with gifts. Even Aphrodite, the mighty and most beautiful of all the goddesses, got a glimpse of her, but only out of jealousy. Then, very soon, people stopped worshiping Aphrodite and the visits to her temple were nil. They were worshiping Psyche instead. Blinded with rage and the assumption that she was being purposefully insulted, Aphrodite complained to her son, Eros, and plotted with Apollo, the god of the oracle. A careful plan was laid out as how to handle Aphrodite's crisis.

On earth the parents of Psyche were trying to deal with their own dilemma of the future of their alluring daughter. The two older daughters of the king and queen were already married, but with Psyche, men were intimidated by her beauty. She was worshiped and loved by them, but they were terribly afraid to ask for her hand in marriage, thinking they weren't good enough for her.

Accordingly, the king sought the oracle of Apollo regarding the future of Psyche. Deceitfully and in league with Aphrodite, Apollo told him that it was the destiny of Psyche to marry a dragon, and that she must be given the appearance of a corpse and left on the top of a hill facing a valley. From there, fate would take its course.

Eros's part of Aphrodite's plan was to shoot one of his arrows so that Psyche would fall in love and marry the ugliest and meanest man in the world. Eros, who was always up to mischief, agreed to help his mother. Then it all went wrong, and Eros never shot a single arrow. When he saw Psyche lying on the bier, he immediately fell in love with her and made his own plan contrary to that of his mother's.

When the mock funeral of Psyche was over and the mourners went sadly away, the south wind carried her safely to the vicinity of Eros's palace. Psyche woke from the death-like sleep and found herself in this strange place and soon wandered off and found her way to the palace of gold and marble. It was there that the most unimaginable things began to happen. First, she saw a table set for a feast with no visible servants and no other living person to partake. The place was filled with music and singing. Being hungry, she sat down to eat alone, and then there were the voices of the unseen servants telling her that the house was hers, that they were her servants and there to do and fetch whatever she asked. There was no need for her to be afraid of anything, the voices added.

She went to sleep, but in the middle of the night, she awoke by the presence of someone in the bed beside her. Thinking at first that this was the dragon, she was afraid to move, but finally she gained the courage to reach her hand out and touch the thing. Instead of the rough, leathery skin of a dragon, she felt a soft face and silky hair of ... well, someone. Then there was a voice, a male's voice telling and reassuring her that he was her husband, and that there was nothing for her to be afraid of. In a comforting voice, he told her that the place was hers, just as the invisible servants told her before. From then on, Psyche was relaxed, and she talked with her husband until dawn. The only thing he asked of her was that his identity must remain a secret, and she should never try to look at his face or great misfortune will befall them. When she awoke in the morning, he was gone, and she was alone.

The same experience repeated itself night after night, and during the day, Psyche was alone, so eventually boredom set in as a result of loneliness. The need for human contact was so pressing that she begged her husband to have her sisters pay her a visit. At first he would not agree, but eventually he did, but with one warning: her sisters could never know anything about him.

Again, Eros employed the powerful agent the south wind to bring her sisters to the palace.

Psyche was more than happy to see them, but the questions from the two siblings were endless. Psyche avoided the ones about her husband for as long as she could. The answers she gave were quite vague until finally she caved in and told the truth.

Her sisters told her, "He is that dragon, that monster you were doomed to marry. Hide a lamp and a sharp knife, and tonight when he is asleep, take a look at him, and if he is the dragon, cut his head off, and you'll be free." Psyche agreed and the south wind took the sisters away.

That night when her husband was asleep, Psyche took the lamp and a sharp knife and went to have a look at Eros. Instead of seeing a sleeping dragon, she saw the most handsome boy she ever laid eyes upon. He had flowing hair and a pair of golden wings that were neatly folded as he slept. From the shock of seeing someone so dashing, her hand holding the lamp shook and spilled some of the hot oil on his wing. In agony and fright, he woke from his sleep to see Psyche holding a knife over him and light in his face. "You evil demon," he shrieked. "Why are you trying to kill me?"

In tears she tried to explain, "I thought you were a dragon."

"A dragon, did I feel like a dragon when I took you in my arms? Goodbye, Psyche, you won't be seeing me again," and out the window he flew.

What happened next was tragedy and despair for Psyche. Her life of luxury vanished as if it never happened. She travelled the world to find Eros, but it only led to more misery. In the meantime, the triumphant Aphrodite knew exactly what was going on, and she was very pleased. She sent for the sad and exhausted Psyche and made a deal with her. If she could complete a set of gruesome tasks given to her, then she would be allowed to see Eros. The first of such tasks was to separate grains mixed together, a total of about seven, including wheat, millet, barley, and mustard. They were all piled up in large heaps on the ground and she was to sort them into their respective groups by sundown. Psyche didn't know where to begin, but help was on the way. A friendly ant called an army of other ants, and they completed the task for Psyche.

The tasks got more difficult and dangerous after each one was completed, not by Psyche, but by some other benevolent friend. Then the final one was to go to the underworld with a container and ask Peresphone for an ounce of her beauty. Aphrodite claimed that the burden of nursing Eros during his burn had caused her to lose some of her beauty. So into the dark underworld of Hades she went, amidst great peril, but she gave it her best. She made contact with Persephone and got the jar replenished as Aphrodite wanted, and then started the long journey back. On the way, she felt tired and lay down to rest.

Gradually, Eros was nursed back to health by his mother after the burn, and now his wound was healed. Psyche woke up from her rest and thought she could use a bit from the jar to restore some of her beauty; Aphrodite wouldn't even notice. With much hope, she opened the vessel, but there was some kind of a trick, out came a poisonous vapor that choked Psyche and she fell unconscious.

By then, Eros was able to fly about, and during flight he saw a bundle and realized that it was his beloved Psyche. He breathed immortal breath into her, and she opened her eyes and saw Eros. Their reunion was marvelous. Aphrodite was not happy, but she could not keep them apart anymore. However, they could not be married without the approval of Eros's father, Zeus. So they flew to the throne of Zeus with their story. Zeus gave Psyche the gift of immorality.

The stage went dark and the curtain went down. We applauded as Philippa looked at her watch; it was time for her to go start dinner. I enjoyed the play but couldn't commit myself to start classes before there was some assurance that I would be staying in Greece for a long time. I remembered what they said about languages: if you don't use it, you lose it.

Chapter Twelve

The memory of *Eros and Psyche* stayed in my mind after I went home, and strangely, I was thinking about it one afternoon while I was having tea and dessert on the outdoor patio of a café in Skala. Not long after I sat down, I spotted Zarek and Desirae walking and holding hands. Desirae, of course, was as elegant as ever, with the poise of a Miss Universe beauty contestant. It was no coincidence that they were coming straight towards my table; they knew that they would find me there. I looked away before I met their eyes. "Gloribella?" She tapped me on the shoulder, and I turned around.

"Hey, guys, where are you heading?" I finished my last sip of tea.

"Gloribella …" Desirae hesitated and looked at Zarek.

"Honey," Zarek responded in almost a tone of warning to her and without meeting my eyes.

"Well … I have to share this with someone. Gloribella is cool, I can tell she is."

Zarek sighed and was still unable to look at me. Their

behavior was so strange that I didn't know what to think. Without any further hesitation, Desirae pulled away from Zarek, with her left hand still in her pocket. Then slowly she took the hand out and stretched it towards me. The diamond on her fourth finger seemed astonishingly large as she flashed it before my eyes. "My babe here has just asked me to marry him, and I said yes."

"Wow, it's beautiful! Congratulations to you both and all the best for the future."

"Thank you, Gloribella, but there is something else."

Instinctively, I knew there was more, even before she said so, and that it wasn't going to be pleasant, so I held my breath and waited.

"We're flying tonight to Athens to tie the knot. Zarek wanted a big wedding with all his family and friends, but I'm already in Greece, why wait? We can have a big family event later; I don't want to wait too long."

Zarek remained silent all through her speech. I knew he had some feelings of insecurity in his relationship with her. His concern was that she might not feel the same way about him once she was finished with school. I had only known Zarek for a short time, but I had never seen him so reserved before, especially on what was supposed to be a moment of great happiness in his life. A woman who was almost as beautiful as Psyche from the Greek myth had just agreed to marry him, and there he was standing with this strange and somber expression on his face. Was he in shock or was there something else going on?

"Well, congratulations again." I started gathering up my trash and cup from the table and was getting ready to leave.

"I told you she'd be cool, Zarek, see." Zarek remained silent. "If this was a traditional wedding, I would definitely ask you to be my maid of honor. Gloribella, promise me you won't say a word to anyone," she continued.

"You have my word."

"And your blessing?"

I didn't respond. How could I when the man she was marrying was still silent?

They walked away while I dumped the trash in a bin, and I headed back to the Oils of Patmos, which wasn't far away. There wasn't much time to think about what had transpired when I got there. Uncle Joshua met me at the door. He had insisted that I call him Uncle Joshua from the very first day I entered his house, and if I ever forgot, he didn't hesitate to correct me.

"I was actually waiting on you, Gloribella." There was a serious look on his face but at the same time it was pleasant. Then he read my expression. "You look frightened, as if you had just seen a ghost. What is it?"

I wasn't about to tell him that his nephew had just run off to get married; though, he was reading me quite well. I must have looked a little flushed. "Nothing really, still trying to get used to the mysteries of this place. Every day I experienced something new."

"I can relate. I'm here for years and it still baffles me sometimes. Well, my dear girl, enjoy it, but don't let it engulf you. It's just another place on earth that is different from the rest of the world out there. In the meantime, we have pressing business to do, and I am glad you got here now. I just got off the phone with a potential business partner from New Zealand, Maximilian Rick Sharif. He is an eccentric billionaire who wants to can his sardines in some of our oils. He wants a meeting with us, but he is an across-the-table, face-to-face kind of guy who hates modern-day communication, except for a telephone and fax machine. I want to strike this deal before it gets sour or someone gives him a better offer. I would have sent Zarek, but his girl is here, and I don't think he is thinking straight. I can't go and Mustafa is out of the question. I couldn't risk the prejudice he might face."

I cut to the chase. "Uncle Joshua, if you're asking me to go, I will."

"Would you? Thank you! Along with his other oddities, Maximilian is very picky about whom he does business with. I appreciate this very much and can almost guarantee that you will come back with the signed contract."

"I will do everything in my power to make it happen." I almost call him sir, remembering he was still my boss.

"Okay, then go pack. I'll have to get on the phone right away and make all the arrangements. With a few connecting flights, you should be in New Zealand by tomorrow night, and don't worry about Johnno. Lottie and I will take good care of him until you get back."

It was at that point that I thought about my friends in the business community who were always doing this. They made six-figure salaries but were unable to keep stable family lives and they had poorly raised children.

Uncle Joshua was already on the phone while I was gathering some things from my desk, and by the time I was about to go through the door, he paused his phone conversation to say, "Your plane leaves at midnight."

Back at the mansion, Temp helped me pack, and she gave me a very expensive bag for the trip, along with outfits that were appropriate for the meeting with Maximilian Rick Sharif. After spending some time with Johnno, talking to him, and looking at all his new drawings and origami animals, I left the house. Zarek and Desirae were nowhere in sight, but his aunt was aware that they had left for Athens and had no idea that they were getting married.

Mustafa rode with me on the ferry to the airport in Leros and was my translator during the check-in process. "Once you're on the plane, it won't be a problem. You'll find plenty of people who speak English."

"Well, Mustafa, if I can't find someone who speaks and understands my language, then don't expect me back."

"You'll get to New Zealand and back just fine."

Mustafa was right. Once I got to the business class of Aegean Airlines, everything was at my disposal; Uncle Joshua arranged it all: an English-speaking stewardess, a wide assortment of food and drinks, and USB ports for my laptop. All the comforts were paid for, and I took advantage of them.

Chapter Thirteen

As soon as I was settled, I turned on the laptop and started to read the set of emails that I was so afraid of looking at. The first one in the inbox that caught my attention was from Dragan E. Bradshaw. Nick was arrested on various charges. Apparently, he was operating in a ring and there was still a bigger person at large. There was another detailed paragraph about the crimes and the people who might be involved and how crafty they were. The email ended with:

> Live your life in peace; there is nothing to fear.
> Federal prison will be the home of these people
> for a long time, and I am sorry for your loss.

I closed the laptop and my eyes for a few moments, but those few moments turned out to be longer than I thought. I slept and woke up crying. I remembered something my mother once said: everyone has loss in their life; it is built into the system, but it's how you deal with that loss that matters. Then I thought to myself I was already dealing with my loss and in a positive way.

To continue on the note of positivity, I opened another email from Lauren. She said her pregnancy was starting to show, and with all the symptoms she was hoping not to have. It took me an hour to answer her email, and I sent her the recipes we talked about. She explained that she wasn't a great cook so any advice would help, starting with oven temperatures because she had a tendency to burn things.

Cooking Temperatures

HEAT	FAHRENHEIT	CELSIUS
Very Low	250–275	121–135
Low	300–325	149–163
Moderate	350–375	177–191
Hot	400–425	204–218
Very Hot	450–475	232–246
Broil	500–525	260–274

She continued:

> Then my fresh herbs, they always go bad before I finish using them. What should I do to keep them longer?

My advice to her was to freeze them: Blend the herbs in oil and a small amount of water, then pour into ice cube trays and freeze. Remove from cubes and store in zip-seal bags for future use.

And while I was on the subject of freezing, I told her all unused pieces of ginger could be stored in plastic bags in the freezer.

Lauren also wanted to know how to keep her salad fresh and crisp when made hours in advance. I told her:

> Well, the first trick is to keep it undressed and to place tomatoes in a separate container. The next part of the puzzle is to keep the salad elevated, and the way to do that is to put a saucer upside down in the bottom of the bowl before filling it with the salad. This technique will enable the moisture to run underneath the saucer and your salad will stay fresh for longer.

One of the main recipes that she wanted was:

CALABAZA CORN CAKES

- 2 cups cooked and mashed calabaza
- ⅓ cup cooked cornmeal
- 1 tablespoon garlic powder
- 1 cup milk
- 2 cups corn kernels (cooked)
- 1 cup shredded cheddar cheese
- ¼ teaspoon Mrs. Dash® table blend salt-free seasoning
- 3 stalks scallions (thinly sliced)
- Salt and pepper to taste

METHOD

Combine cooked calabaza and cooked cornmeal in a mixing bowl, along with salt and pepper. Stir in milk, corn kernels, cheese, and scallions, and mix well. Let the mixture sit for 2 minutes. Form 1-inch balls from the mixture and flatten to form small cakes of about half of an inch thick, on a flat surface, dust cakes with flour. In a large, non-stick skillet sprayed with cooking spray, cook cakes over medium heat in batches. Cakes take about 4 minutes on each side to cook. Cook until golden brown. Serve hot.

She also wanted:

SWEET POTATO WHOLE WHEAT PASTA SALAD

- 4 sweet potatoes (diced and steamed)
- 1 16-ounce package whole wheat spiral pasta (cooked and cooled)
- 1 red bell pepper (seeded and diced)
- ½ cup scallion (finely sliced on a bias)
- ½ cup mayonnaise
- 1 cup ranch dressing
- 1 cup real bacon bits

METHOD

In a steamer pot, steam potatoes until they are slightly tender. Remove diced potatoes from steamer and transfer to mixing bowl, along with pasta. Stir in bell pepper and scallion, and let the mixture cool for about 7 minutes, then add mayonnaise and ranch dressing. Refrigerate, and just before serving add bacon bits.

Finally, I sent Lauren a conversion chart that she thought would be helpful to her.

Standard Measurement	
A pinch	⅛ teaspoon or less
3 teaspoons	1 tablespoon
4 tablespoons	¼ cup
8 tablespoons	½ cup
12 tablespoons	¾ cup
16 tablespoons	1 cup
2 cups	1 pint
4 cups	1 quart
4 quarts	1 gallon
8 quarts	1 peck
4 pecks	1 bushel
16 ounces	1 pound
32 ounces	1 quart
1 liquid ounce	2 tablespoons
8 liquid ounces	1 cup

During the hours and countless hours I spent on the plane, I answered tons of emails and sent out recipes to people, especially the friends I made at the mission house.

I opened Vera's email and sure enough, she wanted the three recipes we previously discussed. So, I started with the date blueberry pudding.

INFUSED

DATE BLUEBERRY PUDDING

3 cups fresh blueberries
1 cup pitted dates
1 cup water
2 teaspoons lemon juice
2 tablespoons unsalted butter

6 slices white or whole wheat bread (crust removed)
Butter
Ground cinnamon for sprinkling

METHOD

Search through blueberries for unwanted particles and spoiled berries. Rinse well and set aside in a strainer. Chop dates and check for pits. In a saucepan add 1 cup water and dates; cover and cook for 15 minutes, then add blueberries. Cook uncovered until berries are softened and juices are released. Stir occasionally and cook for another 10 minutes. Remove from heat and cool slightly, then stir in lemon juice. Spread the butter on the slices of bread and sprinkle cinnamon. Spray a loaf pan with non-stick spray and start lining the pan with the slices of bread. Spread berries mixture evenly over bread slices, alternately making sure the top layer is completely covered. Refrigerate for 6–8 hours. Serve with rum and raisin ice cream or whipped cream and strawberries.

Then she wanted a recipe for hummingbird cake but one that would be healthier than the familiar ones.

SUGAR FREE HUMMINGBIRD CAKE

3 cups almond flour
1 cup Splenda
1 teaspoon baking powder
1 teaspoon salt
1 teaspoon ground cinnamon

3 eggs
1 cup vegetable oil
2 cups mashed banana
1 cup golden raisins
1 cup crushed pineapple
1½ teaspoons vanilla extract

METHOD
Preheat oven to 350° and prepare 3 (9-inch) round cake pans by spraying them with non-stick cooking spray with flour. Combine 3 cups almond flour with Splenda, baking powder, salt, and ground cinnamon in a mixing bowl. Add eggs and oil then stir until the dry ingredients are moistened. Stir in bananas, slivered almonds, pineapple, and vanilla extract. Manually mix the ingredients and then pour even amounts into prepared pans. Bake at 350° for 25–30 minutes, or until a wooden toothpick inserted in center comes out clean. Cool cake layers completely before frosting. Spread frosting between layers and all around until cake is completely covered. Store in refrigerator until ready to serve.

Cream Cheese Frosting

1 8-ounce package low-fat cream cheese (softened)

1 16-ounce tub low-fat whipped cream

1 teaspoon vanilla extract

METHOD
Beat cream cheese and whipped cream and vanilla extract with an electric mixer at medium speed until smooth.

And finally, I sent Vera buckwheat black bean stars. I consider buckwheat the star of the grain family, so I decided to re-name this recipe buckwheat black bean stars.

BUCKWHEAT BLACK BEAN STARS

1½ cups chicken or beef stock

1½ cups buckwheat

1 16-ounce can black beans

½ cup low-fat ricotta cheese

¾ cup wheat germ or bran

½ teaspoon freshly ground black pepper

Fresh cilantro to top stars

Low-fat sour cream

Breading Mixture

1 cup wheat germ or bran mixed with 1 teaspoon black pepper for breading stars.

METHOD

Rinse buckwheat in a fine strainer under cold running tap water and remove any unwanted particles, then set aside to drain. In a 1-quart saucepan bring the stock to boil. Add buckwheat, stir and cook for 1 minute on high heat, then lower the heat, cover, and simmer for 8–10 minutes until stock is absorbed. While buckwheat is cooking, drain black beans and reserve liquid for future use. In a large mixing bowl, mash beans with a potato masher and combine cooled buckwheat along with low-fat ricotta cheese, wheat germ or bran, and freshly ground black pepper. Mix into a dough-like consistency, adding the liquid from the beans if necessary. Transfer dough to a cutting board or flat surface. Press dough with a rolling pin to the thickness of ¼ of an inch and use a star-shaped cookie cutter to cut out stars. Dip stars in breading mixture and fry in small amounts of oil or butter until crisp. Serve with sour cream and fresh cilantro.

For another missionary who wanted recipes for vegetarians I sent the following:

GREEN LIMA BEAN SOUP

2 cups green lima beans
6 cups vegetable stock
2 cloves garlic (minced)
1 teaspoon Mrs. Dash® garlic and herb salt free seasoning
⅓ cup olive oil
¼ cup lemon juice
2 tablespoons fresh parsley (finely chopped)

METHOD

Combine beans and stock in a medium stock pot and bring to a boil. Reduce heat and simmer for 30 minutes or until soft. With an immersion or hand-held blender, puree until smooth. Add hot stock if too thick. Stir in garlic, garlic and herb salt-free seasoning, olive oil, and lemon juice, and simmer for 5 minutes. Serve hot and garnish with fresh parsley.

GRILLED EGGPLANT SANDWICHES

3 small eggplants	2 tablespoons fresh basil leaves (chopped)
Olive oil	
1 cup roasted red peppers (from jar)	6½ ounces goat cheese
	Sea salt
1 cup sun-dried tomatoes in olive oil	Thinly sliced multi-grain bread

METHOD

Cut the eggplants lengthwise into slices about ½ an inch thick. Wrap slices individually in paper towels and pressed under heavy weight, such as a brick, for about 1 hour. This will extract some of the moisture in the eggplants. Brush eggplants with olive oil, and on a hot grill, grill eggplant on both sides until grill marks are clearly visibly. Sprinkle lightly with sea salt while on the grill. In the meantime, drain sun-dried tomatoes from oil and set aside. To assemble sandwiches, spread goat cheese on 2 slices of bread, then lay basil leaves, red roasted peppers, and sun-dried tomatoes on bread, then top with grilled eggplant. Close sandwiches and serve warm.

And yet another missionary wanted this:

GARLIC ROASTED SALMON AND BULGUR

12 large cloves of garlic (elephant garlic is a good choice)
¼ cup extra-virgin olive oil
½ teaspoon capers
¾ teaspoon freshly ground black pepper
1 teaspoon lemon juice
2 cups chicken stock
1 tablespoon extra-virgin olive oil
1 onion (minced)
2 pounds salmon filets (cut into 6 portions with skin removed)
1 cup bulgur

METHOD

Roast garlic as discussed on page 170. Divide the roasted garlic into 2 equal parts. In a medium saucepan sauté onion in 1 tablespoon extra-virgin olive oil, then stir in bulgur. Keep stirring for another 30 seconds then add chicken stock and bring mixture to a rapid boil. Cover pot and turn heat to low. Cook for 30 minutes or until liquid is absorbed and grains are tender.

In the meantime, set oven to 450°. In a small mixing bowl, add capers and ¼ cup extra-virgin olive oil. Use a fork to crush the caper buds in the olive oil, then whisk in roasted garlic, freshly ground black pepper, and lemon juice. Whisk until all the ingredients are combined. Lay salmon filets on a baking sheet skin-side down and use a basting brush to coat the salmon with the olive oil mixture. Bake for 15 minutes on one side. Remove from oven and serve with bulgur.

The list of people wanting recipes went on and on, and I managed to answer every single one of them. That was the best way to kill time.

At some point, we crossed the International Date Line, but I had no idea when that took place. The gaining and losing of time followed as we crossed over into Sydney Australia. At the airport, I barely had time to spare before I was on another plane to Christchurch, New Zealand. I couldn't remember how long since I had left Greece, having been on a plane for such a lengthy time.

I checked in the Hotel Novotel at Christchurch and only had about twenty minutes to rest and clean up before my meeting with Maximilian Rick Sharif. He was gracious enough to request to meet me in one of the conference rooms at the Novotel. I was grateful for not having to race around a foreign city within the first hour of my arrival.

Maximilian was already in the room waiting when I got there, and he stood up when I entered. He was tall and lean, with sort of reddish, sandy hair. He was oddly dressed, with a weird color scheme, a plaid blazer of maroon and white and bright blue polyester pants with busy patterns. I could see why Uncle Joshua said he was eccentric. Although his skills in dressing were poor, he was quite jolly, and he had a great personality. "That color looks great on you, Miss Gloribella Frank." he pulled out a chair and waited for me to sit before he took his own chair at the other end of the table, facing me.

"Joshua sent me your picture, so I knew exactly what you would look like. Yes, your picture got here before you. You are beautiful."

I was wondering where he was going with all these compliments as I looked around the room. It seemed like one of the smaller conference rooms in the hotel, yet large enough to seat about twenty to thirty people. Then I noticed something else; the entire room was filled with patterns, not just Maximilian's outfit. The glass on the long conference table was decorative glass. An entire city was engraved along the whole length of the table's surface. The city might have been Christchurch; I would find out soon. I had no prior knowledge about the place except for the little I read in the hotel's brochure. I studied the carpet, and it was the most mesmerizing design I had ever seen as far as rugs go. Squiggly black lines meandering like snakes ran horizontally along the floor. Then the painting on the wall got my attention. It was of a spotted owl of gray and white with piercing eyes staring at me, almost as if it could read my innermost private thoughts.

Maximilian's words of admiration ended abruptly when a young woman about my age walked into the room. She wore a blue evening gown that complimented her eyes, which were another shade of blue, while her blonde hair bounced on and off her shoulders, but the most expensive thing she wore was a pair of heart-shaped dangling diamond earrings.

Maximilian stopped talking, looked at her, and then turned to me. "This is my wife, Eva." Then to her he said, "Gloribella and I were waiting on you, dear. What took you so long?"

Eva did not respond but walked over to me, and with a handshake, she said, "Great to meet you, Gloribella."

Maximilian pulled out a chair for his wife, and looking at the two people directly, I could see an age difference of about thirty years.

"So, how is old Josh doing? I remember the first time he walked into my office, eons ago, proud and ambitious. I knew he was going somewhere, and then that marriage of his to ..." He scratched his head trying to recall a name. I kept quiet while he struggled and then he gave up. "Oh ... whatever her name is. I can't remember anything these days, not even the color of my socks."

Eva smiled and shook her head. "So how did you meet Joshua?" she asked.

"Oh, I met him through his nephew, Zarek."

She nodded as two waiters walked into the room carrying trays, which they set down on the table. I watched as they pulled the covers and towels from the trays. As it turned out, they'd brought in jugs of ice water, crackers, cheeses, and grapes, but there was also a dome-shaped silver platter that was not uncovered. The waiters left us, and Maximilian rubbed his hands together in anticipation, "So, Gloribella, show us what you got."

Well, what I had was the same as all business people have: a video and a Power Point presentation. I could simply tell them in conversation what our business of infused oil was all about, but Uncle Joshua wanted the formal presentation. Since the conference room was equipped with screens and machines, I did what he wanted. I knew it went well when Maximilian told me to stop the projector and then applauded. "Now, let's apply your infused oil to sardines."

The waiters entered the room again and uncovered the silver platter containing sardines on beds of lettuce and red onions. Then I saw the infused oils in small crystal cruets on a tray next to the platter. The waiters left the room after making sure everything we needed was there.

"Gloribella, I really don't have many questions since most things were already explained in the presentation, and what wasn't there, Josh had previously filled me in on, but can you tell me more about this oil we are about to try? This spice and flavor is new to me."

"Well, allspice is from the island of Jamaica, and the Jamaicans call it pimento. It's a rare combination of Mother Nature's, the mixing of three spices that many people love: cinnamon, nutmeg, and cloves. It is grown only in warm climates, and I will provide you with more of its history."

"Thank you, Gloribella. Okay, let's do our sampling, my love," Maximilian announced to his wife.

Eva drizzled some of the infused oil on her sardines and crackers. "Mm! Very good, and I am picky when it comes to my spices."

"Excellent," Maximilian agreed after digging into his. "And this was your creation after you joined Oils of Patmos, this is a new oil?"

"Yes, it is the latest since I started."

He looked at his wife, and she nodded. "Definitely should be part of our brand," she said.

"Okay, I'll contact Josh and will most certainly make my decision within twenty-four hours. He stood up. "Get some rest, my child; we'll make it worth your trip."

I went back to my room and slept the entire night. Waking

up the next day, I was close to brand new when I opened my eyes. As I walked around the room, I noticed that a large brown envelope had been shoved under the door. I wanted to make sure there was no mistake, so I opened the envelope and read the entire contents of the package. First, there was a brief sticky note stuck to the white embossed pages. It read:

> Sorry, my dear, we wanted to see you again but had to run off to a convention in Canada. The contract is signed, as you will see. Thanks for your gracious company last night.
>
> All the best,
>
> Maximilian R. Sharif

Although I had known it was a strong possibility Maximilian would sign, I was proud of myself after I read the contract, and I contacted Uncle Joshua right away to give him the good news. He asked me to fax it to him as soon as I had a chance, and while I was searching for his fax number, I stumbled upon something strange but amazing, the phone number of Hortense from the mission house. She was somewhere in Christchurch, and I couldn't leave without giving her a call.

I dialed the number from the hotel phone and a representative for the organization she worked for answered. The place was a charitable trust that was helping to rebuild Christchurch after the 2011 earthquake. They gave me another number where I could reach her; obviously, a cell phone number.

She was extremely shocked to hear that I was in Christchurch and just minutes away from her. "Gloribella! In New Zealand and Christchurch? Why?"

"I'm on business for a new job I started after I met you guys."

"Great! Such a small world; I never thought I would hear from you on the phone, let alone from this part of the world. How long are you staying?"

"Actually, my meeting is over, and there's not much more for me to do here. I'm taking the red-eye back to Greece tonight."

"Greece? You sure get around. Where are you staying now?"

"I'm at the Novotel."

"Okay, great. We can hang out for a while and have lunch. I wish I could take the rest of the afternoon off, but I have this little part-time job that I have to show up at later, just to make ends meet."

"I understand. I'm not familiar with the place, but tell me where to meet you."

"Oh, no, I won't let you roam all over a strange city. Just meet me by the Queen Victoria statue at Victoria Square. It's very easy to find, not far from your hotel; anyone can show you. It's a beautiful day to take a stroll."

"Okay, I'll find it."

"Okey-dokey, call me if there's a problem."

Surrounded by trees and shrubbery in a park setting, I found the statue of Queen Victoria on top of a monument in Victoria Square. As part of the hotel courtesy, a man named Kyle drove me there, saving me the walk and the anxiety of asking strangers. I was grateful to the kind man, and he was more than happy to provide the service.

It wasn't difficult to separate the tourists from the locals, and if I had waited longer for Hortense, I would have had time to guess who was who as they passed by. I saw familiar things common to many cities and towns, yet of all the things I saw during the few minutes I waited, nothing was more familiar than a woman sitting with her back turned towards me. She wore a blue dress with white polka dots. Quite elegantly, she wore a blue pillbox hat with a veil, and seemed as if she was admiring a bed of marigolds. It was the type of outfit my mother would wear, and as a matter of fact, I knew she had exactly the same apparel. Even at that moment, I still didn't know what had happen to her during the fire in Soy, and I was still yearning to know.

As creepy as it sounds, I started to walk towards this stranger whose face I couldn't see, just to make sure it wasn't her. Before I got close, the woman got up and walk away. "Mom!" I said. The woman kept on walking with no intention of engaging me, and I sped up but not fast enough. Then a busload of children rushed by laughing and screaming, cutting off my path while the woman with the blue veil vanished. There had only been a few times when I felt more disappointed, but I composed myself as I waited for Hortense to show up. I was still early, and she wasn't due for another fifteen minutes, and while I walked around the park listening to the deep accents of the New Zealanders, I called my sister, Mia. I had no idea what time of day it was in Boston, but Mia said it was about noon on Sunday. "Well, I'm glad I didn't wake you in the middle of the night."

"Gloribella, where are you?"

"Christchurch, New Zealand, why?"

"Wait a minute, I don't understand. You're in church? Where?"

I giggled slightly at what she asked.

"Why is that funny?" Mia and I always got into these moments of misunderstanding, which always ended with one of us getting impatient.

"I am in the city of Christchurch, New Zealand, silly."

"I've never heard of it before. What are you doing there anyway?"

"I'm on business for a new job."

"You're not at the restaurant anymore?"

"No, quite a lot happened within a short while. I'll have to fill you in later, don't have the time now. Any word from Mom?"

"Yes, of course. We were all trying to reach you, but it seems like you've fallen off the face of the earth."

"Mia, you're scaring me. What happened?"

"No, she's fine."

I breathed so hard she must have heard it on the other side of the line. "Where is she now?"

"As of this moment, I don't know, but she is with the new boyfriend I told you about."

"The mystery man?"

"Yes. On the day of the fire, she was with him; they were touring."

"So how is her mental state finding out that she lost everything in Soy?"

"She didn't lose anything."

"What do you mean? Soy was burnt to the ground; I went there myself."

"She sold the house a month before the fire."

"What? She sold the house without telling us? That's something we all should have signed off on."

"I agree, but you know Mom. She claimed every penny from the sale is in the bank, in a special account in our names. The other thing I wanted to talk to you about was that she kept our childhood stuff: dolls, report cards everything. I got mine, but nobody knew where to send yours, but as soon as she speaks with you, she'll send them."

"Send what, really?"

"Are you listening to me? I just told you."

I guess I was zoning out from the good news that Mom was okay. It put my mind at ease knowing that the worst didn't happen. We were among the lucky ones in Soy, but all this time I hadn't been sure.

Mia must have read my mind during my moments of silence, because she knew I hadn't hung up on her. "Mom thinks we are blessed."

I didn't comment on what she had said but strayed from the point to something else that was puzzling me. "Any idea yet as to who she is dating?"

"No, not even a picture; the only thing she says is that his name is Stephen Bozwell. Of course I searched the Internet, but I came up with the wrong person. This man isn't listed anywhere, and Mom says he wants to keep his privacy. Now it's started to bother me because he could be a psychopath."

"Well ... could it be that she gave a false name? Remember, it's not unlike our mom to make up stories like that when she wants to hide things from us. She did it all the time when we were kids."

"Yes, but this time is different. We are all adults now. Unless something is wrong with this man."

"I saw a woman today, and I could almost swear it was her, only I didn't see this person's face. What are the chances that Mom and I could both be here and not know it?"

"It is possible since she said she would be going on a world tour."

"Mia, stop, this is just too bizarre. Is Mom even still in the church?"

"No. Before Soy was burnt down, there was a big falling out between the bishop and the new choir director, Dr. Wilson, who was forced to resign. He took almost a quarter of the congregation with him. Mom was among them, and now she is into New Age stuff."

"Wow!"

"The other big shake-up in the church was with Alex."

"Alex? What happened to him?"

"I'm not sure, but months before Dr. Wilson left, Alex announced from the pulpit that he had a lot of soul searching and cleansing to do, so he could no longer serve as their assistant pastor."

"Very strange. I never expected to hear any of this. Check your email tonight; I'll explain my situation. I'm meeting a friend for lunch now but will stay in touch."

"Please do. I'm hanging on a cliff now, and I never like suspense."

Hortense arrived at the exact time we were supposed to meet. She was the same nervous person, quite unsure of herself. "Did you wait too long? It was so hard getting out of that office, but you don't need to hear my problems."

"No, you're good, you said in thirty minutes, and I was on the phone with my sister."

"Oh ... okay, thanks then."

Hortense and I knew very little about each other. Our paths had crossed for less than seventy-two hours, yet it seemed as if I had known her longer. She was like that shy schoolmate you've known almost all your life but still don't really know, always in the background and never up front. We talked about what our lives had become after the mission house and of course how I ended up in Greece.

"Wow, I wish my life was that interesting."

"But it is, Hortense; you just don't realize it."

"I don't know that, Gloribella. Anyway, I wish you were staying here longer. There is a lot to see in Christchurch. I discover something new every day."

Hortense and I walked around the city for a long time until we ended up by the Bridge of Remembrance. Then she asked about Reverend Tanner.

"I haven't seen him since the day I left the mission house, but I'm sure he's fine doing the work of God."

She talked fondly of the relatives who had raised her without mentioning their names, but then changed the subject to the bridge, which had been damaged by the earthquake. Construction workers were quite abundant and the digging noise of jackhammers jarred the nerves as we got close to them. Walking around while we talked made the conversation with Hortense easier. It was less intense and we could pause to comment on the scenery or even changed the subject to the damaged city and the beautiful landscape.

"Your Zarek sounds like a nice guy, getting you this job and everything else."

"He's not my Zarek. He is somewhere honeymooning now with one of the most beautiful women, second to a Greek goddess."

"Sorry, after all you've been through, you deserved happiness; you deserved him."

"Well, we don't always get what we deserve, at least some of us; that's the kind of world we live in."

"Of course, I know exactly what you're talking about. I'm thirty years old with my own share of disappointments, failed marriage, unsuccessful at motherhood, and at forty, when I write my six-volume memoir, you'll read the rest."

"Really. So how are things going for you here in Christchurch? This is different; it is the road less travelled."

"It's not easy, but I have no doubt this is what God wants me to do, help to rebuild lives that were broken, just like mine."

"Too bad I will have to wait to read your memoir. With six volumes, maybe I should get a head start."

"I don't think you need that, and since your time here is short, talking about me is counterproductive. You need to see the rest of Christchurch. I would also like to get to the healthy foods we talked about at the mission house. I still can't believe you're really here."

"I remember you wanted a list of the forgotten grains and information about them."

"Yes, thank you. I always wanted to try something new but had no idea what was out there."

I reached into my bag and found my notebook and turned to the pages I had marked. "Do you know where we could find a photocopier around here? It would be much faster than writing them out."

"Sure, let's go." We walked to a sort of variety store, and along with the copying of the information, we had coffee. The list included amaranth, one of the powerhouses of proteins. Great for baking and widely used in desserts.

Then there was the golden grain, quinoa, the only plant that contains the nine essential amino acids.

Buckwheat was prominent on the list, and not actually a wheat, but related to other plants such as sorrel, rhubarb, and dock. It was a great substitute for rice.

The trip back to Patmos, Greece, was just the reverse of going to Christchurch a few days before in terms of travel time. After a while, my fellow passengers close-by felt like roommates. I had become so aware of their habits, that I could almost predict what their next move was going to be. There were no major events that I could recall, since I slept through most of the trip as if I was drugged. When I was awake, I dealt with as many emails as I could. One such email was from Uncle Joshua telling me that he would send Mustafa to pick me up at the airport.

Chapter Fourteen

About half an hour before the plane descended into Leros airport, I started to think about all that had happened from the time I left Greece to the present touchdown. I tried to figure out what this trip was all about. Was it just to get a contract, which was great! Maximilian even promised to name the new sardines he'd manufacture Gloribella. What did I learn? Well, like a tape recorder, it was all there and would come back when the tape got to that point. I didn't have to racked my brain so hard; I just needed to wait.

"It is a fair day with temperatures in the seventies," the captain on the plane was saying, and he said he hoped we'd enjoyed our trip. After being checked through, I walked out of customs and headed for the exit where Mustafa should be waiting, but strangely, the person waiting wasn't who I was expecting; it was Zarek who stood there. I was very curious as to why he was there, but it was obvious: Mustafa couldn't come, so out of loyalty to his uncle, Zarek took leave from his new bride to pick me up. Well, I could have managed on my own.

Zarek smiled when he saw me, but I did not return the warmth. I think I was still stinging from the fact that he didn't tell me he was planning on getting married, even after we'd shared so much in the past.

"I know that you were expecting Mustafa, but we switched places."

"Frankly, yes. I thought you were on your honeymoon."

He paused to look more directly at me, trying to read my expression, almost as if he wanted to ask, who are you? Another moment of awkward silence followed before he said, "No, I'm not."

Neither of us said anything else, but then he took the initiative to ask, "Can I take your bag?"

I had no reason to refuse, since I had been carrying around the same stupid overnight bag for what seems like an eternity. I gave him the bag and we walked away in silence. I realize that this was totally unlike me, but I was also tired and jet-lagged. Even an hour of sleep in a real bed would help. Before I could think of something to break the silence, which was becoming overwhelmingly uncomfortable. Zarek asked, "How was your trip?"

"It was good. Somewhat interesting and strange."

"Uncle Joshua is very excited about the new contract you got him. You were perfect for the job; Maximilian R. Sharif can be quite a handful, but in the presence of a beautiful woman, he is putty. Why did you say the trip was strange?"

"I saw a woman who I thought was my mother and never got a chance to verify if it was her."

"Sorry, that hurts, and yes, strange, but what would your mother be doing in that city?"

"It's a long story."

"We have time; the ferry won't be here for another thirty minutes."

I thought about telling him the whole story of what I learned from Mia, but then I felt like our friendship wasn't the same anymore. I decided I wouldn't discuss personal things with him. I would stick to business, the business he got me into. If he didn't trust me enough to tell me he was getting married, why should I bare my soul to him? Why would it matter anyway? He was under the spell of his beautiful wife. He broke through my thoughts. "Sorry I couldn't go with you."

"What?"

"Sorry I didn't go with you," he repeated.

"How could you? You weren't here; you went to Athens to get married to your fiancée on the same day."

"I am not married, and I never said I was going to, did I?"

"Excuse me? What? What do you mean? I saw the ring, the engagement ring, and at the house, Aunt Temp said you and Desirae went off to Athens. What are you saying now?"

"Look, Gloribella, it wasn't what it appeared to be. I allowed myself to be caught up in something childish and irresponsible."

"Come again, irresponsible?"

"Well, it started out silly. We were walking along the harbor in Skala when Desirae picked up a ring somebody had lost, a cheap piece of costume jewelry that looked real. Seeing you that afternoon fueled this supposed joke of hers. After testing it on you, and much to my displeasure it seemed to work, she began to change this joke to reality. I am by no means a weak person, and family means a lot to me, but by the time we got to the house, I was thinking maybe this was my last chance to ... I don't even know what."

"I don't know, you two seem perfect together," I said, a bit frazzled.

"But there was one underlying factor that was keeping me back the whole time, not only the idea of eloping. I am not an eloper by nature. Something else started before Desirae got to Patmos."

"What was that?"

"Well, if I can get through relating this ridiculous experience without feeling like a total idiot, I'll tell you. So, to continue, Desirae realized that I was hesitant throughout her entire game and asked me if I was in love with her. It was a very frightening question because I realized at that moment that I wasn't. It was a very strong physical attraction that I had for her. Something that would have cost me dearly in the long run, but it wasn't love. From then on, everything went downhill. I could not make right the wrong I did, according to her. We were exactly here in Leros when she walked away from me, catching the plane back to the States instead of Athens. The last thing she said before she walked away was to accuse me of cheating. She claimed that I am in love with this person and refused to marry her for that reason."

"And is that true?"

"Yes."

"You ... were cheating?"

"No! Heavens, no, but I couldn't marry someone I wasn't in love with."

"Sounds odd, but may I ask who this person is; although, it's none of my business."

"It's you."

"Me?"

"Yes, it was always you, from the day you entered that boat, you entered my heart and my life. So, the million-dollar question now is, do you feel the same way about me? And even if the answer is no, it still won't change my love for you."

We were still walking towards the dock for the ferry back to Patmos, and I saw the boats in the water and an avalanche of memories came rushing back towards me. Each significant event in our lives so far, seemed to be centered around boats and the ocean. Even more memorable, were the words of Hortense: "Your Zarek sounds like a nice guy, after all you've been through, you deserve happiness; you deserve him." He had shown nothing but love and kindness, never a moment of despair, but endless hope instead. I could not think of a better person to love. "I feel exactly the same about you," I answered, knowing very well this was not the time to pretend or play games.

Without saying anything, he dropped the bag and pulled me close to him. I could feel his heart pounding in his chest and the warmth of his breath passing over my neck. It was a moment I didn't want to end, but our ferry was pulling into the harbor, and I wanted to be back in Patmos.

On the ferry, Zarek sat close to me, taking my hand tenderly. "Are you tired?" he asked.

"I was, but not anymore." I felt a sense of warmth and safety with him that could not be easily explained; it was a drug that pharmaceutical labs could never manufacture, and if they could, it would not be cheaply retailed.

I thought it was time to give something back, something tangible that he could appreciate. On my last day in Christchurch, after I left Hortense, I went shopping. On an impulse, I bought a gift with no particular person in mind. It was a green and silver Swiss Army Knife with a handle of bone. The engraving was a symbol of New Zealand, the unfurling fronds of the baby fern. According to the girl in the gift shop, it meant new life, growth, strength, and peace. This particular design was a key-shaped figure with two distinctive fronds coming together to form a heart on the bow of the key. "It is the perfect symbol and gift for someone you love," the clerk informed me. I was sold the moment I saw it. Carefully, she packed it in a black velvet case for me.

I placed it in his hand, and like a child, he excitedly took and opened the gift, "Sweet, very, very nice. I always wanted one of these, ever since I was twelve." He turned it from side to side, admiring the craftsmanship and trying to figure out the design. It took him only a minute or two to make the connection with New Zealand's national symbol. I told him the deeper meaning of the ferns.

I wasn't quite sure how long the ferry ride lasted, but it seemed very fast. People were all around us speaking different languages, or it could all have been various dialects of Greek. There was only one voice I was really concentrating on and that was Zarek's. He whispered in my ear, "I love you, always have."

"I love you too." I couldn't say I was totally surprised; the signs were there.

"Is there any reason why your mother would be in New Zealand?"

It was time for me to tell him everything, before we got any further in what we had started. "My sister said she's on a world tour. Recently, she met a man with lots of money, and I'm told that they are taking advantage of it."

"And this stranger, did she see you at any point?"

"Difficult to tell. She might had seen me long before I saw her. Whoever the person was, she got up and walked away, then the kids got in my way, and that was the end of that. My mother also sold the house in Soy before the fire; none of us knew that."

"Wow, is she clairvoyant or what?"

"Not that I know of."

"Gloribella, now that you're my girl, I should also tell you about my family, the secrets that we all were keeping."

"Secrets? Okay, you have my attention."

"Well, as you know Uncle Josh is my father's younger brother, but what you didn't know was that Aunt Tempest is my mother's youngest sister."

"Well, it doesn't get more uncle and aunt than that. So, Temp is actually the short for Tempest, wow!

"Correct. Anyway, here is the deal. They are not married; they just live together, well, in sin according to the church. It's just not announced. Agatha R. B. Cross is my uncle's lawful wife."

"Amazing, I would never have thought of that in a million years. Agatha?"

"The problem is, she swears that she'll never grant him a divorce."

"But why? Obviously, he doesn't want to be married to her anymore."

"You're right. They can never be in the same room for five minutes without an argument."

"So why is she holding on to something that doesn't exist, a marriage?"

"Well, she's crazy and spiteful, and the fact that he wanted to marry Aunt Temp makes it worse."

"I'm sure there is some legal way to get this divorce if they haven't been living together for a while."

"It's been about fifteen years, since when Mustafa was a little kid. He's their son."

"Mustafa ... ? He's their son?"

"Yes, but that's another story. When the business was in trouble and Uncle Josh almost went bankrupt, Agatha bailed him out by putting a large amount of cash flow into the business. They made a deal: she would stay on the submarine and in their New York apartment until the loan was paid back and he would stay in Greece with his mistress. The house is family property bought by my grandfather. He offered to pay her back several times, but she refused to take the money, and for the sake of Mustafa, Uncle Josh decided to keep the peace."

"So it's kind of blackmail?"

"Exactly."

By the time we got to the Port of Skala, we had exchanged quite a few family stories, but Zarek had one more surprise in store for me, and that one I didn't expect. We got off the ferry and decided to walk. I needed to stretch my legs before we called Mustafa to pick us up. We got as far as the restaurant in Chora where Zarek and I first had the ice cream cones. We went inside, and there were about a dozen people there, some of whom Zarek had known over the years. After we were seated and the waiter brought us water, Zarek took my hand in front of the people he knew then went down on his knees, and everyone stopped what they were doing. "What's going on?" I asked.

He reached in his pocket and took out a ring box and opened it. The diamond seated in the little case almost took my breath away. I wasn't new to rings and proposals, but nothing had ever felt as right in a long time as that moment was. "Gloribella, I can't think of a better time to do this than now. I don't think we need a long courtship and years to know each other. This is it for me. Will you marry me?" Most of the people around us were recording the moment on their cell phones.

I remembered that it was just a few days before that that I thought I had lost him to a woman who had outranked me in beauty and in charm, so there and then I said, "Yes, of course I'll marry you."

The small audience cheered, and one woman who was

watching and recording from the beginning held up her phone. "I'll send it to you, just give me your number before you leave," she said.

The restaurant, which had seemed dead before, suddenly came to life with chatter in both English and Greek and whatever other tongues were mixed in. I couldn't tell what they were saying, but I knew they were all wishing us well, and that was all that mattered.

That night at the house they threw us a party to celebrate my safe return from New Zealand and the engagement. Philippa made a wonderful meal, and to start us off she served roasted garlic and pumpkin soup.

ROASTED GARLIC AND PUMPKIN SOUP

1 head of garlic	4½ cups chicken broth (heated)
Olive oil	3 tablespoons heavy cream
Kosher salt	½ teaspoon freshly ground black pepper
4 cups kabocha pumpkin (cubed)	Scallion for topping
1 small white onion (diced)	

METHOD

There are two ways of roasting garlic. Method 1, peel away the outer papery layer and skins off the garlic, leaving the cloves exposed and place in a sheet of foil. Pour 1 teaspoon olive oil over the garlic cloves with a sprinkle of salt and close the foil. Set oven to 400° and roast garlic for about 30 minutes. Method 2, cut garlic into two equal halves, leaving the skins on the cloves intact. Place the two halves on a sheet of foil. Drizzle with the same amount of olive oil as in method 1 and sprinkle with salt, close the foil, and place in the middle rack and roast at 400° for about 40 minutes. Cool before opening foil.

While the garlic is roasting, steam pumpkin in a steamer for about 20 minutes until tender. Add onion during the last 5 minutes of steaming to slightly soften the onions. Remove pumpkin and onions from steamer and transfer to a medium pot. Add hot chicken stock, heavy cream, roasted garlic, salt, and pepper. Using an immersion blender, process mixture until smooth. Cook for another 5 minutes, stir continuously. Serve in soup bowls and garnish with scallions.

Following that, Philippa served a slow cooker leg of lamb that was amazing. This was her recipe.

SLOW COOKER LAMB

1 5–7-pound leg of lamb (bone removed)
1 teaspoon sea salt
Black peppercorns (about 12)
8 cloves of garlic
10 sprigs fresh thyme
2 sprigs fresh rosemary
1 onion
2 stalks celery (chopped)
2 carrots (sliced ½-inch thick)
¼ cup beef broth
2 tablespoons grapeseed oil

METHOD

Have bone removed by a butcher and tie the lamb with cooking twine. Massage meat with sea salt. In a large skillet drizzle oil and brown lamb on all sides. Cover the bottom of a slow cooker with onion, carrots, celery, and beef broth. Place lamb on top of the onion mixture, then arrange peppercorns, garlic cloves, thyme, and rosemary on top of and around the lamb. Cook on low setting for 6–8 hours. Turn the lamb only once halfway through the cooking process. The lamb is cooked when it's tender. After cooking, remove lamb from slow cooker and wrap in aluminum foil and cool for 15 minutes. Slice meat against the grain.

This dish was served with a wild rice arugula salad.

WILD RICE ARUGULA SALAD

2 cups wild rice (cooked)
3 cups arugula
1 red onion (chopped)
1 large seedless cucumber
   (diced ¼ of an inch)

1 tablespoon lemon juice
3½ tablespoons extra
   virgin olive oil
Pinch of salt

METHOD

Whisk lemon juice, extra-virgin olive oil, and salt in a large salad bowl, then mix in onion and cucumber. Gently fold in arugula leaves, followed by wild rice.

They certainly knew how to throw a party on short notice and quite successfully, or it was probably already planned, unknown only to me. I didn't ask; I was just too happy to experience love, family, and friendship.

The stamina and enthusiasm of Joshua John Cavallo, otherwise known as Uncle Joshua or the man who kept the Oils of Patmos afloat and flourishing, seemed more content than I'd ever seen him over the short period since we had been introduced. He was happy for my help with new ideas and more so that I would soon be part of his family. Our lives continued at an even pace for a while, and then Zarek and I set a wedding date. We did not want a long engagement, and as Zarek jokingly said, he was afraid I might change my mind.

Aunt Temp was a great wedding planner. She took care of all the arrangements, and the fact that she knew the monks at the monastery helped us a great deal. She was the seamstress who had the job of sewing their religious garbs, and therefore, we had no trouble getting their main chapel for the ceremony. The guest list was quite long, but only my immediate family, my siblings, were willing to fly to Greece for a wedding, especially since I called off a previous one not too long ago. I had no desire to open up this whole can of worms once more. My mother's whereabouts were still a mystery, and she couldn't be reached.

Chapter Fifteen

We were pronounced husband and wife one Saturday afternoon in the historic chapel, of all the places on earth I was married in one of the most sacred spots in Christendom, a place that was declared a World Heritage Site, talk about fate. The great bells tolled, and we walked under an arch, and while cameras were flashing, a woman walked up to me, obviously one of the guests. She was elegantly dressed with bright red lipstick that matched her shoes. She kissed me on the cheek and pressed a little pendant into my hand; it was beautifully carved with an eye in the center. It was a protection from the evil eye, and obviously something she strongly believed in. "Thank you, thank you so much," I told her. With a husband by my side, I felt really protected, but could always use another eye. Zarek had no clue who the woman was, and it took me a minute or two after she left to figure her out. It was Elsada Welch, out of her mythology costume.

The reception was held at one of Patmos's luxurious hotels on the waterfront in Skala, and from there, we were to actually go off to Athens for the honeymoon. The event was everything I had hoped for since I was a little girl, and looking back that day, I was so happy that I didn't marry Nick. I didn't know many people there. I would say they were all in some way connected to Zarek, either by blood or as acquaintances of Uncle Joshua and Aunt Tempest's, but it felt as if they were people who had always been a part of my life.

The event started winding down at about 2:00 a.m. and Zarek and I retired to the honeymoon suite. Late the next day, when we woke up to a new life, I was thinking of sailing off into the sunset, as the cliché goes, with the most handsome man in the world. We opened up the laptop to look at the wedding pictures that were uploaded by the photographer. It seemed as if there were hundreds of pictures, and we were going through them one by one when an email alert popped up. That was the last thing I wanted to see or think about at that moment; opening up an email now was like opening the door to our room and inviting strangers to come in and invade our privacy. All I wanted to see and hear was right next to me, nibbling at my ear and making crazy promises I knew he'd never be able to keep. Yet the email alert kept popping up and annoying the life out of me. At that point, I had two choices, shut the computer off or look at the stupid thing for just a brief second and then go back to the wedding pictures. Zarek made the choice for me. "Open that annoying garbage or I swear I'll put it out of its misery."

I clicked on the mouse and the sender came to view, Reverend Tanner, it read.

"Who's Reverend Tanner?" he asked with a tone of authority while knitting his brow. Now that he was the new husband, he wanted to know everything and everyone in my life.

"He is the pastor from the mission house that I stayed after the fire in Soy."

"So what's the urgency now?"

"I'm about to find out." I read the email with my heart skipping beats, and it read:

> Gloribella, I wanted to reach out for a while now, but I lost your contact information, and it took me some detailed inquiry and cross-referencing to find it. Anyway, vital information has surfaced regarding the child. Please contact me as soon as possible.
>
> Reverend Tanner

I read it twice, and so did Zarek. Prior to our wedding, we had discussed the future and Johnno. He had become a big part of our lives, and we wanted to keep him if we could, but not knowing his age or anything about him wouldn't help. He had a past, he was somebody's child, and that fact couldn't be erased. Johnno was the greatest mystery I had ever encountered in my life. Now this was the big revelation we were hoping for, and despite the possibility of a happy ending, I was scared.

We stared at each other for a moment without saying anything, then I breathed heavily. "I have to make this call to the preacher."

He nodded and handed me the phone from the bedside table, and after waiting several minutes on the line, an international operator got me through to the Reverend Tanner. Communicating across time zones was something totally new to me.

His wife, Sister Bertha, answered the phone and passed it to him.

"Hi, Reverend Tanner?"

"Yes, Gloribella. So nice to hear from you!" Then there was a pause. Zarek put his face close to mine so he could hear the preacher's voice.

"Gloribella, is this an international call?"

"Yes, Reverend Tanner, I'm in Greece."

"Greece, huh. I just want to let you know that I've found the little boy's relatives." We paused and Zarek got up off the bed and hissed, then made a deep sigh.

"Is that so, Reverend?"

"Yes, his name is Johnno. Where is he now?"

"He is here with me in Greece."

"Goodness Savior! We have a big problem on our hands. You need to get the child back here in the US right away. How did you get him a passport?"

I suddenly froze with fear. Zarek saw and came over to me. "What is it? Let me talk to him; give me the phone." I gave him the phone.

"Hi, Reverend Tanner, I am Zarek Cavallo, Gloribella's husband. We recently got married and I am responsible for bringing Johnno to Greece. Just give me a couple of days and I will bring him safely back to Truro. My wife and I love Johnno, and I think he feels the same about us. Whoever is asking for him, just tell them he is in safe hands and will be back as soon as possible."

I wasn't sure what Reverend Tanner's reaction was, but Zarek hung up the phone soon after that. He got dressed within a few seconds, kissed me, and was walking out the door.

"Where are you going?"

"I'll be back soon, baby. I have to go see Uncle Josh." He dashed out of the room, and I sank into the bed, pulling the covers up to my chin. I never felt so helpless and stupid in my entire life. I wouldn't ever say I regretted coming to Greece; what I was sorry about was my failure to take Johnno's situation more seriously, to look at the bigger picture. Now I had to trust that Zarek could do something before this whole thing mushroomed into a terrible mess. While I was thinking about what I could do since this was my responsibility in the first place, I fell asleep and dreamed I saw a wasteland of frogs. That was the only mark that I had actually slept.

Zarek was back in the room with tea and other stuff that tasted good. Food and cooking were my thing, but this time I didn't pay attention; I only knew it was good and sweet. I was more interested in how to get Johnno to America. Zarek was in a good mood. As a matter fact, I had never seen him really angry, only upset.

"So what happened?"

"I saw Uncle Josh and he is already on top of it, even as we speak. I left him on the phone. As you know, he has connections with people in high places, people like the ones you saw in New Zealand. So don't worry about it. You and I are going back to the States tomorrow. We'll catch a flight in the morning. Johnno will leave later with my mom; separate flights, that's all. Uncle Josh is a very smart man and knows what he's doing. Uncle Josh said we are a married couple and shouldn't start out with problems. Come on now, baby, finish your tea and stop worrying your beautiful mind. We have to check out of here to go pack for the trip back to America."

As a special service to the bride and groom, the hotel chauffeured us back to the house on the hill in Chora. I spent the entire evening with Johnno, playing board games and taking him to some of his favorite sites in Patmos before he left. Mustafa drove us some of the way, and then we walked to the rock of Kallikatzous, where some of the most rare and interesting birds bred. I let him walk around and do his stuff and collect his usual treasures, knowing he might never be back on the island once he was reunited with his family. It was quite a bittersweet day for me.

We left the house shortly after dawn, when the roosters in Patmos were crowing and the dew on the grass was still heavy, and of course Mustafa was driving us to catch the ferry in Skala.

It was not a flight that I enjoyed; I was quiet for a long time after we left Athens for Boston. Zarek was reading a copy of one of the Athens newspapers, and eventually he became aware of my silence. Eyeing me, he said, "What is it Mrs. Zarek Cavallo thinking about now?"

"A variety of things."

He folded the paper, tossed it in the overhead compartment, and put his arm around me, stroking my hair. "Do you want to talk about it?" Everything about him was comforting.

"Who were all those people at our wedding except for your immediate family? I didn't know a fraction of them."

"That's Greece; everybody is family there. It was nice to finally meet your family. Do you think they like me? Especially your brother Owen. The guy looked like he would take me down if I ever hurt a strand of your hair."

"That wouldn't be Owen, that would be me."

"Woohoo! Take it easy, baby, take it easy. I would have loved to meet your mom too."

"She probably wouldn't have come anyway."

"Yes, I remember, you didn't marry her boy, Alex, and I'm glad you didn't. You have much better taste than that," he laughed.

As the plane soared through the sky and through time, we joked. It was a beautiful, intimate moment for us that I froze with a photograph. I tried to get him to talk about his sister, but it was still a painful, sensitive subject, so I left it alone. I didn't want anything to change between us.

Chapter Sixteen

That was basically how it all began. I mean, being married to Zarek. We landed in Boston and dared not go to Truro until Johnno was there by my side. We checked into a hotel and kept on checking our voicemails and text messages for news of Johnno and Lottie's arrival. We were assured that they would be on their way as soon as the consulate gave clearance for him to travel. Of course, Uncle Joshua was working on it, so we waited two more days, and my anxiety level was the height of Mount Everest. Zarek gave me strong shots of vodka to make me sleep.

On the third day, Uncle Joshua called us to say the consulate needed Johnno's full name, date of birth, and the names of his parents or guardians. This new development sparked off a series of email correspondence between Reverend Tanner and me. The first email came back from the reverend with his full name and his date of birth, but the name of his parents could not be disclosed until he was safely back into the country. Reverend Tanner said it was for legal reasons, so Zarek and I should give our names as his guardians. We forwarded the information to Uncle Joshua.

On the fourth day, I told Zarek that I needed some form of distraction or else I would lose my mind; this wait was killing me. He had no idea what to suggest, so I went out to search for an apartment to rent. I didn't want to stay in the hotel anymore, and he agreed and didn't argue with me. It took me only a day to find a place in the Boston area that didn't require a lease. The next day, we went out to look at furniture, beds, tables, a television, the whole works. I got curtains, and then I did something even crazier; I went to an animal shelter to adopt a pet, talk about a diversion. The first animal I looked at was a very unusual, raggedy dog. I'd never seen one like that before. The color of his coat was a beautiful shade of gray, almost like slate, and his face was the most delicate shade of white, like a precious shell found on the beach. The balance of his coat looked like a woolen sweater coming out of a washing machine. When I approached the dog's cage, it immediately came up to me, whining and wanting to get out. I put my hand out, which he licked, then he barked and whined. The shelter volunteer took him out of the cage, and that was the dog I took home.

On about the sixth day, because I'd lost count of this very stressful spell, Uncle Joshua called to say he had cancelled plan A and was moving on to plan B. There was too much red tape, and some of the many questions had no answers. We told him about renting the apartment and just trying to make things as normal as possible. "Congratulations, you are a young couple starting to live your life. Time waits for no one. I got this."

I didn't know what other action was necessary; actually, there was nothing I could do. I had made a terrible mistake that I wasn't sure could be corrected. I decided to bury my problem in the joy of cooking for Zarek. I certainly cooked a lot of meals, but I clearly remember the day I made the classic fried chicken in grapeseed oil.

FRIED CHICKEN IN GRAPESEED OIL

3 pounds chicken, cut into pieces
Freshly ground black pepper
1 package Goya Sazón
1 quart buttermilk
2 teaspoons hot sauce
1 bay leaf
3 cloves garlic (smashed)
3 sprigs fresh thyme
1 cup whole wheat flour
1 cup pancake mix
1 cup bran
1 tablespoon baking powder
1 tablespoon onion powder
1 teaspoon salt
1 teaspoon black pepper
Grapeseed oil and margarine for frying

METHOD

Massage chicken pieces generously with black pepper and Goya Sazón; place on a baking sheet, cover loosely with plastic wrap, and refrigerate for 1 hour. Combine buttermilk, hot sauce, bay leaf, garlic, and thyme in a large zip-seal plastic bag. Add meat and make sure it is completely covered in the buttermilk mixture. Seal and refrigerate for about 4 hours. Mix all dry ingredients, flour, pancake mix, bran, baking powder, onion powder, salt, and black pepper, in another zip seal plastic bag.

Fill a deep cast-iron skillet with grapeseed oil and margarine. Heat over medium heat and insert a deep-fryer thermometer. When it registers 350°, remove a portion of the chicken from the buttermilk mixture to a wire rack and let the excess liquid drip. Transfer the chicken to the dry mixture bag. Seal and shake the bag to fully coat the meat with the seasoning. Shake off excess dry seasoning and transfer to a rack.

Use tongs to lower the chicken into the hot oil, with much care to avoid splashing. Take note of the dropping temperature and adjust the heat accordingly. Fry and turn only as needed until golden brown. As a precaution to prevent undercooking, transfer chicken to a wire rack in an oven of 400° and cook for about 5 minutes. A thermometer should register 160° in the breast and 170° in the legs and thighs. Remove chicken to a clean rack, (not paper towels). Fry in batches. This fried chicken is always good with rice and a salad.

The dog kept me busy and reduced a bit of the stress and anxiety, because as it turned out, Zarek was also having trouble, not just about Johnno, but his sister, who was confirmed missing. She had never been gone for so long without contacting her family or friends. So we had another issue on our hands.

The nameless dog I adopted was quite friendly, but most days he would just sit on the mat at the door as if he was waiting for someone just as much as we were. We were fortunate to become instant friends with the couple in the apartment next to ours, Fabio and Winnie. We would chat almost every day and had been to each other's apartments. They were very good with animals, especially dogs and offered to take care of our dog if we ever went away. That in itself was a blessing because, sooner or later, we would have to be away and couldn't take the dog with us. So in preparation for that, I let them take the dog on frequent walks so he would get used to them.

On the day that was the two-week anniversary of when we came to Boston, Fabio offered to take the dog out for a walk. He was going to the store to pick up milk, so he would save us from going out if we didn't want to. I accepted the offer gladly, because I was in one of those moods of not wanting to see people. After Fabio was gone with the dog, I lay on the couch, and Zarek came to lay next to me. It was less than five minutes later that the doorbell rang, and I thought that Fabio had returned for something. I got up to answer the door, and to my shock, it was Uncle Joshua smiling from ear to ear. I thought to myself that it couldn't be bad news if he looked that happy.

A little girl was standing next to him with her wheeled backpack in one hand and in the other she held a doll. She rested the backpack on the doormat and I looked down on it. Pictures of the Cinderella story were illustrated on both sides of the bag. I looked back at the girl. She was an odd-looking child, the type I had seen on very rare occasions with their parents in the mall. She wore a bonnet with little curls hanging down, and to match the bonnet, a long floral dress touching a pair of white shoes with bows. She had on glasses with thick lenses, the Coke-bottle kind. She was certainly a sight to behold, but the most frightening part of those brief moments was realizing Johnno was not with them. I tried to open my mouth, but it remained shut, as if I was suddenly paralyzed.

Zarek came leaping to the door, scanned the spectacle with his mouth wide open, stared at his uncle and then back at the little girl, then settled his glare on Uncle Joshua, as if to say, have you lost your mind, old man?

"This is Effie," Uncle Joshua finally said. "Are you gonna invite us in?"

"Of course." I stepped aside to let them pass.

Effie picked up her little bag quite gracefully and entered the apartment. "Uncle Joshua, where is Johnno?" I asked impatiently.

"Well, my dear, Effie is Johnno."

"What?"

He pulled the bonnet off Effie's head, and the drop-curls still hung from the bonnet. Then he removed the Coke-bottle glasses from her eyes, and then he removed the additional makeup the child was wearing, and within seconds, the mystery started to unravel. Effie was indeed Johnno. I almost squeezed him to death with hugs; Uncle Joshua as well. "Thank you, thank you! I don't know what I would have done without you in a situation like this."

"You would do fine. You're smart, beautiful, charming, and you make my nephew happy. You'd have figured it out once your head was cleared."

"Uncle Josh," Zarek cut in, "what happened here? Did you bring Johnno on the plane like that?"

"No, Zarek, your uncle is getting old, but not yet senile. We came on a yacht. I wish I could give the full story with all the details, but I have to be at the airport soon. Killing two birds with one stone, as they say. From here I am heading to Texas. Nice apartment, by the way. My friend is waiting in the car, so I'll take a rain check on the tour. Here is the abbreviated version of what happened after you guys left Patmos.

"Some people I thought were my friends got really difficult to deal with and were making a big thing out of the situation, so I walked away from them. It took me an entire day to sit down and think this through, and then the answer came to me. I remembered that a pal of mine had a daughter who was about the same age as Johnno. He owed me a favor and was more than willing to come to my aid when I call upon him. His daughter, Effie, is autistic, so I hired a make-up artist to do the transformation, changing Johnno into what you just saw. We sailed for America on the yacht, and when we got to the border, the officials came on board to check everyone who was there. When they came to the new Effie, she was at her little desk drawing and coloring with her crayons and markers. The officer loved her drawings, and my friend explained to the man that Effie is autistic and very talented. He checked her passport, and the new Effie offered him an origami paper airplane. I'm very sure the officer was being polite when he looked at her and took the airplane and said, 'Thank you, Effie.' That was the end of that, and we breathed a sigh of relief."

"How did you get Johnno to cooperate?"

"Simple, Gloribella, I told him it was a game, and if we won, he would get to see you and Zarek within a very short time, and you guys would take him out to have a vanilla shake as the prize. After that, it was a done deal. Lottie was too nervous to come, and this was something I preferred to handle by myself."

The doorbell rang as Uncle Joshua checked his watch. He was about to wrap up his short visit. Zarek moved to answer it, and it was Fabio returning the dog after their walk. As Zarek and Fabio started to talk in the doorway, the dog suddenly sprang into the apartment in the direction of Johnno. "Alabaster!" Johnno exclaimed. The dog jumped up into his lap and licked his face, then bounced to the floor and began to do a happy-dog dance. It repeated the antic several times before settling down on the couch next to the boy. We all stood still, astonished as we watched the two of them. Upon hearing Johnno's gleeful cry, "Alabaster," I realized that it was the color of the dog's face, a shade of white. I wondered, was that the dog's name? I didn't recall having heard the name at the animal shelter. Again I pondered, who did the dog belong to, Johnno?

"It's an amazingly beautiful dog, but, kids, I really must go now. Well, keep me in the loop, and I'll call from Texas. I'll only be there for a few days, then I'm expected back home. Bye, Johnno. Thanks for being such a good sport; you're a winner."

"Bye, Uncle Josh," Johnno said without taking his eyes off the dog.

As soon as Uncle Joshua was out the door, I took up the phone and called Reverend Tanner. As I listened to the phone ring, I watched the dog and Johnno bonding or renewing their friendship. My attention was so taken up with them that I almost didn't hear when Reverend Tanner picked up and said hello. He said he would be at the mission house or the church, and whenever I got there, someone would be available to let me in. A member of Johnno's family would also be there to meet with us.

We caught the ferry from Boston to Cape Cod as soon as we left the apartment, as that was the fastest way to get to Truro. Car service was readily available, and we were at the missionary church just as the minister was finishing up with the Wednesday evening service. "The harvest is plentiful, but the laborers are few," he ended while we waited at the back of the church. He saw us as he was coming down the aisle to shake hands with his congregation, who were hastily leaving the sanctuary to get home. Reverend Tanner was a man of short stature and going bald, but what was left of his brown hair he kept very short, which gave him a youthful appearance. He came to us directly while some of the people squeezed past, but not before a quick handshake and, "Thank you for coming. God bless you, Sister Victoria," or, as the case might be.

"Gloribella, my dear sister. Finally, you made it." He looked at Zarek. "Nice to meet you in person." He shook his hand cordially. "And, Johnno, how are you, my little man? Long time no see." He bent slightly to shake the boy's hand.

"Fine," Johnno said, petting the dog as he glanced up at the reverend for only a second.

"And the famous dog that I never met but heard of only briefly, this must be him." Reverend Tanner adjusted his glasses as if he wanted to get a better look at the dog.

Zarek looked at me, but I shook my head slightly. I had no idea what was going on with this unusual dog.

"Blessed Savior, this is such a joyous occasion with a hopefully happy ending." Reverend Tanner looked at the painting of Jesus on the cross on the wall in front of him. "We should have a real celebration; Sister Florence is waiting at the mission house."

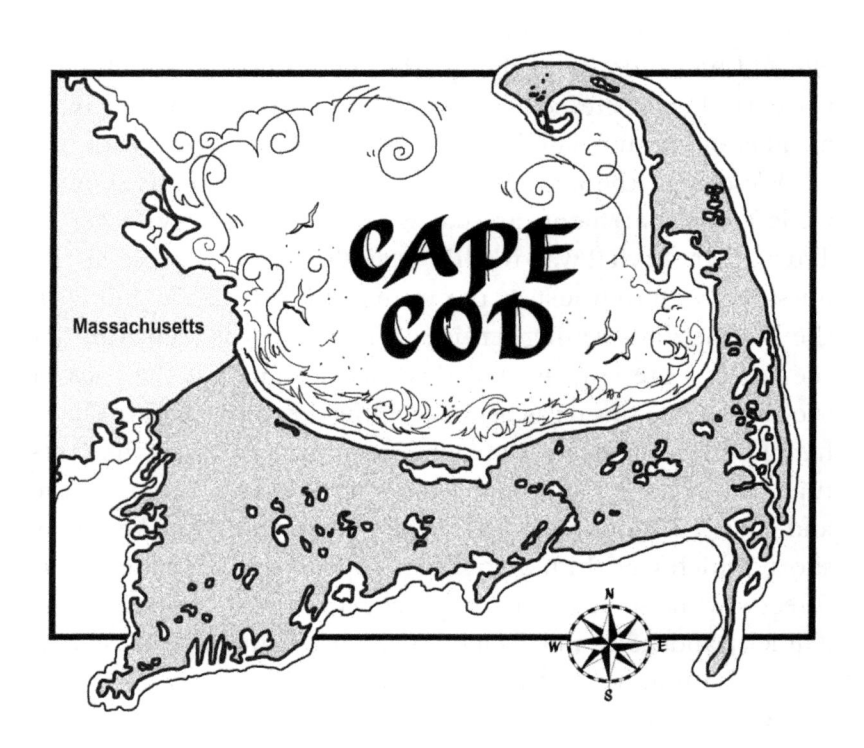

Chapter Seventeen

The mission house was only a few blocks away, so we all walked the short journey, and as we entered, an old and familiar sense of serenity greeted me. The place was just as it was a few months ago; the only difference was the absence of the people I met there. This time a lady was waiting for our arrival; she was sitting in a rocking chair talking to the minister's wife when we entered the room. No part of her body was exposed except for her face; she was even wearing a pair of white gloves. She took them off to shake our hands.

Sister Florence was Johnno's aunt, and considering how she was conservatively dressed in a hat and long-sleeved dress, and the way they referred to her as sister, she fit the description of the term church lady. Johnno didn't run to greet her, which I thought was odd, since she was a blood relative whom he knew and hadn't seen in months. Initially, she took his hand and led him away to have a private conversation, but due to his lack of response she gave up and came back to join us. Not long after, Sister Bertha invited Johnno to the playroom, which was the dream world of a child. The place had shelves and boxes of children's books for every age, along with toys, games, musical instruments, and a rocking horse, all arranged in one large space.

Every room in the mission house seemed to evoke some kind of feeling, some form of memory for me. The Tiffany lamps and tables with the crooked legs, the Brentwood rockers, and large Bibles in every room reminded me of my grandmother's house. I would race my sister, Mia, for the rocking chairs and would rock so fast that Grandma Ruth's biggest fear was that I would land on my face during the frantic rocking.

We did not sit in a circle as we did the last time I was there. I was glad for that; it wasn't my favorite way to sit in a group. The candles that burnt dimly in the room were all of different heights and colors, yet they created the right mood for the moment. The chairs were so comfortable that I could have fallen asleep within seconds of sitting down, and I was starting to drift down memory lane quite a bit when the voice of Sister Florence jolted me to the very important present.

"Johnno is the only child of my niece, who we fondly call Joy. Shortly after he was born, my niece had a nervous breakdown. The doctors said it was depression. No big surprise there, old problems mixed with new ones stemming from childhood are sure to manifest into something bad. My sister died when Joy was only a little girl, and I helped to raise her; I did the best I could, considering that I had my own children.

"She got a good education; I worked two jobs to make sure of that. As a result of her mental state, she walked out of her marriage, which had lasted only about ten months, just long enough to give birth to Johnno. Well, she was a fighter; she got over the depression and went back to school to get her master's degree while I raised Johnno. Her ex-husband didn't want the child; he didn't have the patience with him, and he didn't understand him. As it is plain to see, Johnno is a child with human needs, and hunger for the love I couldn't adequately provide. He is very smart, but was diagnosed with Asperger syndrome; though, with help and proper training, he can be functional."

Sister Florence paused as she became overwhelmed and was choking up a bit. She dabbed at her eyes with tissues she took from her purse while the minister's wife brought her a glass of water. Reverend Tanner took her hand. "It's okay, Sister Florence. Take your time; you're in good company here."

"Thank you, Reverend." She regained her confidence to go on with the story of Joy and Johnno. "I got full custody of Johnno and raised him up to this point, but of late, his favorite thing is to run away. I am not young anymore, and Johnno knows it. With the help of my pastor, I was looking for a nice couple to adopt him, people who can give him the care he needs. That is not easy to find these days. I almost had a heart attack when he went missing then someone led me here to you, Reverend Tanner."

The pastor nodded in agreement.

"My dear, Miss Gloribella, I can't thank you enough. I could have gotten into serious trouble, not to mention the fact that Social Services could have come down on me, and he would have been placed in foster care."

"I can't take all the credit. Johnno found me; I didn't find him, and a number of other people helped me, especially my husband here."

"That's why I was thinking, Miss Gloribella ... Well, it's obvious that I can't take care of him anymore, and it's only a matter of time before they force me to give him up, and possibly to the wrong people."

"Sister Florence, if you don't mind me asking, where is your niece, Joy?"

"As of this moment, my child, I don't know. She never calls, and nobody write letters anymore these days. My daughter knows how to contact her on the Internet. I don't know the first thing about computers; never used them in my day and have no desire now."

"So, what are we saying here, folks? Are we travelling down the path of compassion as far as this child is concerned? He needs us, every one of us in this room," Reverend Tanner cut in.

"Well, Johnno will always be special to me. I met my wife

on the same day he ran away and she found him. If it wasn't for that, I would never have met her, and Johnno has been part of our family ever since," Zarek added.

"God moves in mysterious ways," Sister Florence said.

"Sister Florence is looking for a home with good parents for Johnno. He is already strongly attached to you God-sent people. I can't think of a better match," Reverend Gregory Tanner concluded.

I took Zarek's hand. We both knew that we wanted to keep Johnno from the very beginning; there was never a question. He squeezed my hand in agreement, and we said yes, we would like to keep Johnno. We only made one request: we wanted to meet the boy's parents and get their side of the story. We didn't want any unpleasant surprises four years later when he was already established in our lives. The person who would lead us to them was Sister Florence's daughter, Selena Rose.

Sister Bertha brought Johnno back into the room with the dog leading the way but still not very far from the boy, and so we launched into a discussion about this dog and its identity. I gave my side of the story, that I found him at an animal shelter in Boston and also in the absence of Johnno.

"Well, my dear," Sister Florence informed us, "the dog belonged to him. That's his therapy dog, Alabaster. The thing never left him, but somehow, they got separated. He used to wear a collar with identification, but I can see he isn't wearing it now. That won't explain why it ended up in Boston. The only way for you to find out is ask at the shelter."

"Well, here is another piece of the puzzle, Gloribella," Sister Bertha cut in. "The night you collapsed here at the front door, we heard a dog barking, and when I went out, Alabaster was there. He took off immediately as soon as we make eye contact. I never saw the dog again until now, and I wanted to mention it before, but something else more pressing always came up; as you know, this is a mission house."

We went back to our apartment in Boston, taking Johnno with us. Sister Florence was afraid to keep him. She did not want a reoccurrence of what we just went through, and we all agreed to keep things as stable as possible.

Well, starting out as a new family once more, I had to feed them with only the best, and these were some of the things I made:

BUFFALO CHICKEN ZUCCHINI BOATS

- 4 zucchinis (sliced in boat-shaped halves)
- Olive oil
- 2 cups cooked chicken (shredded)
- ½ cup chopped scallion (halved)
- ½ cup whipped cream cheese
- ½ cup buffalo sauce
- ½ cup sharp cheddar cheese (shredded)

METHOD

Use a spoon or melon baller to scoop out the zucchini halves, leaving them somewhat hollow but firm enough to stuff. Freeze the scooped out parts for soups or stews. Place zucchini boats on a large baking sheet covered with parchment paper and brush each boat with olive oil. Bake for 15 minutes at 350° Remove from oven and set oven to broil. In a mixing bowl, mix chicken, half the scallion, whipped cream cheese, buffalo sauce, and sharp cheddar cheese. Fill each boat with the mixture and return to oven. Broil for 5 minutes on low. Turn to high for 1–2 minutes if you need to brown the boats more. After baking, garnish with chopped scallion.

COCONUT BUCKWHEAT WITH CILANTRO AND LIME

- 1 tablespoon butter or margarine
- ¾ cup onion (chopped)
- 1 cup coconut milk
- 1¼ cups low-sodium chicken broth
- 2 tablespoons fresh lime juice
- 2 tablespoons fresh orange juice
- ½ teaspoon sea salt
- 2 cups buckwheat

3 tablespoons cilantro (chopped)

1 teaspoon fresh lime zest

METHOD

Rinse buckwheat in a fine strainer under cold running tap water and set aside to drain. In a saucepan, sauté onion in butter for 3–5 minutes then combine coconut milk, chicken broth, lime juice, orange juice, and salt, and bring mixture to a boil. Stir in buckwheat and reduce heat to low. Cover and simmer until the liquid is absorbed in about 20–25 minutes. Remove from the heat and let sit for 10 minutes. Remove cover and lightly fluff with a fork. Add the cilantro and lime zest to the buckwheat. Adjust seasoning to taste.

CORNMEAL CRUSTED CHICKEN DELIGHTS

20 pieces of chicken cutlets (about 1¼ inches long)
20 strips of bacon
2 tablespoons soft cream cheese

1 tablespoon pimento (minced)
½ cup grated sharp cheddar
Splash of hot sauce
½ cup yellow cornmeal

METHOD

Before preparing chicken, heat oven to 400° and have a baking sheet with a wire rack ready. Pound chicken cutlet with spikey face of a mallet and lay them out flat on another baking sheet. In a mixing bowl, mix cream cheese, pimento, sharp cheddar cheese, and hot sauce. Spread a thin layer of the mixture on each cutlet and roll up the cutlet. If needed, pin with toothpicks to secure. Wrap each roll-up with a strip of bacon and make sure the chicken is completely covered. In a shallow dish, pour cornmeal. Then dredge each roll in the cornmeal, carefully shaking off the excess. Place the chicken on the rack and cook until each cornmeal chicken delight is golden brown and the bacon is crispy on the outside. Cooking time is about 20–30 minutes.

FRESH DILL SALMON DIP

1 8-ounce tub sour cream French onion dip
1 16-ounce can salmon (drained, bones and skin removed)
1 tablespoon fresh dill (chopped)

METHOD

In a mixing bowl, combine sour cream French onion dip, salmon, and fresh dill. Fold the ingredients together gently, cover with plastic wrap, and refrigerate for 1 hour before serving. Serve with whole wheat crackers.

SPICY LENTILS WITH BUCKWHEAT NOODLES

1 cup lentils
2½ cups water
¾ cup feta cheese
1½ cups pasta sauce (with peppers, extra virgin olive oil, sea salt)
1 12-ounce package buckwheat noodles

METHOD

Carefully pick through lentils for stones that may be hidden among the grains. Rinse with cold water and drain. Bring lentils to a boil in water and cook for 5 minutes. In the meantime, heat pasta sauce in a saucepan. Remove lentils from heat and drain, then transfer to sauce and cook for about 30 minutes on low flame until grains are tender. Stir in feta cheese and remove from flame.

Buckwheat Noodles

Cook according to package instructions and serve with spicy lentils.

I even made greens, a recipe that had been in my family for as long as I could remember.

CROCKPOT KALE

1 large bundle of kale
2 smoked ham hocks
10 cloves garlic
1 onion (chopped)
3 small tomatillos (sliced)
1½ tablespoons olive oil
1 tablespoon Lipton Recipe Secrets, beefy onion
1 teaspoon black pepper
¼ cup low sodium chicken stock

METHOD

Thoroughly wash kale under cold running water then set aside in a strainer to drain. In the meantime, cover ham hocks in boiling water and cook for about ten minutes. Remove ham hocks and place at the bottom of a slow cooker then add 5 cloves of garlic. Shake off excess water from kale and place in a large bowl. Coat the kale with olive oil, Lipton beefy onion, and black pepper. Layer the slow cooker with the kale and chopped onions, tomatillos, and remaining garlic cloves. For extra moisture, pour chicken stock over the kale and close the lid of the slow cooker, then set it for 8 hours on low heat. Cook until ham hocks are tender and meat falls off the bone. Remove all bones and mix the meat with the kale. Serve hot as a side dish or with rice.

*Please note that collard greens and mustard greens can also be mixed with the kale.

One of the most awful states in life is waiting, even for a day was horrendous. I was waiting to hear from Selena Rose, so while that was happening, I picked up where Lottie had left off with home schooling Johnno. Since money did not grow on trees for us, and we weren't independently rich, Zarek had to go back to work. I begged him to be safe and return to us as soon as possible He went back to the boat, starting at the dock where we met in Truro, and from there he followed the same familiar path back to Greece. I continued as a researcher and a consultant for Uncle Joshua, even though I wasn't in Patmos.

As I watched the amazing friendship between Johnno and Alabaster, I understood why Fabio and Winnie thought they could work with children. This couple had a zeal for doing good and were quite positive, even in daunting situations. They thought Johnno's temperament, along with Alabaster's, could have a favorable effect on other children, especially those who were unwell. Winnie, who was a pediatric nurse, offered to sign them up with a program she was involved in called Animal Assisted Therapy if Zarek and I agreed. I also kept in mind that at that point, Johnno had zero friends of his own age and was constantly around adults. I ran the idea by Zarek when we spoke on the phone. "Go for it," he said. "It can only make him a better person."

After the initial training and the pairing up with a social worker, every Friday I took Johnno and Alabaster to the hospital for the sessions with the children, and it went well, and as a result, his communication skills were sharpened and I noticed that he was less withdrawn. Alabaster was quite accommodating with the children; he allowed his head to be petted as long as Johnno was there. It turned out to be quite a positive experience.

About two weeks after the initial contact with Selena Rose, just about the time when Zarek returned from Greece, I got a response. She lived in Foxborough, about twenty-two miles southwest of Boston. She was a mother of three with a dog and a canary, and she lived with her husband, who worked for the New England Patriots. We agreed to have lunch at a downtown restaurant in Boston that served some of the best meatloaf I had ever had, and this was the one Selena Rose and I ordered: goat curry meatloaf over basmati rice.

GOAT CURRY CHAYOTE MEATLOAF

1 large chayote (peeled and shredded)

2 cups chicken stock

½ cup onion (chopped)

2 garlic cloves (minced)

¼ cup green pepper (minced)
½ cup uncooked bulgur
1 teaspoon ground thyme
½ teaspoon salt
1 tablespoon curry powder
1 teaspoon black pepper
1 large egg (beaten)
1 pound goat meat (coarsely ground & 95% lean)
1 tablespoon grapeseed or any other cooking oil for frying

METHOD

In a medium saucepan, bring chicken stock to boil, add chayote, and cook for 7 minutes. Remove from heat, drain the liquid, and set aside to cool. Preheat oven to 375°. In a large skillet, heat grapeseed oil and add onion to the hot oil. Sauté onion for 1½ minutes then add pepper and garlic; continue cooking for another minute before adding curry powder, black pepper, thyme, and salt, then cook for another 2 minutes. Remove from heat and set aside to cool. In a large mixing bowl, add beaten egg and onion mixture from the skillet, and thoroughly mix together. Add goat meat, bulgur, and chayote to the mixture. Mix and fold it all together, but do not overmix. Pack mixture in an 8x4-inch loaf pan coated with cooking spray. Bake at 375° for 1 hour and 10 minutes. Let meatloaf stand in pan for 10 minutes before removing.

Selena Rose basically filled in the gaps that were too painful for Sister Florence to talk about. Selena Rose was a very beautiful woman, but a skimpy eater, hardly ate any of the food, a total waste I thought, but the conversation we had was quite interesting. "My cousin Joy was raped when she was fourteen years old by someone we actually knew. The bastard is in prison now, and may he rot in there forever. Joy never quite trusted men after that. I was quite surprised when she got married, not to mention had a child."

Then from her purse she whipped out an envelope and

handed it to me. The letter was sent to her to be forwarded to me. It read:

> Dear Gloribella, congratulations! I heard you got married, and I wish you and your husband all the best in life. I just wanted you to know that Aunt Florence has full custody of Johnno, and if you want to adopt him, it is fine with me, whatever she says goes. I had long ago given over the rights of his welfare and upbringing to my aunt, and therefore, you need no further clarification from anyone else to move forward with your plan. Please never worry about his father. He has never been part of his life and never will be. Your husband, Zarek, can now fill that void that was vacant for so long. I am not capable of raising children.
>
> Love,
>
> Joy

I read the letter with trembling hands and took a deep breath at the end. I felt peace and rest as if I was awfully tired. It reminded me of climbing a tower and pausing at the landing next to the top just before the view. I knew it was not over, but this was the first stage before we could finally refer to Johnno as our son. The letter was very personal, as if we had known each other at some point in time, so I tucked it away really carefully. I planned to make several copies as soon as I got a chance just in case the original got lost or misplaced.

The papers for the adoption of Johnno were filed not long after that, and then came another waiting period. I hosted a series of parties to catch up with old friends and relatives almost every week, just to keep myself busy. My ex-boss and people who were friends of mine became frequent guests at these parties I hosted. On some Friday nights when they came over, I would name the night fritter night. Fritter nights were all about fritters, and there were a variety of them. These were just a few of the fritters we made:

ZUCCHINI LENTIL FRITTER

- 2 medium zucchinis (shredded)
- Sea salt
- 1 tablespoon margarine
- 1 small onion (finely chopped)
- 1 clove garlic (minced)
- ½ cup lentils
- 1½ cups chicken stock
- ½ cup yellow cornmeal
- ½ cup whole wheat flour
- ¼ teaspoon baking powder
- ½ teaspoon freshly ground black pepper
- ¾ cup buttermilk
- 1 large egg (beaten)
- Grapeseed oil for frying

METHOD

Pick through lentils for stones and unwanted particles, then rinse in a strainer in cold running water. In a small saucepan, bring chicken stock to boil then add lentils and minced garlic. Cook lentils until tender, about 10 minutes. Drain excess liquid and set lentils aside. Combine shredded zucchini with sea salt in a bowl and let sit for 10 minutes. Transfer to a strong kitchen towel and squeeze out as much of the liquid as possible. In a large mixing bowl, add whole wheat flour, cornmeal, and baking powder. Mix until the baking powder is completely blended with the flour and cornmeal mixture. Mix beaten egg with buttermilk then add to the dry ingredient bowl and mix. Add zucchini, lentils, onion, and black pepper. Stir until everything is combined. If batter is too thick, add a few teaspoons of water until the desired consistency is achieved. In a large cast-iron skillet, heat about a ¼ cup oil and 1 tablespoon margarine over medium heat. You can add more as necessary later. For each fritter, measure about a ¼ cup of batter and add to oil. Flatten with a spatula. Fry in batches of about 4. Cook fritters until golden brown, then transfer to paper towels. Sprinkle with salt and serve warm.

GRILLED EGGPLANT FRITTERS

- 2 eggplants
- 1 tablespoon kosher salt
- Olive oil
- ¼ cup whole wheat flour

¼ cup wheat germ
½ cup bran
2 tablespoons chick pea flour
1 teaspoon baking powder

1 teaspoon lemon juice
2 eggs lightly beaten
1 teaspoon Mediterranean seasoning (salt free)
⅔ cup grapeseed oil for shallow frying

METHOD

Slice the eggplants about ¼-inch thick and sprinkle with salt. Wrap eggplant slices individually in paper towels and press under heavy weight, such as a brick, for 30 minutes. Carefully rinse off some of the salt. Pat and press dry with more paper towels. Prepare and heat grill, then brush with olive oil to prevent sticking. Grill both sides of eggplant, getting as much char on the slices as possible. Remove from grill, cool, and mince with a sharp knife. Combine all dry ingredients in a large mixing bowl and mix thoroughly. Add eggplant to mixture, followed by beaten eggs and lemon juice. Thoroughly mix the batter, adding teaspoons of water to add more moisture to the mixture if necessary. Heat oil in a large cast-iron skillet. Add 2 tablespoons full of the batter to the hot oil for each fritter. Cook fritters over medium heat for about 3 minutes on each side until golden brown.

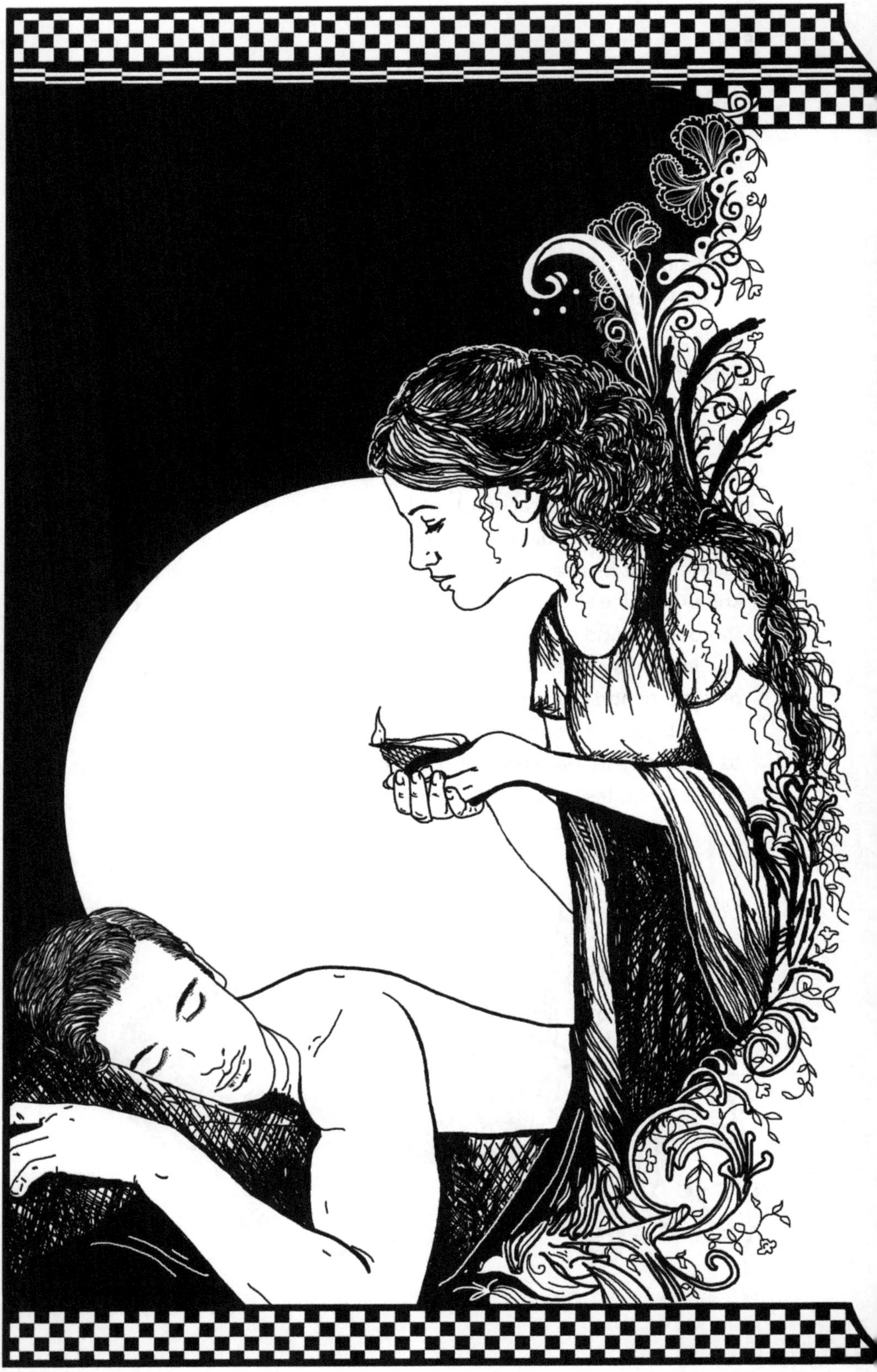

Chapter Eighteen

I literally heard about the play approximately forty minutes before curtain time at a drugstore checkout line. Two women were talking about how they wished they didn't have to miss the final performance of *Eros and Psyche*. They were quite polite when I butted in on their conversation to get all the information. Getting to the theatre was like a race against time, and I was late every step of the way. I was the last person to get a ticket, the last person to be seated, and the list goes on. I had no program; it was the final performance, and therefore, I had no idea who the actors were. Besides liking the story, I just wanted to see how it would be done by the professionals and with the English translation.

Well, I wasn't disappointed. It was just amazing. The acting was exceptional, and since the theatre was larger, the production team had more space to spread out, and it brought the myth to life. It was obvious that whoever the cast and crew were, they had a broad range of experience. With the costumes and makeup, I was transported to another world and time that was so different from the one we lived in now. The actor who played Aphrodite was outstanding and had a voice that I almost thought I knew in one scene and then in another I was unsure. It was just good acting all around.

Zarek came to pick me up after the play was over, and as we headed down the highway for home, we became stuck in late-evening traffic. I hadn't seen him all day, but we had spoken on the phone a couple of times.

"So how did you like it? Did you get a chance to talk to her?"

"Talk to whom?"

He looked at me and realized that I had no clue what he was talking about.

Being on the other side of town, there was only a fifty-fifty chance that I would ever make it there on time. I called Zarek to tell him about the play and to ask him to look up some information about it for me. He promised he would, but by the time he called back with the information he pulled from the Internet, I was already seated inside the theatre.

"Your mother played Aphrodite. I recognized her from photographs, and they had a picture of her on the page, and of course, the name Estella Frank ... it was hyphenated with something else I can't remember right now."

Although I was sort of in shock, I managed to open my mouth. "You said hyphenated ... she's remarried?" I paused and pull forward in my mind the actor who played Aphrodite ... "Well, what can I say; good makeup and brilliant acting can be very convincing. It would have been nice to talk to her."

"I'm surprised. You're usually more perceptive, babe," he complimented, and then changed the subject to something he has seen earlier that day. But no longer fully listening, my thoughts drifted to wondering how well my mother was doing in her new life, remarried, and back to the career she always wanted to jumpstart. I remember how she always blamed us kids for holding her back, and when she was frustrated with our father he would be verbally attacked with her sharp words too.

"Baby, I'm sorry you keep missing your mother," Zarek cut through my thoughts. "It's like she has this radar that knows exactly when you are around." As ridiculous as that sounded, it was beginning to feel true. "Do you think she is still punishing you for turning down her matchmaking bid?"

"It is quite possible that she hasn't forgiven me. One of her favorite sayings was 'honor thy mother and thy father.'"

"Well, too bad for her. I have forgiven you and that is that."

It was a beautiful day when I took Johnno and Alabaster to the park to play. The boy and the dog were in a world with room for no one else. Johnno had a ball and he would throw it and Alabaster would run and fetch it each time. I had wondered about the dog ever since Reverend Tanner's wife told that story about what must have been Alabaster barking outside her house. I was curious, and the only way to get some form of clarification was to go back to the shelter where I got him. How could this be the same dog? It was too strange, almost impossible.

The verification was satisfying after I spoke to someone at the shelter. The dog was picked up late one night by a police officer driving from Truro to Boston. She had a friend who worked in the animal shelter and just thought it was the right place to take the dog. The date she found the animal was the same time I was staying in the mission house. That was all the information they had, and since Alabaster had no identification, there was nothing else they could tell me. It was just another part of the whole series of events that could not be explained. The most beautiful part of it all, was the emergence of Zarek, and I often thought of him as this beautiful plant that grew out of a place where vegetation growth was almost impossible.

It was the day after the adoption was officially over and all the red tape had finally been removed that Zarek heard from his sister. She found out through social media that he had married. She was awfully sorry that she had missed his wedding. Zarek was extremely angry at her and kept the conversation with her at a minimum. His answers to her questions were simply yes or no. After he hung up the phone, he was fuming. He thought she was such a selfish person who had no trouble walking away from her family and letting them worrying. Danielle begged him to allow her see me and Johnno and said she would love to be invited to the party we were planning for Johnno. His response was, "Whatever."

Johnno didn't have many friends that we knew of, except of course, Alabaster. He did not have many at the hospital where he visited with the dog, and besides, they were sick children; most of them could never leave their rooms.

We turned to Sister Florence for help since she knew everything about him, and she was very helpful. "Yes, he had friends," she told us. "But they have no idea where he is. They are mainly from the school he attended in Truro," she continued.

She also did not think their parents would allow them to attend a party all the way in Boston. Gaining that bit of information, we decided to have the party in Truro just so that his friends could attend. The planning took several weeks to get off the ground, and we found a great venue. It was a playland setting, a place called The Mended Anchor, and we got the ballroom downstairs at a good price. There were two things about the place that caught my attention when I first went there. The first was a huge anchor in the main lobby that was broken and welded back together. But the main attraction was the staircase leading down to the gigantic ballroom. It was an enormous crystal vase starting at the first floor with the stairs inside. I watched everyone I invited filter and trickle their way down that architectural marvel to the ballroom. Before they entered the floor, they seemed to move in slow motion, and inside the narrow part of the vase, people's figures got all contorted, as if they were walking through a hall of mirrors.

There were many surprises that night, and it started out with watching people I didn't invite trickle their way down. I knew who they were, but inviting them to something like that wasn't part of my thinking at that time. Pilar was the first one to arrive, and she was as beautiful as ever; the nun's habit seemed to add even more charm to her personality.

The party was about Johnno, so of course his friends had their own section of the room for play and whatever they wanted to do. Sister Florence was very good with the follow up; all seven of Johnno's friends were there. They were strange children like Johnno, but in a very sweet and innocent way. Five boys and two girls around his age of eleven. Most of them carried their pets as companions, which gave them a sense of comfort and perhaps security. One of the two little girls reminded me of Effie, Uncle Joshua's creation. She had her pet rabbit with her, which she pushed around the room in a baby's stroller. The rabbit laid still and enjoyed the ride.

The first shock to come that evening was when Hortense entered the mouth of the vase and drifted down the stem. I didn't invite her because New Zealand was a long way off and quite an expensive trip. Well, part of the job of a missionary was constant travel, so Reverend Tanner must have told her about it. She was a very sweet person anyway, and I didn't mind having her there.

Then my mother entered the staircase followed by Alex, the man she'd wanted me to marry. So now this was really turning into something beyond my wildest dreams.

Fittingly, I cordially welcomed them all with hugs, and we talked and laughed for a while, and they took drinks from a waiter who was walking around with a tray. There was plenty of room and food, so it seemed to be open to whoever showed up, invitation or not.

While we were all talking and sipping from straws, my mother took my hand and said to the others, "May I talk to my daughter for a moment? We need to catch up; it's been a while."

"Please, please," they all said. I looked at Zarek invitingly, but he shook his head, meaning I should go along without him. We went to the far end of the room.

"Gloribella, you look great! Much more beautiful too. You aren't pregnant, are you?"

"No, Mom, I'm not."

"Sweetness, I was so stupid. I hope we've passed all that ... nonsense now and can move on to a new, clean page."

"Mom, whatever happened in the past is long gone. We've missed out on a lot of years, and yes, this is a new page."

"That is so true, my baby girl."

She hadn't called me baby girl since Mia was born and I was no longer the baby. As embarrassing as it was for her to call me that as an adult, I took it as her way of making peace.

"So how have you been, Gloribella?"

"Well, I have a great job in Greece, which I'm doing long distance. I got married, as you know, and tonight we are celebrating the presence of Johnno in our lives. Yet there was a very stormy patch in my life with Nick, and after I walked away, good things started to happen."

"Well, I'm very proud of you, and I take no credit for your accomplishment, but I always boast to people about my beautiful daughter Gloribella. I missed your wedding because I was getting married probably around the same time as you, and there were several little things to be straightened out before. It was a shock to me when Alex asked me to marry him." She stretched her finger out to show the large rock, the type that I would never have imagined to be my mother's style.

I just didn't know what to say after Alex came into the conversation. Since it was a moment of reconciliation, I could not wait too long to congratulate her and a few seconds had already passed. The uneasiness of the situation was punctuated when gunshots reverberated throughout the room and everyone became still until they realized it was coming from the children's table, where they were playing a video game.

"Look, sweetheart, I don't expect everyone to understand this; sometimes I don't understand it myself. God knows we must have been attracted to each other and just didn't know it."

"Mom, it doesn't matter as long as you and Alex make each other happy. That's all that's important."

"It does matter what my children think of me, especially since I was pushing for you to marry Alex. Gloribella, you must have thought I was a terrible mother. And then when he asked me, I needed your blessing more than anyone else's, but I couldn't wait too long; men are very sensitive when it comes to that matter. Then there was the question of my age. How many more chances do I have?"

"Mom, congratulations to you and Alex. You would have gotten my blessing then and you are getting it now, twice."

"Darling, Gloribella, your guests are waiting on you, so I will come to the point quickly, and later you will be filled in on the details of me and Alex. I am very proud of you; your compassion and understanding surpasses that of anyone I have ever known. Thanks so much."

As she was moving along to greet Pilar, who according to her religious order was now Sister Perpetua, Selena Rose walked up to me. She had been waiting for a while to talk to me and her mother was with her. "Gloribella, we need to talk to you. There is something you need to know, but if it's going to be a problem or interrupt Johnno's party, then it can wait," she interjected.

If what she had to tell me would hurt, regardless of when and where, the result would be the same. They had been very nice people from the very moment I met them, so I couldn't imagine anything unpleasant at such a time. I looked up at the staircase for just a moment and saw Uncle Joshua, Philippa, Lottie, and a young woman I believed to be Danielle entering the vase. "Well, if this is going to hurt, it may as well be now. The wait will be far worse."

"No! No, it's not like that," Sister Florence said. "It's just a matter of sensitivity and timing, and we didn't want anything to spoil such a lovely evening."

Just as if he had read my mind from across the hall, Zarek appeared. "Can I help with anything, babe? I'm starting to feel like a useless husband. You've been doing all the work."

"Sister Florence and Selena Rose have something of a sensitive nature to say, so I am trying to decide if now or another time would be better."

"We would rather hear it now than later. I don't think anyone can take another day of suspense. Let's get everything clear and in the open, so we can start with a clean slate when we leave here tonight."

Selena Rose spoke first. "What we wanted to say is simply that Joy and her ex-husband are here."

"Johnno's mother and father? I thought they didn't want to go public. It's been a secret so far; why did they decide to show up now?"

"I can assure you, my dear Miss Gloribella," Sister Florence took on that tone of reverence she sometimes slipped into, "they invited themselves, just to mend fences and not cause problems."

"Whatever it is, let's get it over with; the sooner the better," Zarek said

We followed Sister Florence and Selena Rose up the stairs to an area where food was served. Four people were sitting at the counter, two women and two men. The first couple in plain view were strangers but the other two were Hortense and Alex having a conversation.

"There they are," Sister Florence said.

"Who? Where?" I asked.

She pointed. "Joy and her ex-husband, Alex." Sister Florence's words hit me like a bolt of lightning.

"That's Joy and her ex? I know them both, but that's Hortense and ... well Alex, who is now my mother's current husband."

"This is what I was afraid of, Gloribella. It is a strange connection; some of it I recently just found out myself."

In disbelief, I said, "Sister Florence, are you telling me that they are Johnno's parents?"

"I'm afraid so, my dear."

"But why call her Joy when her name is Hortense?"

"Nobody in our family calls her that. It says it on her passport yes, but from when she was a child, we all called her Joy because of her disposition."

Alex saw us first and he got up from the stool and walked over. Joy reluctantly followed. The awkwardness of the situation could be measured in the hesitation of her steps. For a while, we just stood there in silence; I was at a loss for words.

Alex, who was a leader by nature and by trade, broke the silence. "It is warm in here. We should go outside for a breath of fresh air." He stepped ahead.

I think we were all relieved to leave the room and step into the salty air from the sea. We were so quiet that our individual heartbeats could be heard without the use of a stethoscope. Whatever we wanted to say was said in our thoughts. It was amazing how the welfare of a child could elicit so much drama.

Alex once again broke the silence. "You know, I've been a preacher for over twenty years now, and this is the first time my own sermons caught up with me in such a real way. I should have used all of that advice I gave people, but I didn't. So most people would say to me, 'well, Pastor you are a hypocrite then.' No, I'm not; I am a human being with weaknesses, but that is no excuse. I can't say for sure why I couldn't be a father to Johnno, why I couldn't care for him when he needed me. And why I couldn't be more supportive to Joy during her rough patch. Anyway, I won't turn this into another meaningless sermon; what's the point? But one thing I want to say is, thank you, Zarek for being the father Johnno never had; you are by far a better man than I could ever be. Man, I just met you today and you're great. And, Gloribella, I don't know what to say. How did this all boil down to this day? It can never be explained, but I want to thank you. I knew there was something different about you from day one. I had many conversations concerning you over the years, but none of that matters now.

"Joy, I have said this many times today, but now I will say it before all these people: I am truly sorry. I should have been the husband whom I preached about in my sermons."

Joy, or Hortense, started to cry she was so moved by Alex's speech, and I took her in my arms. Poor thing, she needed a shoulder to cry on. "I am sorry for everything," she said between sobs. I knew what she meant. She had every opportunity to tell me she was Johnno's mother and she didn't. What could I say? It was already done.

We rejoined the party, and I was determined to not let anything prevent me from having a good time, so I stashed my emotions for another day and place. I mingled as the host, going from table to table and chatting with each guest for a little while. Then I went to my own table, where the Cavallo family was seated. They were the ones from Greece plus the cousins living in the Cape Cod area. As I was about to sit with them, Zarek whispered in my ear, "You think your family is messed up, just listen to mine."

Danielle was seated there watching her brother, almost every move he made, but he paid very little attention to her. Finally, she said to me, "Gloribella, can you tell your husband to stop ignoring me. I know exactly what he is doing."

Every person at the table looked in her direction and then at Zarek and eventually at me.

Zarek couldn't help but to respond. "I am not ignoring you, Danielle. I am just tired of your crap."

"Well, I'm trying to talk to you, but you won't give me a chance. You're treating me like I am this monster. None of what I want to say to you can be said at this table, since it could be used against me. The only person who can hear about this is your new wife, and it's only because she doesn't know me well enough to pass judgement."

I took Zarek's hand and stood up. He reluctantly moved his limbs as we strode to another location in the room not far away from where Johnno and his friends were having fun with their pets and games.

"Okay, Miss Danielle, this better be worth my time or I'm deleting you from all my contact lists," Zarek spewed.

"I was working, but still, that's not an excuse for not shooting you a text. I already apologized to Mother, and I told her I would buy her whatever she wanted."

"So where are you getting all this money now? Selling drugs?"

"No, Mr. Perfect. Gloribella, how do you put up with him?

My friend, who went to another Ivy League school, hooked me up with a fertility clinic. They only screen donors who ... okay, are freaks like us ... We have very high IQs. Do you see where I'm going with this?"

"Yes, and it's making me sick, minute by minute," Zarek said.

"Okay, when you pass out, I'll call 911. I have it on speed dial." She continued, "I had a baby."

"So where is it?"

"I was paid to have it, duh! A childless couple paid me $1.5 million plus an apartment in LA to have their baby. So for nine months I was pampered, fed, and kept away from stress. I didn't even do my own laundry."

Zarek raised his hand to interrupt, but she stopped him. "Let me finish. Half of that money is already in a special account, a kind of annuity, so that's my safety net in all of this. Everything is legal. I will have no contact with this child, who has half my DNA. I will still need to find a job to maintain the lifestyle I have become accustomed to. But at least for now, I don't have to break my neck."

"So you're telling me this now why?"

"I said I was kept away from stress, and that included judgement, which this family is noted for."

I stepped on Zarek's toes under the table before he could say anything else. He sneered, kissed me on the cheek, and returned to the normal kind person that he was. "Okay, you're lucky my wife is a very sweet girl; she wants me to be just as nice as her."

"Without a doubt."

"Any more surprises that we should know about?"

"Well, let's see, I will probably marry into royalty soon and move to one of the richest parts of the world." She smirked and rose to leave Zarek and me alone at the table.

The night ended with music and dancing, and even Sister Florence, the most conservative person in room, went out on the dance floor when a tune from the forties came from the sound system.

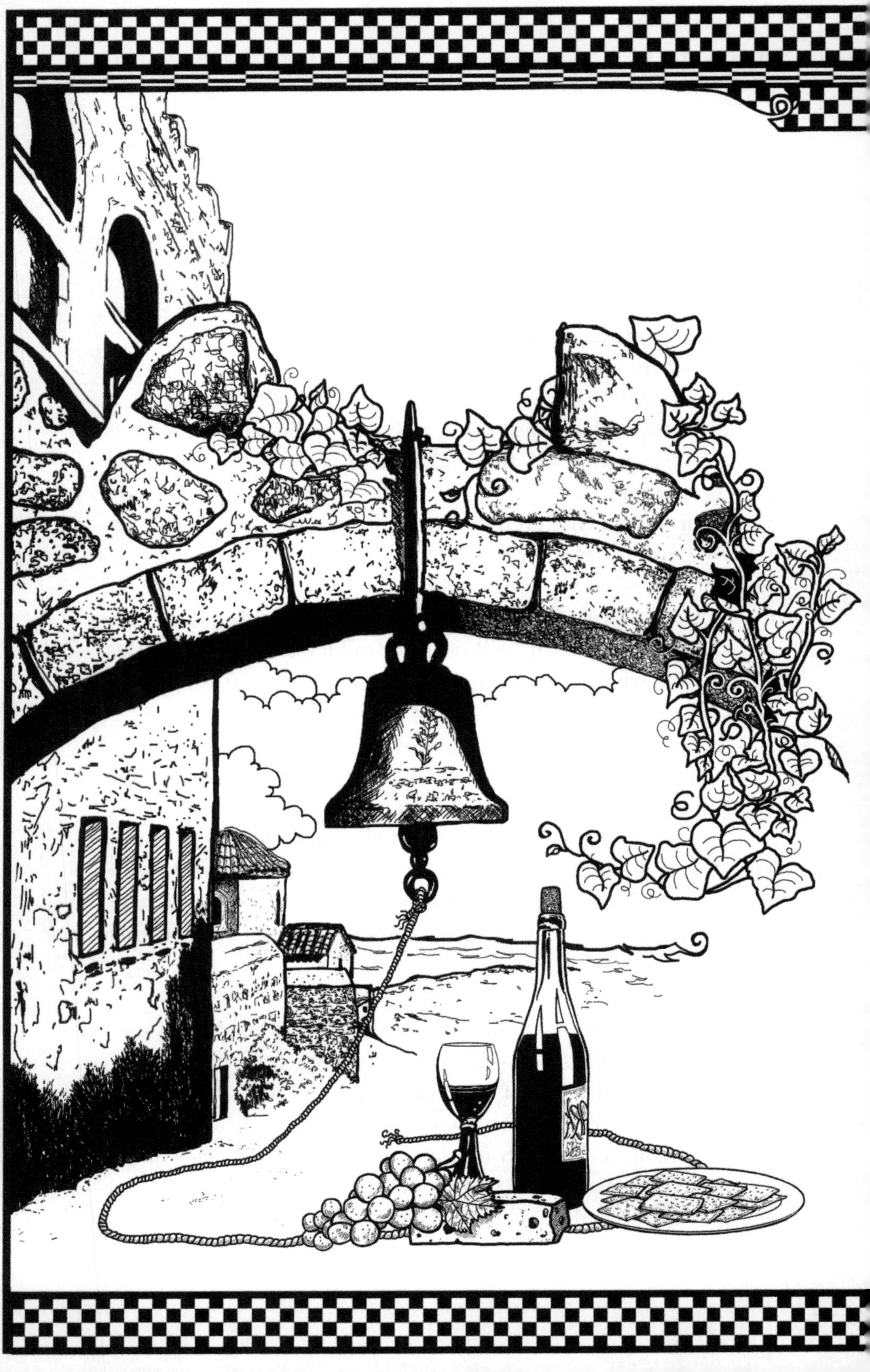

Epilogue

Two months later, Zarek and I and Johnno and Alabaster were on a flight to Athens, Greece, and from there, we would catch a red-eye to Leros. We would see the sunrise in Patmos once more. But most important of all, it would be Easter week, and from what I was told, Easter in Patmos was unique and cannot be duplicated in any other part of the world.

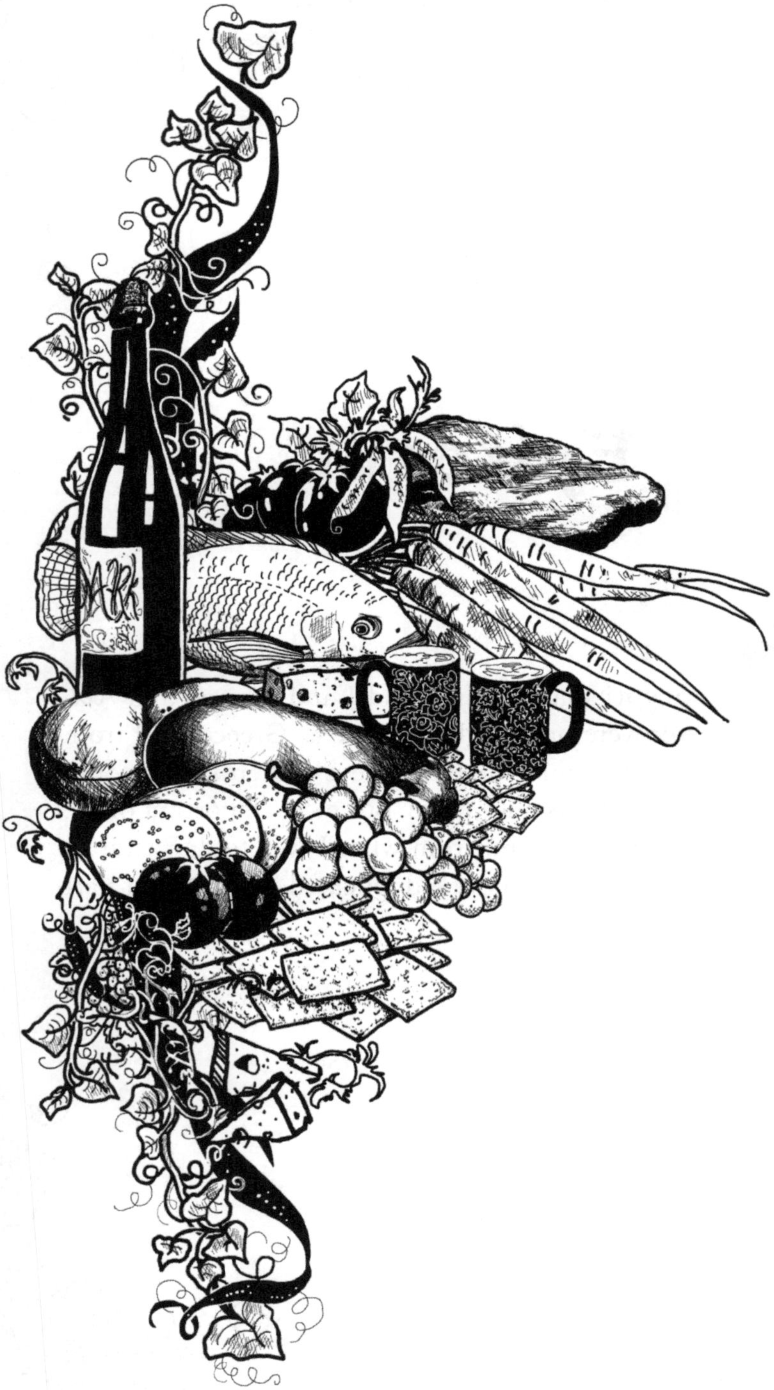

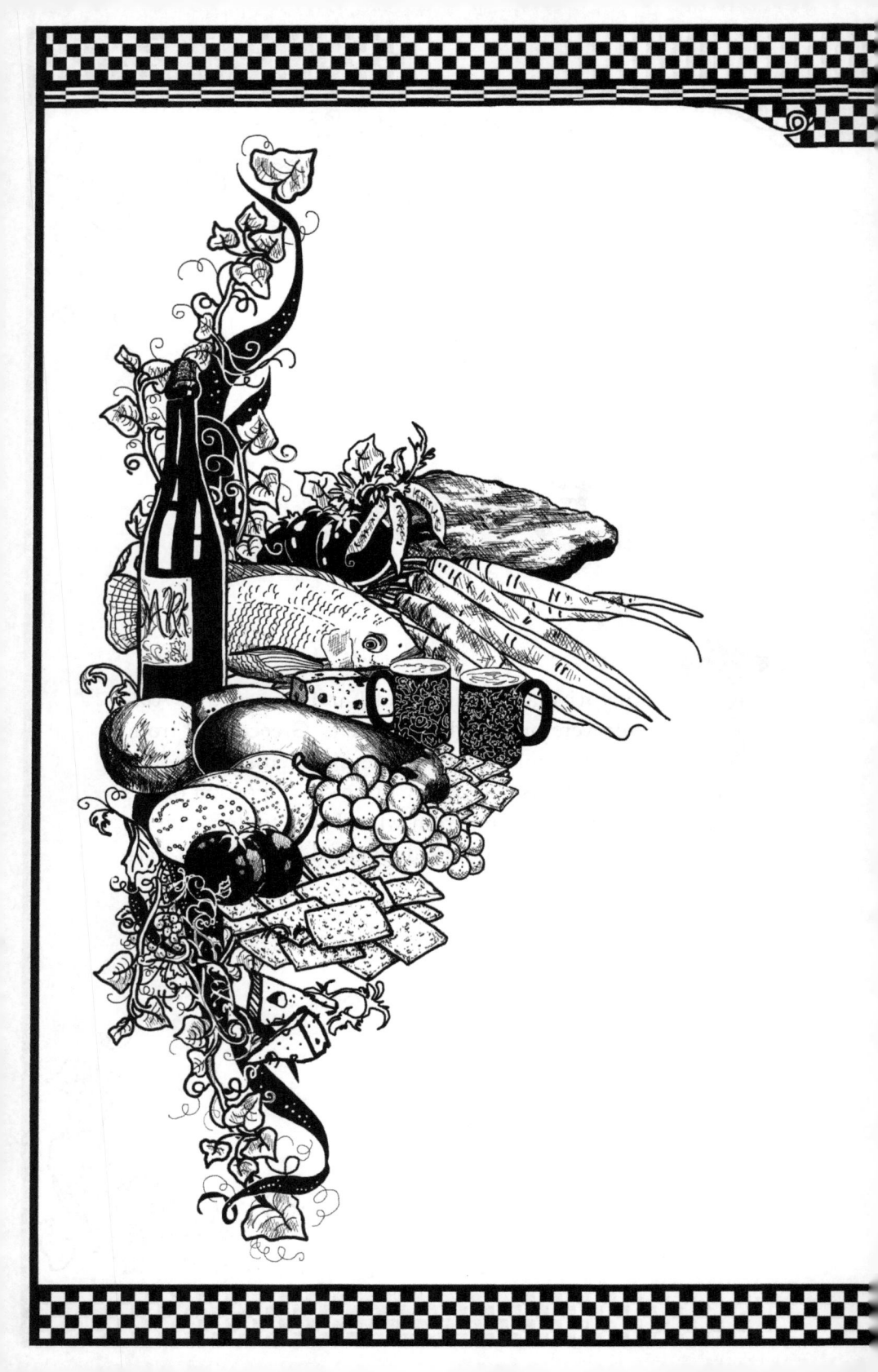

Recipe Index

Ackee and Codfish	83
Almond Mango Bars	119
Basmati Rice	37
Bean and Pepper Stuffed Bell Peppers	118
Beef Pumpkin Savory Pie	93
Beef Pumpkin Soup	28
Buckwheat and Black Bean Muffins	34
Buckwheat Black Bean Stars	148
Buckwheat Edamame Salad	21
Buffalo Chicken Zucchini Boats	191
Calabaza Corn Cakes	145
Caper Sauce	47
Cauliflower Crust Pizza	75
Cilantro Rice	115
Coconut Apple Pancakes	13
Coconut Buckwheat with Cilantro and Lime	191
Columbus Day Hash	117
Cornmeal Crusted Chicken Delights	192
Cornmeal Porridge	12
Crispy Fried Tilapia	47
Crockpot Kale	194
Curried Beef	67
Date Blueberry Pudding	147
Dates and Rum Bars	128
Dipping Sauce	19
Eggplant Mozzarella Sandwiches	35
Fish and Baked Sweet Potato Chips	63
Fresh Dill Salmon Dip	193
Fried Chicken in Grapeseed Oil	181
Fried Green Plantains	41
Garlic Roasted Salmon and Bulgur	151
Ginger Beer	37
Glazed Carrots	48
Goat Curry Chayote Meatloaf	195
Grapefruit Bubbles	120

Greek Macaroni and Cheese	92
Green Lima Bean Soup	149
Grilled Eggplant Fritters	198
Grilled Eggplant Sandwiches	150
Grilled Snow Peas Buckwheat and Salmon Bowl	122
Grilled Zucchini Brown Rice	117
Infused Water	xv
Jerk Turkey Bowl with Buckwheat Edamame Salad	20
Jicama Carrot Salad	121
Kabocha Pumpkin Salad	31
Lemon Carrot Cake	94
Mango and Strawberry Trifle	22
Mushroom Celery Rice	68
Mustard Mackerel and Banana	115
Orange Cran-Apple Splash	121
Origami French Toast	129
Origami Pancakes	129
Party Bacon Sandwiches	123
Peach and Mango Delight	123
Pepper Pot	125
Pickled Cucumber Salad	34
Pickled Red Onions	121
Popcorn Turkey	113
Pork and Beans Croquettes	30
Pot Roast Pork	xiv
Poultry Brining	32
Pulled Pork and Plantains	45
Quiche in Mugs	61
Red Kidney Beans and Pork Belly Stew	36
Rice and Peas	xiv
Roasted Cauliflower Stuffing	118
Roasted Garlic and Pumpkin Soup	170
Roasted Sweet Potato Salad with Bacon	120
Rum and Raisin Banana Mango Cream Pie	35
Salmon Burgers	116

Sausage and Black Bean Casserole 92
Scotch Bonnet Curry Goat Wrap.. 112
Slow Cooker Lamb...171
Spicy Lentils with Buckwheat Noodles....................................... 193
Spinach and Feta Cheese Lasagna Rolls 44
Split Pea Curry 69
Sugar Free Hummingbird Cake... 147
Sweet Potato and Salmon Cakes 29
Sweet Potato Ham Casserole.. 91
Sweet Potato Whole Wheat Pasta Salad..................................... 145
Tuna Cucumber Boats 31
Turkey Teriyaki and Cilantro Rice..114
Tzatziki Sauce.. 46
Vegetable Fries 18
Watermelon Delight 105
Wild Rice Arugula Salad 172
Zucchini Lentil Fritter... 198

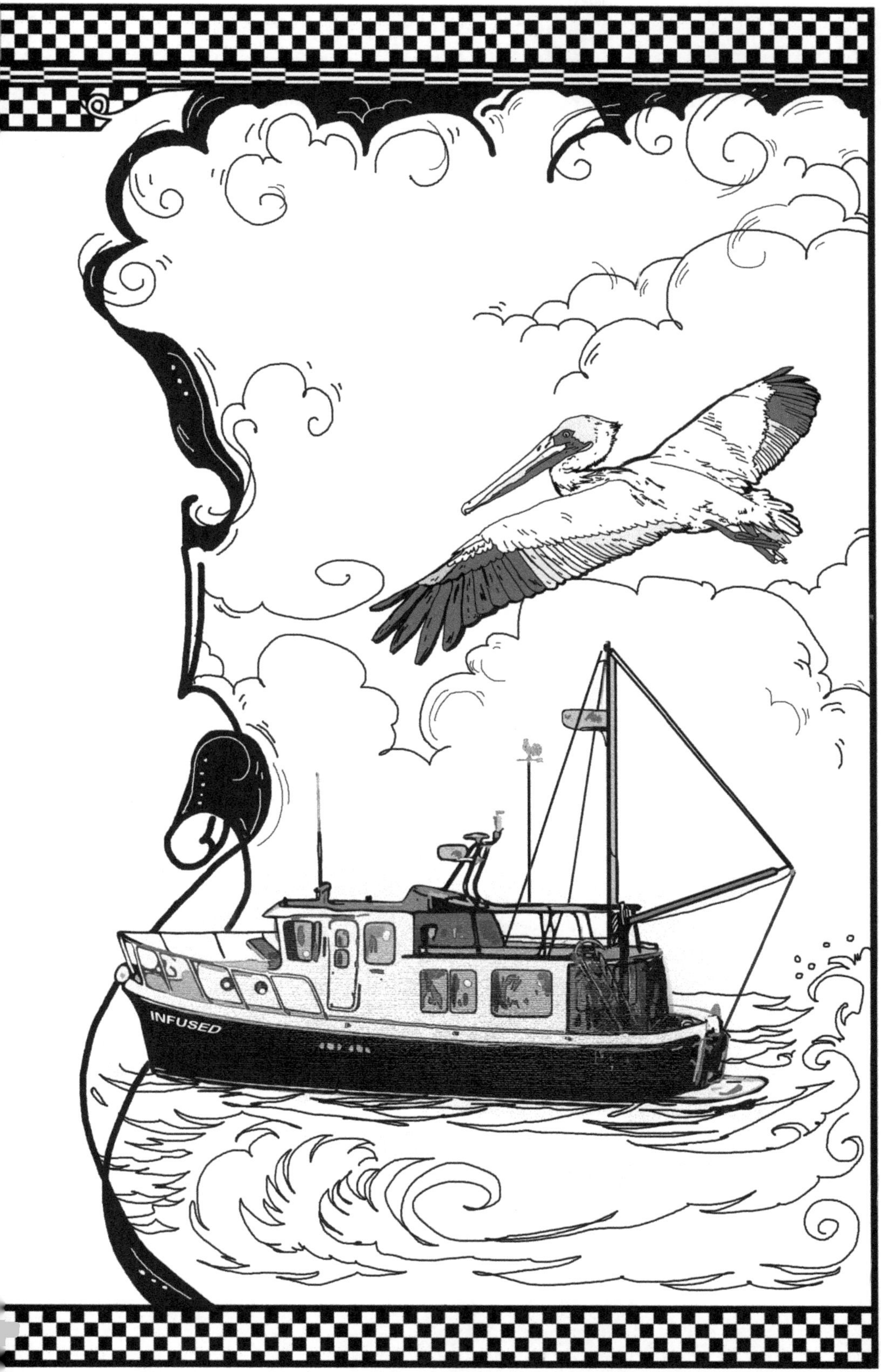
INFUSED

CPSIA information can be obtained
at www.ICGtesting.com
Printed in the USA
BVHW090210121121
621365BV00015B/643/J